Si

St

Over 100
Great Novels
of
Erotic Domination

If you like one you will probably like the rest

New Titles Every Month

All titles in print are now available from:

www.adultbookshops.com

If you want to be on our confidential mailing list for our Readers' Club Magazine (with extracts from past and forthcoming titles) write to:

SILVER MOON READER SERVICES

Shadowline Publishing Ltd
No 2 Granary House
Ropery Road
Gainsborough
DN21 2NS
United Kingdom

telephone: 01427 611697
Fax: 01427 611776

NEW AUTHORS WELCOME

Please send submissions to
Silver Moon Books
PO Box 5663
Nottingham
NG3 6PJ

Silver Moon is an imprint of Shadowline Publishing Ltd
Darkest Dreams first published 2003 Silver Moon Books
ISBN 1-903687-37-3

Darkest Dreams

By

Tessa Valmur

Also By Tessa Valmur

The Art of Submission
Bought and Sold
Darker Dreams
Tanya's Torment

CHAPTER ONE

'So how can I help you Miss...'

Serena smiled and glanced around the man's office. Her search for Lara had brought her here to the Dreamscape Institute and she knew she was clutching at straws. She doubted the man now sat opposite her could help her but she had exhausted all her other leads. She was almost certain that she was probably wasting this man's time and her own. Being *almost* certain though left a sliver of doubt in her mind and a hunch, call it female intuition, had brought her here.

'Miss Fairfax: Serena Fairfax. I am a close friend of Lara Lustral, I believe she was a patient here?'

'Client,' the man corrected, smiling disarmingly. 'Yes, that's right. She came here for maybe half a dozen sessions a few weeks ago. How exactly can I help you Serena?'

'Well, Lara has gone missing. She's vanished without trace. We were very close and I can't believe she wouldn't have told me what she was up to. The Police think she's slipped abroad with some man but I can't buy that. She would have at least told me her plans, we shared our secrets you see.'

'I see.'

The man gave a wry smile and the merest knowing nod. Serena watched him pick up an old fashioned silver pen from his desk. For a moment she thought he might be about to write something but he merely pressed one end of the pen against a clean pad of paper and let the smooth steel tube slide through his fingers. He then deftly rotated the pen through a hundred and eighty degrees and repeated the movement. Again the man smiled before glancing at the pen and carefully placing it back down on the mahogany of his desk.

'And you think that somehow I might be able to help you?'

His tone was smooth and faintly patronising. Serena watched him lean back in his chair and regard her thoughtfully. The intensity of his gaze made her acutely aware of the thinness of her Lycra top and the shortness of her skirt. She was accustomed though to men's lascivious gazes – she well knew how desirable her body was and now she didn't give a second thought to this man as he allowed himself a leisurely appraisal of the her.

Somewhere in Serena's family there had been Asian and Italian blood that accounted, she supposed, for her a tanned, olive complexion and dark hazel eyes. Her hair, dark red with copper highlights fell straight to her shoulder blades. Or if she swept it forward, to just above her breasts, which were firm and generous. At just over five feet tall and delicately built, Serena knew she looked like every man's fantasy teenage girl. Twenty pushing seventeen, Serena would think to herself, smiling, as she'd admire her reflection in the mirror of her bathroom.

Serena had cultivated a penchant for playing the vulnerable little girl who liked to drink too much at parties and end up helpless before the determined advances of the opposite sex. With her wide innocent eyes, her tight little waist and her heavy but firm breasts she drew men like bees to a honey pot. She had lost count of the number of times she had ended up in bed with a man, breathlessly begging him not to be rough with her while secretly loving how she invariably got treated.

'I was hoping Doctor MacKennan that you might be able to help me in some way. You see, I basically know why Lara came here. What she was seeking…'

Serina let her sentence hang unfinished and for a split second she imagined she saw a flicker of alarm cross the man's face but then she decided, as he furrowed his brow and seemed momentarily absorbed in thought, he was merely giving serious consideration perhaps as to how he could help her.

'Well as you know Lara came here to indulge in her dreams. That is the purpose of the Dreamscape Institute,' the man said. 'You're thinking that perhaps in her dream world there might be a clue as to where she has really gone?'

'Precisely,' said Serena, smiling at the man and now suddenly filled with confidence that at last she might be getting somewhere in her search for Lara.

'Come back tomorrow morning Serena at ten thirty. I have a free hour then and I'd like to do anything I can to help you.'

'How can I thank you Doctor?' she let her sensual mouth curve into a smile but this time she kept her lips parted a little and allowed the man a glimmer of her tongue tip as it licked thoughtfully across the gleaming white edges of her teeth. Serena stood up and MacKennan rose and shook her hand.

'Until tomorrow then Doctor.'

Turning on her high heels she walked out of the man's office and out of the gleaming chrome and tinted glass of the Dreamscape Institute.

* * *

MacKennan lingered for some time at his desk after the young woman had left. He was disconcerted by her visit but at the same time he couldn't help smiling to himself at the possibilities her visit might afford him.

MacKennan had created and run the Dreamscape Institute for five years now, having opening it in 2022, the year that the European Union and Russia had merged to become the Northern Confederation. Just as the Confederation had flourished and prospered whilst the rest of the world's fortunes had in comparison declined, his own personal circumstances had improved beyond his wildest dreams. Originally his plan had been to trade on his wealthy clients deepest fantasies. The powerful computer directed dreamscape machine could allow people to realise their dreams. Or to be strictly accurate, it gave the impression that they were actually living their dreams. In a world were money could buy anything MacKennan charged highly for his service which gave wealthy individuals the chance to control and play out their dreams so convincingly that they would believe that what they dreamt was reality.

So that was how it started and quickly MacKennan had found a recurring theme and common type of client: wealthy, spoilt young women who were sexually ravenous. They craved more than their safe, cosy lives gave them and they were ready to pay for the sexual escapism that the Dreamscape Institute offered. However less than a year ago MacKennan had found a new return upon his investment that brought rewards a hundred fold more than he had enjoyed until then. Once under the influence of the Dreamscape, his client's dreams could be subtly controlled and whilst asleep and dreaming they were completely at his mercy. When he found a wealthy young woman fantasising that she was abducted and sold into slavery it was not so very difficult for him to actually turn her dream into reality.

The barbarian nations, MacKennan had discovered, were ready to pay handsomely for the sort of slave girls that MacKennan could offer them. The first young woman he had found a buyer for over the Internet and as the woman's dreams showed her furtive desire for such subjugation he'd quickly stifled any qualms he'd begun to have when he received pre-payment for her. Briefly he'd contemplated not shipping the girl to her buyer once he had the money in his bank but he decided making an enemy of a South American warlord was inadvisable regardless of how many miles away he might be. So MacKennan had found an exporter happy to take cash payment and ask no questions and the girl, drugged and bound was dispatched in amongst a consignment of goods destined for the lawless jungles of steamy South America. It was about a month later that the Warlord had sent MacKennan another e-mail with a photo attachment. The picture showed the girl, naked and kneeling submissively. Her skin was now deeply tanned and glistened with perspiration. Her slim arms were pulled tightly behind her back and bound together with rope at her wrists and above her elbows. The expression on her face made MacKennan shake his head with wonder and momentary surprise and he found himself gazing at the picture for several long minutes. Though obviously in some discomfort from the way she was bound, the girl was looking eagerly at whoever had taken the photo. More than excitement though showed in her expression; her eyes were bright with fervour and appreciation of how she was being treated. There was no doubt in the viewers mind from her look, that she was actually enjoying the experience of being held naked and bound.

MacKennan glanced at the accompanying e-mail and shook his head in disbelief. His client was delighted with his purchase and had a friend he wished to give another girl to as a present. Could the Doctor arrange for another shipment? Just two days ago a charming young girl had taken her first session at the Institute. In her dream she had been a secret agent who had been captured by her enemies and within an hour of starting her dream she was being tortured to divulge secrets. Tortured in a most interesting way… She would be perfect, MacKennan had decided and thinking about how much money he'd make from this new client, he'd begun to ponder just what possibilities lay in this new development his business seemed to have taken.

MacKennan smiled to himself. Those early days seemed a long time ago now and back then it had all been more exciting… the danger seemed greater because he was learning as he went and he never knew what might happen or go wrong. Now though the business, his secret business, was well established and skilfully wrong. He left no margin for error, there was now too much at stake. Lara Lustral, this new girl's friend had been quite the most stunning girl he'd abducted up until now. She had also had a most interesting dream and he had thoroughly enjoyed adapting it to suit his own dark plans and personal dreams. Lara Lustral had been a pleasure indeed for him to deal with and now there was the prospect of submitting this new girl, Serena Fairfax to the same fate!

Tapping a security code into one the drawers of his desk MacKennan opened it and retrieved the file of the young woman whose fate had been to be sold to one of the most tyrannical and sadistic dictators on the African continent. On the inside left sleeve of the file was a photo of the young woman. Lara Lustral at twenty-six, looked like every man's dream eighteen year old girl. A perfect size ten, her narrow waist accentuated her generous breasts that were as firm and pert as a teenager's. Her legs and arms were slim and smooth; her skin a light chocolate brown with a coppery shine. Her hair fell in soft loose curls almost to the swell of her firm and rounded arse. It was the colour of burnished gold; the fashion colour of the summer of 2027. Lara's fantasy had been born from her name, when she dreamed at the Dreamscape Institute she imagined herself to be Lara Croft to the Tomb Raider heroine who had been famous back in the year 2001 when she had been born. But for Lara Lustral there was to be no escape from the adventure she had dared to embark upon. MacKennan smiled ruefully as he began to recall all the sexual suffering and torment he had forced her to endure. And to think she had kept coming back to the Institute and paying for more! A natural submissive, she had deserved the fate he'd delivered her.

Putting away the file MacKennan took a remote control from another desk drawer and flicking a switch brought a large visual display screen on the wall opposite to life. After first pressing a button on the edge of his desk which locked his office door he then keyed in his security pass code on the remote that gave him access to all the data and imagery that the Dreamscape Institutes L2 computer stored in it's memory. After keying in more security codes, which only he knew he then settled back to watch the screen.

In the centre of the bare stone walled, windowless room there was a stout wooden table to which a naked girl was tied .The girl was sat astride the narrow table, jerking her arms ineffectually against the ropes that bound her wrists against her waist. Obviously panicking at what was about to befall her she struggled frantically trying to pull her legs free but there were ropes around her ankles that held her legs firmly against the sides of the table. Watching over her was a man and two young girls. The man was dressed in the white coat of a doctor, the girls in black leather bustiers, short black skirts and high, black boots.

The captive girl's shoulders were drawn back by a rope bound around her arms above the elbows and the tension this placed upon her body served to thrust forward and expose her generous breasts. A rope was bound in a figure of eight around her breasts and from this another was fastened and ran forward to a securing hook at the front of the table. There was a cord bound around her mane of golden hair and this was pulled tightly backwards and fastened to another hook at the rear of the table. Between the two opposing pulls exerted on the girl's tethered body she was forced to maintain a sitting position. Although her breasts were so tightly bound by the rope they showed crimson, her nipples were a darker purple as each was caught in the cruel grip of a tiny clamp from which short, heavily weighted chains dangled.

'Stop it! Please…'the girl begged.

The man fingered her sex making her gasp.

'Very wet aren't we? You can't help it can you? This is just too exquisite and you want to come now don't you?'

'Yes… uhh…yes…'

The captive girl's eyes were wet with tears of shame and pain.

'Okay then, you've been a good girl. I'll let you come and then you can have a rest before we play another game.'

One of the black clad girls handed the man a tub of glistening gel and dipping his fingers into it he then stroked the tethered girl's sex again.

'Mmm…too hot… uhh…stop it…please…'the girl begged, tossing her head from side to side and jerking ineffectually at the ropes that bound her.

'Desperate for it now, aren't you?'the man smiled with satisfaction.

'Yes, yes… please…'

'Please what? Do you need to come? Would you like it if I

fucked you?'

'Yes...please... fuck me...fuck me...'the girl sighed breathlessly.

'Okay girls, take the nipple clamps off, leave her on her back and pull her arse down to the edge of the table.'the man grinned with satisfaction and his two accomplices swiftly set to work. In no time the captive Lara was unfastened, dragged down the table and her slender legs quickly spread and bound, her arse left thrust out over the edge of the bench. A rope was threaded through the collar that was around her neck and tied so that she was prevented from lifting her head more than a few inches from the table.

'Fetch a silencer Suzi, I think Lara may soon be needing one,'the man ordered, his hands stroking and caressing the exposed arse. The captive Lara moaned feverishly as he then began kneading the pert globes of her rump and sliding his fingers into the crevice between them until his fingers sunk into the girl's sex. Lara groaned, tossing her head from side to side as best the collar allowed.

'Time to have your silencer fitted Lara, there's a good girl.'

One of the girls held Lara's head still and the other forced a rubber gag upon the defenceless girl. The broad pad of rubber was tightened against the girl's mouth by a strap around her head effectively muzzling her. The rubber muzzle had a circular opening in the middle and through this a soft ball of rubber was fed into the helpless girl's mouth. The ball was connected to a rubber pad that loosely rested against the hole in the muzzle. The pad itself had a strap and like the muzzle this was now swiftly fastened at her nape.

'Does that feel nice?'

'Nnnhh!'

'Now it's time for Doctor MacKennan to look after you. Would you like to see the treat that the Doctor has for you?'

Lara's response was irrelevant. The man moved around the table until he came into clear view of Lara. The man's genital organs were massive beyond belief and Lara jerked urgently but ineffectually against her restraints in alarm at what was going to happen next.

'Nnnh!'

Her muffled protest was still audible until one of the girls in black smiled apologetically and gave a small valve protruding from the mask a slight twist allowing air to rush into the rubber ball until it expanded as far as the girl's mouth permitted.

'Something the matter Lara?'

Lara blinked back more tears in dismay and though she looked beseechingly at her tormentors not a sound now emerged from her gagged mouth.

'Well Lara, I'm sure you'll enjoy this as much as I will.'

The man moved back down to the end of the bench. The girl tugged her legs against the straps but without effect as she felt the man's hands stroke between her thighs. The young vixens in black smiled with obvious relish at her plight. Their wide, expectant eyes betraying their blatant excitement and delight as the man's massive cockhead was slowly forced into the bound victim's exposed sex. The tethered girl's limbs writhed and twisted, beads of sweat running down her face and slender collared neck as the shaft of the cock ploughed deeper into her.

'What a deliciously tight little thing you are Lara! And so compliant!'

The man laughed as he unhurriedly withdrew his cock then drove it into her again. The girl twisted her wrists against the ropes, jerking her arms desperately. It was clearly evident that the man's organ was so large it was as much as she could bear. The man showed no restraint though and allowing the full length of his shaft to slide into the girl he calmly fucked her, even though with her tearful eyes she was silently begging him to stop.

MacKennan adjusted his position in his chair to ease the pressure of his trapped erection. Using the remote control he paused the image on the screen and stared at it, even now still wondering at the sort of girl who enjoyed being treated in such a fashion. Well, perhaps not exactly like that, he admitted with a rue smile. Lara had a pretty extreme penchant for being roughly treated but in truth MacKennan had subtly manipulated her dream, making her taste just a little more sexual torment and pain than she might have wanted. Still, the truth was that she had wanted to dream something like this and he had merely taken her a little further than she might have done on her exploration of her submissive nature. Keying in a few more numbers he replaced it with another image. Whilst his client had been asleep, MacKennan had secretly filmed her whilst he had personally enjoyed her body whilst she had been in a drug-controlled sleep.

On a leather couch under a bank of green lights lay a sleeping girl. She looked almost identical to the girl who MacKennan had just been watching except that her arms were perhaps a little less well muscled and her breasts while generous were not as large. Doctor MacKennan and two nurses were stood over the girl whose slender body was covered only by a white towelling robe. There were fibre-optic wires taped to the girl's wrists and neck. The two nurses carefully removed the wires from one wrist, slid the sleeping girl's arm out from her towelling robe and then reapplied the wires. They then did the same with her other arm and with their patient still asleep they calmly opened her towelling robe exposing, her whole naked body. With the Doctor stood watching, the nurses proceeded to gently lift the sleeping girls arms gently back above her head. Rubber cuffs were then fastened around her wrists and fine cords clipped to them. The cords were thread through concealed rings at the top corners of the couch and as they were drawn tight the girl's arms were edged a little higher and further apart. She did not wake though and the nurses proceeded to spread and secure her legs in an identical fashion.

The doctor began fingering her nipples, delicately at first then more assertively, coaxing them to a state of erection before instructing the nurses to 'peg them'. Small steel clasps were clipped to her nipples and although the sleeping girl moaned faintly and her arms slid across the leather couch as much as the restraints allowed, she did not wake. Adhesive tape was then pressed across Lara's mouth and the rear section of the bench lowered, leaving her rump just balanced over the edge. The doctor then stood at the end of the couch and unfastening his trousers he withdrew his tumescent cock. It was as unnaturally large as the man's in the previous dream sequence. Calmly he slid his cock into the sleeping girl's sex.

MacKennan sighed and stood up, switching off the tape he locked away the file on Lara Lustral and left his office. Taking a lift at the end of the corridor, he pressed a button marked "Basement Two". In a few seconds the lift door glided open to reveal a plain, white tiled corridor ending in a smoked glass door. Behind the glass door stood a man, dark suited and idly leafing through a magazine. MacKennan punched in a security code and a yellow light flashed on the doors electronic lock. The other man keyed in a number on the lock on his side and a second yellow light started flashing along side the first. He then keyed in a second number and the lift door behind them slid shut and a red light lit up above the lift door.

'Lift secure. One in the corridor, Doctor MacKennan.'

Whilst the man spoke into a microphone attached to lapel of his suit jacket, MacKennan knew the security precautions were excessive but he was taking no chances. Of course the highly valuable computer main frame, which he'd developed was housed behind this layer of protection, so the security was easily explained to the curious. However, the real money making side of his business was here too. Well out of sight and closely guarded because it was totally criminal.

The smoked glass door slid silently open. MacKennan stepped through and the door glided shut behind. Only by glancing at its edge, as it was momentarily open was its strength revealed: four centimetres thick bulletproof glass.

'Where's Jemma?'

'In Discipline I believe, Doctor.'

MacKennan nodded and making his way past a door marked "Office – Security Cleared Persons Only" he strode purposefully down the corridor past further doors marked "A", "B" and "C" until he reached a door marked with a simple "D". He keyed a number into the door lock and the door glided open. Inside, a metre beyond him was another door. Once he had stepped inside and he'd closed the first door, the second door slid open automatically. MacKennan walked into the room and smiled at the girl who had only a few weeks previously come to the Dreamscape Institute as a prospective new client.

'Hello Jemma, how are we feeling today?'

Dangling from two fine ropes that were clipped to broad leather cuffs around her slender wrists, a blonde haired girl hung from her outstretched arms, her bare feet just touching the floor. The girl looked forlornly at him, tears running down her pretty face as she shook her head abjectly.

'Something the matter my dear?'

The girl groaned in response, unable to speak because of a ball-gag whose crimson sphere filled her mouth, forcing her jaws acutely wide.

MacKennan stood before the girl and gazing at her, smiled with satisfaction. The nipples of her pert little breasts were erect and glistening and he knew what effect that the gel they had been smeared with would be having on her. He walked slowly around his tethered victim, noting the red whip lines across her back and then he saw the flared end of a butt plug protruding from between her taut buttocks which also bore several crimson whip marks. Putting his thumb tip against the end of the rubber plug he could feel the vibrations from the device ripple through his hand. Having become pleasantly aroused from watching the tapes of Lara Lustral he had determined that he would take his time and enjoy himself with his latest acquisition. Now, the sight of the distressed and helpless Jemma was deliciously intoxicating only too much so. He could have taken as long with her as it pleased him, he had planned to subject her to a slow and excruciating hour of torment but now he suddenly found that his self-restraint had all but evaporated. The sight of the helpless girl tethered before him was too much and he quickly unzipped his trousers and drew out his cock.

He was achingly hard and aroused after watching the film of Lara Lustral and his mind was full of what he wanted to do with the young woman who had just visited him. Serena Fairfax would be next but until he had her under his control he would have to satisfy himself with Jemma.

'It's alright now darling Jemma, I'm here to look after you.'

As he spoke MacKennan unfastened the strap that was tightly buckled at the girl's nape then he eased the ball free from her mouth. The girl was too breathless to speak at first and stroking his hands down her bare flanks he could feel her trembling.

'Have they left you like this for very long?' MacKennan soothed.

'Yes…yes…'the girl sighed, her voice was ragged and husky and when MacKennan moved his hand up to gather the swell of her right breast, she sighed appreciatively, her back arching.

'Poor Jemma, you must be feeling so aroused…'

MacKennan lightly trapped the girl's swollen nipple between a finger and thumb drawing a deep groan from her. The ointment that had been smeared across her nipples was Gelphax, a potent sexual stimulant used in small quantities in arousal creams. MacKennan though had illegally bought it in its pure concentration and one of his nurses had smeared some on the girl's nipples. Applied to a girl's sex it would bring her swiftly to intense orgasm. On her nipples though it would simply keep the victim acutely aroused for several hours until the effect slowly wore off. He knew that Jemma had been tied and subject to the gel for over an hour now. Combined with the persistent vibrations rippling through her body from the butt plug she had been kept teetering on the edge of a climax all that time. All it would have taken to make her orgasm would be a little stimulation of her sex, but this had been denied to her for nearly an hour and now the girl was desperate for sexual gratification.

'Please Doctor MacKennan, make me come…'Jemma pleaded as soon as she had recovered her breath.

'Is that what you want Jemma? Would you like it if I fucked you?'

'Yes… oh, yes…'

The girl nodded urgently, dragging her arms down against the cords that held her suspended and twisting her lithe body in an attempt to see the man who was stood behind her.

'But you know Jemma that your little pussy is really too small for my cock, last time I fucked you I seem to recall you were soon begging me to stop because I was too big for you.'

MacKennan glanced down at the suspended girl's body. Her young breasts were delightfully pert, the erect nipples fully swollen and shiny from the gel.

'I don't care… got to come…please…'the girl begged.

'And you're certain your pussy would like to feel my cock deep inside it?'

MacKennan stroked his hand down the girl's thigh and as she twisted suspended from the ropes he saw her young sex, the pink lips distended and her clitoris hard with arousal.

'Yes…yes…'

'Very well then, since you've asked so nicely.'

MacKennan flicked the switch at the base of the butt plug to stop it vibrating and then sliding his finger tips around the flared base he pulled it from the girl's arse. Grasping the girl's hips from behind MacKennan pulled her backwards until his hardened cock slid between the globes of her little arse.

'Uhh, yes…'the girl sighed.

Wiggling her rump in encouragement Jemma gave a contented moan as MacKennan found her vulva with the tip of his massive shaft and guided it into her moist folds. As the head of his cock sank into the girl's sex she groaned feverishly, then as his shaft began to slide deeper into her, her sighs of pleasure trailed away and she began to whimper plaintively.

'Uhh…too big…gently…please...'

'Hush now… keep still Jemma, there's a good girl.'

MacKennan pushed his shaft a little further into the tightness of the girl's sex.

'Too much…'she sighed breathlessly. 'No more…please…'

'You want me to stop? Are you sure?'

MacKennan withdrew his cock, glancing down at its glistening length, slick with girl's arousal juices. He knew she was now so hopelessly aroused she'd beg him to fuck her even though he was too big for her comfort.

'Shall I stop then Jemma?'

As he posed the question he rubbed his cockhead back into the slick folds of her vulva and the girl moaned uncontrollably.

'Well…'he prompted.

He'd make her beg for it again and this time after she'd consented, just to make things even more exquisite for himself and even more agonising for her, he would jam the butt plug back into her arse so that her sweet little pussy found it even harder to accommodate his cock once he drove it inside her.

'Well Jemma, shall I stop?' he asked impatiently.

'No…no…just…'Jemma shook her head despondently, 'I need to come… please just make me come!'

'If you want to come darling you have to let me fuck you. No pain no gain. It's your choice. So, how badly do you need to come?'

Jemma hung her head back and gave a defeated sigh.

'Well?' MacKennan prompted.

'Fuck me. I want it,' the girl admitted shamefully.

MacKennan smiled to himself and guided his tumescent cock head slowly back into her sex. With less than half his cock buried in her pussy, the girl was soon trying to pull her body away. MacKennan grinned with amusement.

'Something the matter darling Jemma?' He asked sarcastically.

'No...'Jemma gasped before biting down on her lip to stifle a cry as he pushed his cock still deeper into her.

'Hush now... nearly there...'

MacKennan smiled sadistically and allowed a little more of his massive cock to slide into the girl's body. He glanced down and grinned maliciously as he saw that now only a little more than half of the length of his member now embedded in her sex. Jemma was panting hard.

'There... I'm right inside you and doesn't that feel good?'

'Uhh...yes...'the girl sighed.

'Do you want to change your mind Jemma?'

The girl shook her head negatively. She was breathing in short urgent gasps and as he slowly withdrew his shaft a little she glanced up at her tethered wrists and outstretched arms.

'I didn't hear your answer Jemma; do you want to change your mind?'

'No,' the girl answered petulantly.

MacKennan withdrew his cock completely then allowed the massive head of his shaft to nudge again against the girl's sex. Jemma moaned and tried to thrust her rump backwards in encouragement.

'So you really want this then Jemma? You want me to shaft you don't you, your desperate for it aren't you?'

'Yes... please do it!'

'Do you promise not complain once I start fucking you, then?'

'I promise...'the girl answered breathlessly.

'Would you like it if I gag you again then you can't tell me you've changed your mind, can you?' MacKennan suggested, both his hands stroking down the ribcage of the petite girl who dangled helplessly before him. Jemma sighed but said nothing. He knew what was going through her mind: last time she had been desperate for it but once he'd started to fuck her she was soon begging him to stop. Now, once more she was aching for sexual gratification but all too aware of what exquisite pain would come with it.

MacKennan smiled and moved one hand up to caress the swell of one of her breasts. Lightly trapping her nipple between a finger and thumb he drew a gasp of appreciation from her.

'Well?' he prompted again, 'Would you like me to gag you?'

'Yes...' Jemma sighed, nodding her head.

'Keep still then, there's a good girl.'

As he spoke MacKennan took the ball gag from his pocket. Pressing his body close against her naked back he brought the rubber ball up against her mouth and held it against her lips.

'Come on now Jemma, open wide, you'll not get too come unless you let me give you a good shafting.'

With only a slight hesitation the girl opened her mouth and allowed him to press the rubber sphere between her jaws until it filled her mouth.

'Uhhh...'

'Good girl...'

The girl's breathing was faster now. He stroked her hair reassuringly.

'Sure you want to be gagged?'

His cock gave a twitch of eager anticipation as she gave a consenting nod and he drew the leather straps across her cheeks and a second later had them buckled snugly just above her nape.

MacKennan laughed softly as he pressed the butt plug up against crater of her anus. Jemma shook her head urgently to signal her objection but ignoring her MacKennan mercilessly rammed the butt plug into her arse.

'Right then, now it's time for that shafting you're so desperate for.'

Wide-eyed with alarm, Jemma gave a muffled, plaintive groan as she felt the head of his cock plough slowly into her pussy.

'There's a good girl... now keep still.'

Holding the girl's slender waist he drew her back onto his cock. As the head sank into her he immediately felt the increased tightness of her sex caused by the butt plug filling her anal passage. She pulled ineffectually against the cords that held her arms outstretched above her head and began struggling as his cock sank progressively deeper into her helpless body.

'Does that feel good Jemma? You want it so badly don't you?'

MacKennan smiled with satisfaction; half of his massive organ was now buried in the young girl's tight little pussy and she was twisting frantically in his grasp. Though the rubber gag all but silenced her he could just hear her incoherent pleading. He caught hold of her hair and drew her head back so that he could see the expression of wide-eyed alarm on her pretty face. Pushing with his hips he ground the remainder of his iron hard shaft into her.

'Poor Jemma, would you like me to stop?'

The girl looked balefully at him but when she shook her head it was negatively and he grinned with satisfaction. The horny little bitch wanted the pain as much as the pleasure… well, that suited him perfectly.

Jemma gave a muffled sigh, tears filling her eyes as he pulled his shaft almost completely from her. MacKennan then rammed his cock back into the girl right to the hilt so that his balls slapped against her pert rump.

'Nnnhh!'

Withdrawing his shaft again he quickly ploughed it once more into her defenceless young body.

All Jemma could do was writhe and twist helplessly. Barely louder than the faint sound of the creaking leather of the cuffs around her wrists, MacKennan could just make out the girl's muffled crying. How pleasing a beautiful young girl looked, he thought, her eyes brimming with tears and her pretty mouth filled and silenced by a ball gag.

Chapter Two

Serena had chatted with Lara several times about the other girl's experiences at the Dreamscape Institute shortly after Lara had starting going there. It was amazing, she had told Serena, though when pressed to elaborate, Lara had become deliberately vague.

Serena had first met Lara at a party a couple of years ago and although they had known each other only this short length of time their friendship had quickly developed and deepened. They soon became inseparable party animals and their collective stunning looks assured them a healthy supply of fit young men to satisfy their insatiable sexual appetites. Less than a month after they'd first met, one Sunday morning Serena had woken up in Lara's bed.

Between the two girls naked bodies was a young man and Serena smiled as the memories of the previous nights antics came back to her. Serena had scarcely started kissing the sleeping man's flaccid cock before Lara woke and joined in. As Serena licked and sucked his cock back to a fresh state of hardness, waking the man in the process, Lara sat behind her and reaching between her legs began to masturbate her pussy. Serena was soon madly excited and encouraging the young man to fuck her senseless.

'Take her from behind while I hold her still,' Lara ordered the young man, snatching hold of Serena's wrists and pulling her arms out in front of her. With Serena still kneeling, the man clambered eagerly behind her. Serena gazed at the older girl sat before her, whose hands tightly pinned her own wrists against the bed. She felt the man's hands coax apart her buttocks and as she and Lara locked eyes the man slid his cock easily into her aching pussy. Moments later Serena was panting wildly and then her orgasm whipped through her, delicious as ever and heightened by the man continuing to pound his cock back and forth into her throbbing sex.

After Lara had watched the man come she separated him

from her friend, sucked his cock to stop his erection subsiding and told him to take her straight away. Serena lay watching Lara as the man rode her and once Lara was satisfied she caught hold of Serena's wrist again and led her from the bed, leaving the man without so much as backward glance. Ushering Serena into her walk-in shower she then rubbed liquid soap lovingly over every inch of her body before dropping to her knees and under the cascading jets of hot water, she bathed Serena's exquisitely tender pussy with skilful strokes of her tongue until Serena was forced to rest her back against the tiles and moan softly as she was brought to another delicious climax.

'Don't you feel sorry for people who have to spend their lives doing crap like work instead of being able to enjoy themselves everyday?' Serena asked dreamily.

'No!' Lara laughed contemptuously. 'I never give it a thought. Delta and Beta class scum are meant to work and Alpha girls are meant to be able to laze around at home all day pleasuring themselves!'

'So do you like to pleasure yourself?' teased Serena.

Lara laughed and pushed Serena back against the tiles of the shower wall. Her eyes sparkled with excitement as she spoke.

'I've found a new way of pleasuring myself,' she announced cryptically.

'Well?' Serena demanded impatiently.

'Have you heard of the Dreamscape Institute?'

'No... what is it?' Serena asked, gazing down at the other girl's magnificent breasts and feeling a pang of jealousy, even though her own were better than most.

'I started going there last week... the experience is unbelievable.'

That had been some weeks previously. The last time Lara had spoken to her about the Dreamscape Institute was by phone early one morning. She had announced that she was going back to see Doctor MacKennan later that day.

Cryptically she had said that she knew she was going to get what was coming to her, but that was what she wanted. Just before she put the phone down, Lara had laughed and told her that whatever happened to her it didn't matter as it was all in her imagination anyway. She hadn't seen her since.

With those words still echoing in her head, Serena walked into the reception foyer of the Institute and announcing to the receptionist that she had an appointment with Doctor MacKennan, she found a reclining seat of soft leather beside a small fountain flanked by high palm trees. Thirty feet above her the domed glass roof gave the impression of a beautiful cloudless summer's day. This was an illusion though created by a weather simulator. She had walked in from a chill autumn morning, grey and damp. Within the Institute though it was always hot and sunny and to enhance the tropical ambience, artificial parrots of stunning reds and greens, flew overhead between the trees.

'Serena Fairfax, good morning to you.'

The Doctor had appeared silently from behind her, his approach masked by the giant ferns and exotic trees that dotted the spacious marble foyer.

'Good morning Doctor.'

Serena stood up and shook hands.

The man was tall and though perhaps thirty years her senior she found herself wondering briefly what he might be like in bed. He was not unattractive and she sensed he had a quiet but forcefully assertive side to his character that she would probably like. Serena liked her men hard and forceful, like her sex and as she followed the Doctor across the foyer and down an opulently decorated corridor, she idly fantasised about letting him fuck her. As he led her into his office she glanced at the broad expanse of his mahogany desk and imagined herself bent at the waist, face down over the desk as he took her impatiently from behind. All she would need to do was give him a few encouraging signals and she knew like every man she'd had, he would be unable to keep his hands off her slender, young body.

'I've been giving some thought to what you said yesterday Miss Fairfax.'

'Serena, call me Serena, please.'

The man nodded, gesturing for her to sit down. Leaning back in his leather chair he smiled then he glanced down at a slim file that was the only item on his desk.

'My problem though,' his smile became apologetic, 'is that I have to respect my clients' confidentiality. It would be quite improper for me to allow anyone else to view the recording that the computer makes of a client's dreams. You appreciate that?'

'Yes,' Serena nodded.

'What I could suggest is that I admit you for a session at the Institute but when we link you up the L2 Computer which runs the dreamscapes, I could pre-program the computer with the landscape scenario that was the setting for Lara's dreams.'

'You mean...' Serena licked her lips expectantly, her pulse suddenly quickening.

'When you go to sleep, in your dream you will find yourself in the place where Lara was when she was dreaming. You could then search for any clues that might help you and you'd remember them when you woke.'

'And it would work?' Serena asked suddenly incredibly excited at the prospect of not only getting a chance of experiencing what Lara had talked so enthusiastically about but to actually be able to follow in the footsteps of her imagination. A dozen questions poured into her consciousness and leaning forward she blurted out the first things that had come to mind.

'What would it cost? Would I find Lara's dreams persona there? Could I talk with her? Can I control the dream? Can anything go wrong because it isn't my dream?'

The man opposite her smiled disarmingly and shook her head. When he told her the cost she gave a dismissive gesture to reassure him that such a small amount of money was of course irrelevant. Very briefly it occurred to her that his fee for one session was nearly as much as a Delta person earned in a year but for Serena it represented no more than what she might spend on cosmetics or clothes in a month.

'Would you meet your friend? Well, you would have to catch her up, if you see what I mean? She is several weeks ahead of you and moving through four dimensions. I think it would be a challenge and I'm not even sure of the correct answer. Let's wait and see, shall we?'

'Oh, Doctor MacKennan, this would be fantastic! When could I try? Surely the sooner…'

'Alright, I'll organise it for you as soon as I can,' the man laughed. 'But don't you think you should have a taste of what the Dreamscape is really like under normal circumstances first?'

'But why? Is it necessary?'

The man shrugged ambivalently. 'I think it would be good if you had an idea of what to expect.'

'Okay, sure. When?'

'You're a very keen young lady, aren't you?'

'Very,' Serena held the man's gaze for a lingering moment with a smile that she knew was suggestive if not downright provocative. Well, she didn't care, she'd guessed this man fancied her and if she let him think that she might just reward him for being so obliging to her requests, that was fine by her!

'Now, I don't have my next client until midday so if you'd like we could give you a session now.'

'Okay, that would be fantastic.'

'Follow me then and I'll talk you through what to expect on the way.'

Serena followed the man out of his office and down another corridor.

'Well, this is where it all happens.'

MacKennan stepped aside allowing Serena a view of the room they had reached. A broad couch dominated the centre of the room. Directly above the couch was a bank of fluorescent strip lights under a sheet of dark glass. To one side of the couch was a simple chrome and plastic revolving chair and next to it several small trolleys loaded with equipment that gave the room the air of a dentist's surgery. Ranged across one wall was a bank of computer controls, several keyboards and facing these, two large VDU screens, each a metre wide. Serena walked into the room and circled the couch. The floor was fake mahogany and her high heels sounded loudly and the stillness as she circled the couch, licking her lips expectantly as she imagined herself lying down on it, watched over by the doctor. So this was where Lara had spent so many hours indulging in the furtive pleasure of wet dreams. Serena sensed the Doctor was watching her and she wondered what he was thinking. How deeply would she be asleep when she was dreaming, she wondered? Enough probably for him to enjoy the illicit satisfaction of touching her while she was lost in her dreamworld.

The room was pleasurably warm and she found herself looking down at the couch and thinking how inviting it looked. Gingerly she touched the shiny black material, running her hands along the edge, her fingertips exploring, her mind wondering at the possibilities that the couch offered. Perhaps if she was alone long enough with the Doctor she could get him to fuck her? Then of course he would be easier to manipulate and she fancied indulging in these delicious dreams that Lara had talked about – except why pay if she could persuade the Doctor to let her enjoy the Dreamscape Institute for free?

Smiling as she contemplated various possibilities, Serena turned a corner of the couch, her fingertips trailing the leather. Glancing up she saw the Doctor was now behind the range of computer equipment, his head bowed before a keyboard upon which she could hear him tapping buttons. She looked around the room again as she completed her circuit of the couch and was about to step away when her fingertips brushed something cool and hard. Surreptitiously she fingered the object that was just concealed below the edge of the couch, almost covered by the thick folds of padding and leather. She slipped two fingers through it and realised that it was something like a steel ring fastened to the corner of the bench. She glanced up but to her relief the Doctor was still engrossed and quickly she withdrew her hand and only just in time.

'So, shall I talk you through how this works?'

'Please.'

Serena smiled as MacKennan walked around to where she stood. He was much taller than her and now he seemed to stand a little closer to her than he had up until now. Serena was deeply conscious of how he was struggling to not let his gaze linger on the swell of her breasts. She had worn a scoop necked T-shirt, deliberately one size too small, that left her smooth, taut stomach exposed and accentuated the ripe curves of her firm breasts, so firm that there was no need for her to wear a bra so her nipples were clearly discernable pressing provocatively against the tightness of her T-shirt. Her dark areolas were visible beneath the fine white fabric and as she breathed she knew the gentle rise and fall was a magnet for any man who strayed as close to her as the Doctor now stood.

'As soon as one of the nurses is here, they will help you undress. For the session you'll wear just a towelling robe. We have to stick electrodes to you, on the arms and neck usually which will connect you to the computer.'

The Doctor smiled reassuringly and Serena nodded to show she was happy with this explanation. She was in truth secretly thrilled at the excuse to shed her clothes and knew how tempting her naked body would be for him while she was asleep and wearing nothing more than a bathrobe.

'The computer will use electrode impulsing to stimulate or repress certain endocrine glands which will mirror the frequency variations of your dream. We will in effect make your body feel itself at one with your imagination and this will give your dream its authenticity. To make sure you sleep at the right depth to dream we administer a drug called emothome. Normally you only dream during the REM sleep period. This actually lasts a very short length of time just before you wake. We use emothome to suspend you in this condition.'

As the man was speaking the door slid open and a nurse walked in. Startling pretty and dressed in a starched white blouse and short, white PVC skirt, the blonde girl walked confidently across to where Serena stood, a neatly folded white towelling robe held before her.

'I will leave you with Suzi for a few minutes so you can undress then we'll get started,' MacKennan announced. 'For the first session you can create your own dream then for the second session if you're ready, I'll programme the computer with Lara's background dreamscape.'

A few minutes later and with the robe wrapped around her, Serena was lying back on the couch. Above her the strip lights flickered into life and bathed the centre of the room in a pale green light.

'Just relax your arm while I connect these to you.'

As the nurse worked Serena lay watching her, her excitement mounting. What was she to dream, she wondered? She had been so preoccupied with her mission to find out what had happened to Lara that she hadn't given any thought to what she herself might like to dream. The faint sound of the door sliding open drew her attention. It was Doctor MacKennan and seeing her he smiled. Again that faintly sinister smile, but perhaps Serena's imagination was just getting to fevered. She glanced sideways at the wires taped to her wrist. The nurse was applying another to her neck. She felt the sticky plaster being smoothed against her skin and the faint hardness of the slender wire just pricking her skin.

'This isn't going to hurt at all, is it?' she demanded nervously.

'Relax Serena; if you experience any discomfort it will be purely self-induced. You are about to dream whatever you care to fantasise about. You can dream whatever you like. Anything you feel will be only because you want to feel it.'

MacKennan smiled reassuringly, nodded to his nurse, who was now seated bedside the couch as he turned and crossed to the array of computer equipment that was ranked against the wall adjacent to the door.

'Suzi, administer the sedative please.'

It won't hurt at all, unless I want it… Serena thought, as she lay gazing up at the soft green lights. She recalled the feel of the last man who had fucked her and how he had tightly grasped her slim little waist as he'd shafted her. She enjoyed the feeling of being held like that… wriggling ineffectually in his powerful grasp as he'd taken her from behind, Serena bent doggy fashion and obligingly submissive as he had shoved his cock impatiently up her achingly aroused pussy.

'Now Serena, think of something pleasurable to dream. Imagine whatever you like, whatever you desire. I'm going to transport you to the place of your dreams, so you may as well choose wherever you like.'

Serena gazed up at the pale green lights and tried to relax. Her mind was racing. She was still wondering about what had happened to Lara; she was trying to imagine where Lara might have dreamt of; she was frantically wondering where she should think about and already she was starting to feel drowsy. Her mind darted between numerous recent pleasurable times she'd enjoyed; places she knew and loved but she couldn't decide where she really wanted to be in her own dream. She'd thought about this briefly last night in bed and the excitement of the endless possibilities had kept her awake for hours. Finally in a desperate bid to get to sleep, she'd picked up a book. Something she seldom bothered with, except perhaps when she was feeling unwell and was spending a day in bed alone resting.

'Serena, you need to try to focus your mind before you fall asleep.'

The Doctor's voice sounded as if it was coming from a long way off and Serena knew that already her eyelids were too heavy to open again. She was being induced to fall asleep.

She was too tired now to try to think clearly about her possibilities; all the dreams she had imagined indulging in were now beyond her reach. Her mind felt leaden and as if it was being drawn down and down into a blackness. She struggled to climb back into her consciousness step by heavy step but she could only bring herself back to lying in her bed reading last night. Fragments of what she had read came back to her: the novel had been set in the past and was about a teenage girl from a poor family who had been sent into the service of a rich family.

Serena had bought it when she was a teenager, it seemed to echo fragments of her family's history and it was liberally laced with passages that described the heroine's erotic adventures in enough detail to satisfy the already sexually ravenous appetite that the teenage Serena had developed. Reading it late the previous night though, she had found it hard to be patient and work her way through it page by page. In places the spine of the book was well bent back with certain pages well thumbed as in the past, as a teenager, Serena had lain in bed reading it and imagining herself in the heroine's predicament. So it had been all too easy to turn again to the passages that aroused her and slipping a hand under her duvet she had quickly brought herself to a pleasurable orgasm. Just like old times, she had thought, discarding the book and curling up, a pleasurable glow suffusing her satisfied body.

CHAPTER THREE

The abrupt jolt of the carriage drawing to a halt woke Serena and quickly she nervously peered out of the window. A row of stone cottages faced her. She leant across the carriage seat and peered out of the opposite side. A long, whitewashed stone building with a roof of grey slate stood alone, a painted wooden sign swinging wildly in the wind over its low front door, proclaimed 'The Filly' and though the paint work was old and cracked, Serena could clearly make out a man in riding breeches and boots stood whip in hand, grasping the reins of the pony while a young girl stood watching, wide eyed in alarm as the man made a threatening gesture with his raised whip. Serena was unsure from the way the scene was painted whether the man was actually about to whip the pony or the young girl and she was still pondering this when the near toothless grinning face of the coachman's boy appeared suddenly before her.

'This is it then!' he bawled through the glass of the window before his upside down head disappeared from view and a clattering above her served as the prelude to the horrible grinding noise of her trunk being dragged half off the carriage roof.

Alarmed at the prospect of all her worldly belongings being scattered in the mud as the oaf pushed her trunk from the carriage, Serena flung herself out with as much speed as her long dress allowed. The rain was coming in horizontal sheets and the wind snapped and tugged at her skirt, bonnet and shawl as she struggled to keep her feet on the slippery cobbles.

'Be careful with that!' she ordered which as much severity as she could manage. Being a timid eighteen-year old daughter of parents whose humble work placed them almost at the bottom of the social scale of Edwardian England, Serena's voice sounded woefully pathetic and pleading and the young lad just laughed as he jumped down from the carriage and dragged her trunk down, allowing it to land with a sharp crack on the rain washed cobbles.

'End of the line then Miss. Take care now, bit wild these parts!'

With a harsh laugh that disintegrated into a hacking cough the youth clambered back onto the coach and with a flick of his whip the driver urged his horses forward leaving Serena standing beside her trunk in the middle of the deserted street.

Serena glanced despondently around her. It was already dusk and the rain was coming down in torrents and here she was stranded most likely because the coach had been delayed and she had undoubtedly missed the transport her new employer had arranged for her. Sir Hugh de Breville's secretary had written informing her that the Exeter to Plymouth carriage would have brought her to Farleyhampton by three thirty. He would have a pony and trap sent to meet her at 'The Filly' and bring her on to Sir Hugh's shooting lodge high upon the moor. Now it was well after five and probably nearer six and there was no sign of any pony and trap and she was well and truly stuck, with not even enough money in her purse to secure a room for a night at the inn. With her waterlogged clothes dragging at her like a leaden weight, Serena grasped the leather handle at one end of the trunk with both hands and began to drag it across the cobbles towards the sanctuary of the inn.

'Quite what do you think you are doing?'

Serena swung around at the first interrogative sound of the imperious voice. Pushing her damp hair clear of her eyes she saw a tall, young man standing not three yards behind her. He was dressed in riding breeches, tailcoat and a hooded cloak that fell to the spurs of his riding boots.

'You'll be the Fairfax girl I should venture?' the man said, looking her up and down.

'Yes… Serena Fairfax, are you…?'

'Edward de Breville. Follow me, I'll instruct someone to fetch your trunk.'

'Thank you sir.'

'You can reserve that title for my father. You need only call me Master. Understood?'

'Yes, I'm sorry sir,' Serena apologised, 'I mean Master.'

Once inside the inn the young man swung around and looked her critically up and down.

'Shut the door fast, this place is cold enough inside as it is. So you are new to domestic service and your father is a blacksmith?'

'Yes, Master.'

'An honest enough occupation.'

The young man snatched up a small brass bell and gave it an impatient ring.

'I let my valet off to get himself a pint and some supper. We had expected to be back home by now.'

The young man stepped a little closer to Serena and looked down critically at her as she stood shivering, a pool of water collecting at her feet.

'You look very wet girl.'

As he spoke the young man lifted Serena's shawl away from her and letting the sodden garment drop to the floor he gazed at the damp bodice that clung across her cleavage. Serena's breathing quickened and for a moment she was too shocked by the man's brazenness to respond. Then before she could find suitable words to try to defend her honour, distraction came in the form of a wheezing old lady in a dirty grey apron whose white hair was drawn back in a severe bun and whose fat bow legs finished in clogged feet that heralded her approach with a scraping and clattering on the inn's flagstone corridor.

'You rang, Master de Breville?' The woman made a poor attempt at a curtsey and shot a curious glance at Serena as she spoke.

'Tell my man that there is a trunk lying outside that is to be fetched upon the trap. And quick about it. We leave immediately.'

* * *

By the time they left the village of Farleyhampton it was utterly dark. The lad driving the trap obviously knew the road well enough for he encouraged the pony with his whip to hurry as best she could up the winding lane that grew ever steeper as they climbed from the valley and up onto the moor.

'And how far is it to Highmost Romanway?' Serena asked as they at last reached a level stretch of road and the precipitous climb seemed finally behind them.

'Six miles. We'll be there within an hour, God willing and the devil permitting.'

Serena saw Master Edward de Breville exchange a mischievous glance with his manservant.

'And I understand that your family use the house for only a few weeks each year?' enquired Serena.

'Just for the hunting season. My grandfather built the hunting lodge on the site of an old farm that was made with stones from a Roman signal station. The hill behind the hunting lodge is the highest point on the moor for miles around and the Romans had a road that crossed the moor. You can still follow it for most of the way if you know the way and don't mind getting your feet a bit wet.'

'But my mother was led to understand that you could offer me a full time position here, even though your family home is away in Oxfordshire?' said Serena.

'That is true enough,' the young man answered, 'I use the place myself often enough at other times for my own pleasure that it serves me to keep it occupied and warm.'

'But surely I would not be expected to live there alone, Master de Breville?'

'Heavens no; there is Adam who looks after the hounds and old Betty his wife who would help you. She would keep the place clean for us if she was a bit more able but she's too old now. Too old by far. If she were a horse, I'd have had her shot a year or two ago by now.'

The young man gave Serena a cold grin as he drew a hip flask from his waistcoat. After he had taken a large gulp from the silver flask, he smiled at her and as he spoke she caught the smell of whisky from his breath as he leant closer to her than she found comfortable.

'I want some fresh young girl at Highmost to welcome me. A hot bath, warm towels, a devoted servant who knows what her master expects of her. I want to be able to bring friends and for them to be well entertained. For me, Highmost is where I come to indulge myself and to escape from the dreary day-to-day nonsense of balls and recitals, dinner parties and dances. I trust you will be willing to demonstrate your devotion as a servant?'

'I should hope so, Master,' Serena answered demurely, casting a furtive glance at man sat next to her. There was, she thought, something disconcertingly suggestive about some of Master de Breville's remarks to her. The young man was handsome enough and though obviously far above her social station, Serena couldn't but help wonder whether he might have a notion of seducing her. Her mother had warned her of such possibilities, reminding her of how pretty she was and how wealthy men were wont to use young girls in their pay for their own carnal pleasure. Carnal pleasure… Serena repeated the words to herself, remembering how the man had lifted away her rain-drenched shawl and gazed so brazenly at her. He had not been the first man to do this though and Serena was well aware that her cleavage was more generous than those of most girls her age. Perhaps it would not be so bad a thing to be taken by this man; there were other girls in her home village who were her age and who had already lost their virginity and they told her that although there was some pain there was a great deal of pleasure in the act. So much so that one of her friends now couldn't help herself but eagerly sought out any willing young man as often as she could.

In the end the journey to the hunting lodge took nearer to two hours since at one point a hunting owl flew close to the carriage, startling the poor pony and sending the trap nearly off the road. The road, such it was, from the village was only stone paved for the first half a mile where it passed the Church and Rectory, thereafter it was only a dirt track. Where it crossed streams there were only fords and no bridges whatsoever and once up on the moor the track became rutted and very poor. When the owl flew into the pool of yellow light cast from the carriage lamps and the pony shied, the trap half left the track and its wheels were swiftly well stuck in the peat bog that flanked the road. It fell to the servant to climb down and push whilst Master de Breville held the reins and gave the pony a good whipping until she dragged the trap clear of the treacherous peat bog. Throughout the episode Serena sat saying nothing but watching the young man as he used the whip on the pony and remembering the sign hanging before the inn, she found herself wondering what it was in her that made her imagine that the man in the painting might have been intent on whipping the girl. What sort of imagination did she have? Serena asked herself. This was England not some Barbary land where women were perhaps treated in such fashion. She had been silly to even momentarily misinterpret the painting, she told herself as the trap resumed its journey and ahead of them in the distance the lights of their destination shone, a faint twinkling isolated against the inky blackness.

The hunting lodge of Highmost Romanway was sheltered in part from the howling winds that whipped across the high moor since it nestled in a fold between two high ridges and the house was further protected by an encircling ring of ancient rhododendrons and a few stunted trees.

The trap halted at the front door and jumping down, Edward de Breville, promptly marched into the house, whose broad front door was held open by a waiting servant in the attire of a butler. With scarcely a backward glance de Breville told Serena, " John will show you to your quarters".

The servant John aided by another young lad, who Serena guessed from his smell must have been the stable boy, carried her trunk indoors and up a twisting flight of stairs and along a corridor to a low doorway. The corridor was narrow and seemed to almost lean somewhat. The floorboards were painted dark brown and a dark red carpet runner ran the centre length of it, its frayed edges suggesting that it had been cut to serve and had once been used elsewhere. One paraffin lamp lit the corridor and the windows were shuttered against the cold night.

'This is your room. I'm in the room next on left so if you're needing anything, just knock. I'm happy to help you settle in; only just remember, one good turn deserves another.'

John's sarcastic tone did not go un-noticed on either Serena or the stable boy who sniggered until silenced by a cuff around the ear from the other youth.

'Thank you,' Serena answered as the lads closed the door behind them and left her alone.

In comparison to outside and the journey across the moor the bedroom seemed pleasantly warm, thanks to a small peat fire that was glowing merrily. There was a single bed with a simple brass bed head, a dressing table and stool, a threadbare oriental carpet in the middle of the little room and a cushioned armchair that fifty or a hundred years ago may have graced a drawing room but was now sufficiently worn out to be relegated to staff quarters. On the dressing table there was a large china bowl of water that was luke warm and a large jug and a bar of soap. Serena quickly took off her wet clothes and stripping down to just her knickers she proceeded to wash herself. There was a key in the lock of the door but it refused to turn but she reassured herself that anyone would knock first, though she couldn't imagine herself being troubled now. It must be nearly nine at night and the other servants would most likely be busy with the de Breville's dinner.

Serena had scarcely finished washing when with no more than a peremptory knock the door flew open and Edward de Breville stood regarding her, an amused grin on his face as Serena struggled to cover her chest with her arms.

'Master de Breville, please!' she begged, floundering for

words and for some piece of clothing that she might use to cover her naked body.

'Calm yourself girl.'

Stepping into her tiny room, Edward de Breville pushed the door shut behind him with the heel of his riding boot.

'But you should not...'stammered Serena, glancing across to where her trunk stood open and her dry clothes were. But already the man was between them and her and even as she tried to reprove him for his unseemly intrusion the man advanced upon her and catching hold of her wrists drew her arms away from her body so that her breasts were exposed for him.

'Very pretty and most generous for such a slender young thing, now keep still girl.'

Serena was too shocked to make any further objection as, letting go of her wrists, the man stroked the back of one hand across the swell of her breasts, his knuckles lightly brushing her nipples and sending a delicious shiver through her body.

'Stand still girl and let me look at you properly.'

Serena stood rooted to the spot as the man circled behind her, her own breathing quickening as his breath came warm against the back of her neck. When she felt him gathering her long hair with his hand she gave a plaintive whimper of nervousness but the man ignored this and with her hair grasped firmly he drew his hand down forcing her head to tilt backwards.

'You're better than I'd dared hope, Miss Fairfax.'

Serena swallowed the lump that had risen in her throat as, with his other hand, he stroked her neck and then caressed her jaw, encouraging her to open her mouth for him.

'Very good teeth and such soft lips...you're a fine example of what I look for in a servant girl. I think you are going to please me greatly Serena.'

'But sir, I don't...'

'Be silent. I wasn't speaking to you, I was merely speaking my thoughts about you and you forget your instructions already: I told you to address me as Master not as Sir. Such disobedience deserves a gentle punishment I think. Take hold of the bed railing with both hands.'

Serena glanced at the brass rails that ran between two brass posts at the foot of the bed and which matched the bed head.

'Do as I say girl!'

For a second Serena hesitated, weighing choices. If she refused he might dismiss her from his employment. What would she do then? She didn't even have any money to make the journey home. And besides, if she obeyed, then maybe he would favour her... perhaps she might even turn the situation to her advantage?

'Good girl,' commended the young man as Serena dutifully took hold of the brass rail with both hands. She was shivering with nervousness but hoped he would think it was because she had no clothes on except for her knickers. Glancing down she could see the man's booted feet close behind her and she noticed that stuck into one boot was a short riding crop.

'Now take a step away from the bed and spread your legs a little apart.'

Serena did as she was instructed, her heart hammering now with excitement. There was something deeply arousing about being disciplined in such a fashion and already her cheeks were suffused with a warm glow of eagerness and guilt at being made to behave in the way that he was demanding of her.

'Now, this is to teach you to remember your instructions!'

Slap!

'Oww!'

Serena gave a cry of alarm as the man's hand slapped down hard against her bottom. Wide eyed in alarm she looked over her shoulder at him but she did not let go of the brass rail.

'I didn't give you permission to cry out. You have to learn to take your punishment in silence!'

Again the hand smacked down on her bottom and this time even though she tried not to make any noise a chocked cry of pain escaped her lips.

'Very well…'

The man stepped closer behind her and loosening the cravat from his neck he caught hold of her chin with one hand and with the other encouraged the silk between her lips and into her mouth.

'Uuhhh…'

The sensation of the soft material being insinuated into her mouth to her shame did not revolt her but only served to heighten her arousal and docilely she allowed the man to fill her mouth with the soft folds of silk. When the next stinging blow fell across her rump her cry was well muffled. Staring down at her outstretched arms, her hands tightly holding the brass rail, Serena stood, legs trembling as three more sharp blows were delivered to her rear.

'Good girl, now don't move.'

Dutifully Serena remained quite still, her body bent forwards, her arms braced against the bed to take her weight, and her rear thrust back and her slender legs well spread as instructed. Her bottom was aching pleasantly and the sensation produced a warm glow deep inside her sex making her wonder dreamily how something that felt like punishment could feel so good. She was pondering this when something brushed her right wrist.

'Keep still,' cautioned the man, sensing she was thinking of pulling her arm away. Serena gazed down at the silk as the man wrapped it several times around her wrist and then around the brass rail she was grasping. Having knotted the material the man then produced another cravat and used this upon her other wrist in similar fashion. That he had obviously brought two spare cravats with him for such a purpose made Serena realise that this whole episode had been carefully planned. She gazed at her outstretched arms, now securely bound to the bed by the silken bonds.

'Now, the finishing touch my dear.'

Without any further warning Serena felt another length of

silk drawn firmly against her mouth and across her cheeks. Secured with a bow at her nape this cravat now kept the one in her mouth forcibly in place. Experimentally Serena tried to expel the silk from her mouth with her tongue but her efforts were quite ineffective. The man's hands stroked down her ribs from just below her arms to her waist. When she felt the string waistband of her knickers fingered experimentally she pulled urgently with her arms but the silk was tight around her wrists and there was no way she could get free now.

'Nnnnhh!'

Serena shook her head in objection as she felt the waistband of her knickers loosened and then the garment being pushed slowly down, first over the swell of her bottom and then down her thighs.

'Now let's see...'

The man's hands stroked across the swell of her rump and then his fingers slid between her legs, finding the folds of her sex wet with arousal. Serena arched her back in pleasure at the man's touch and pushed her rump back against his caress. The man laughed softly and slid his fingers deeper into her warm softness of her sex.

'Desperate for it, you wanton little trollop aren't you?'

Serena nodded shamefully in admission, the cheeks of her face redder with guilt than the cheeks of her bottom from the smacking she had just suffered.

'Well, you're going to get more than you bargained for my dear little girl. A lot more!'

Something cool and hard brushed against the inside of her thighs and looking back Serena saw that the man had drawn the short riding crop from his boot and was stroking the sensitive inside of her thigh with its tip.

'So tell me, have you been deflowered yet?'

Serena shivered nervously as the man stroked the crop tip up between her thighs until it brushed the soft lips of her sex making her arch her back involuntarily and pull with her hands against the silk ties that bound her wrists to the bedrail.

'Well, have you?' the man demanded.

Serena shook her head and the man gave a low, satisfied laugh. The cool hardness of the leather crop was stroked between the lips of her sex and then pushed a little way inside her making Serena close her legs with apprehension and struggle against the silk that held her arms bound.

'Relax… there's plenty of time for that pleasure and when the time comes I shall not be using my riding whip for such a gratifying task. Now get your legs spread again Serena!'

With a light tap against one leg and then the other Serena was encouraged to part her legs.

'Now, let's see how much discipline you can take.'

Thwack!The hard leather end of the crop struck against the softness of her left thigh just below the swell of her rump causing Serena to jerk urgently and shake her head in objection.

Thwack!

A similar blow fell against her other thigh. Serena glanced over her shoulder, tears pricking in her wide eyes as looked pleadingly at the young man. He grinned unapologetically at her and brought the crop down against her bottom.

Thwack! Thwack!

The stinging pain delivered to both curves of her luscious rear was too excruciating and Serena shook her head in objection, tears now welling up in her eyes and running down her cheeks until they soaked the silk cravat that was gagging her.

Thwack! Thwack!

Harder than the last and delivered at the very point where the rear of her thighs curved into the swell or her bottom, the sharp pain was too much for her and Serena cried out through the gag.

'Nnnh!'

Edward de Breville gave a satisfied laugh and stepping close behind her, stroked his hand across her skin where faint red marks were already starting to show. Serena flinched and tried to draw away and soon she was pressed by his body against the railings of the bed.

'There's no escaping this Miss Fairfax. So you may as well learn to find some enjoyment it. I'm sure that shouldn't be so very hard for a girl with your inclinations.'

Serena wriggled and twisted ineffectually as the man caressed her, his hand sliding around her body and closing over the swell of her breast.

'I think you were hoping all along that something like this would happen to you, weren't you?'

Fingers trapped her nipple and gently at first and then more firmly squeezed until a sharp but piquant ache from her nipple ran through her body.

'You can leave my employ in the morning if you wish. Or you can stay and learn to be my devoted serving girl. But if you stay you can expect some harsh punishment if you don't do just what I expect of you.'

The man drew the riding crop up underneath Serena's chin and tilted her head upwards a little so she was forced to look at him.

'Serve me how I want and I'll see you're well rewarded. Or leave in the morning. The choice is yours.'

The man took a step back and Serena tensed herself in nervous anticipation of another blow from the riding crop.

Thwack!

The pain shot from her achingly tender rump through her body bringing fresh tears to her eyes.

'Do you want to stay?'

Serena gazed trembling at her outstretched arms, her slim wrists bound with the silk the brass bed railing. Her legs were trembling uncontrollably but worse, to her shame she realised her sex was aching with a need to be touched again.

Thwack!

'Well girl, do you want to stay and submit yourself to my demands?'

Serena nodded affirmatively and was rewarded by a scornful

and triumphant laugh from behind her.

'Good girl…'

The hard end of the whip brushed between her legs and instinctively she drew her thighs together.

'No, I want your legs spread Serena… come on now, do as you're told.'

The end of the whip tapped encouragingly against the soft inside of her thighs and dutifully Serena spread her legs. Her reward was to feel the man's hand touch the base of her spine and then slide down between the swells of her buttocks until his fingertips slid into the moist folds of her sex.

'Mmmm…'Serena sighed through the gag as she felt the man's fingers push into her sex.

'You'd like it if I fucked you wouldn't you?'

Shamefully Serena nodded, glancing over her shoulder to look with her wide eyes at the man. The silk covering her mouth was wet with saliva and her cheeks were damp with tears. The man pushed his fingers a little further into her and she gave a muffled cry of pleasure.

'Well, if you take your punishment without complaint then I may just give you the reward you're desperate for. Now bend over!' he ordered, withdrawing his hand and taking a step back.

Serena responded without hesitation and waited for the next blow from the riding crop.

Thwack!

'Uuhh…'

Thwack!

Dragging her arms backwards the silk tightened about her wrists and held her trapped.

Thwack!

'Nnnhh!'

Thwack!

The stinging sensation of the riding crop falling hard upon her tender rump brought the tears flowing down her cheeks but even as she twisted ineffectually against the silk bonds she knew that deep down she was glad that she couldn't escape. Each blow was exquisitely painfully and each blow made her young sex ache more and more with a pleasurable intensity she'd never known before.

Chapter Four

MacKennan smiled to himself as he watched the large visual display screen that recreated so perfectly the dreamscape that his client was experiencing. Serena Fairfax seemed well suited to the role of servant girl in the England of 1905. He wondered how much more well suited she would be to the role of sex slave in one of the Barbarian nations of 2027? He glanced across to the softly lit couch that dominated the centre of the room. His new client lay sleeping under the pale green lights, there was little to indicate her erotic dream except perhaps for the soft sheen of perspiration on her smooth skin and the fact that her luscious lips were parted fractionally and as her head tossed from side to side she made faint sighing noises.

Beside the couch sat one of his nurses, monitoring the client's vital signs and the levels of drugs in her blood stream. The emothome would could her asleep until they chose to reduce the level. MacKennan always told his female clients that the drug would keep them dreaming for up to an hour and then they would naturally have the opportunity to wake up. The truth was quite different. If he were enjoying the situation the client had got herself in, he would top up the emothome level and keep her forcibly held in her dream. Invariably he found that if the woman had chosen to have an erotic dream he could introduce the element of her forced submission and the client would soon be coming back to the Institute for further sessions. Of course every girl had her own subconscious idea of how roughly they wanted to be treated but by manually interfering with the computer programme he could steer the client's dream to suit his own ends. It was only a logical progression beyond making the woman in her dreams a willing submissive, to conditioning the woman in reality into becoming a dutiful submissive. Whilst he might be guilty of abduction, in his defence if the case ever arose, MacKennan had secretly taped confessions from all of the girls he had sold into slavery, that they wanted to be subjected to what he had forced them to endure.

Leaving the computer control desk, MacKennan went across to the couch to inspect the dreaming Miss Fairfax. He exchanged a conspiratorial glance with Zara, his nurse. Serena Fairfax looked deliciously vulnerable as she lay dreaming. The girl was quite petite, very slim and delicate limbed. Her skin was tanned a rich olive brown and her long dark red hair spilled across the black padding of the couch, framing her pretty face. The white robe just reached her knees and confident because of the level of emothome in her blood that she would not wake, MacKennan calmly unknotted the tie at her waist and loosened the robe, until it was drawn far enough apart to reveal a pair of perfectly shaped and quite generous breasts, with wide dark areolas and pert, dark brown nipples.

'Very pretty.'

MacKennan drew the towelling robe further apart, exposing the girl's slender waist and then revealing the thatch of dark hair that nestled between her shapely thighs. Lightly touching the exposed sex lips he smiled when he found they were wet with arousal. Lightly trapping her clitoris between thumb and finger he stroked the little erection of flesh until it distended and glistened invitingly with slickness. The sleeping girl murmured softly in her sleep and her limbs shifted a little, her legs slithering across the couch padding and one of her arms prescribing a crescent above her head, her fingers unconsciously tightening a hold upon the edge of the soft padding. MacKennan ran his thumb down the warm valley between the folds of her vulva and the girl gave another moan and her slender neck arched a little.

'She seems a pretty willing submissive, doesn't she?' MacKennan gave a satisfied nod as he pushed his thumb deeper into the girl's sex and let the rest of his palm settle across the thatch of dark hair between her legs.

'I have to say I feel rather tempted to fuck her right now.'

'Do you think that's wise, Doctor?' the nurse looked questioningly at him.

'You think I'm getting too impatient?'

'She is a very petite girl and unless well prepared she might find you too much. Don't you think a little time spent conditioning her… some Gelphax perhaps? A trial run in her dreamscape maybe, to see how she responds to being fucked by a cock that's so big it makes her feel like she's being split apart!'

'Zara, you make it sound like some hardship for the bitch to suffer?' MacKennan gave a low, snide laugh. 'They all enjoy it, once they've got accustomed to the sensation.'

'And to the pain,' the nurse added dryly, glancing down at the sleeping girl and smiling maliciously.

MacKennan withdrew his thumb from the girl's sex and walked around the couch to where his nurse sat.

'Suck it darling, I know how you like the taste.'

Obeying him without the merest hesitation the nurse took his thumb between her lips and drew it into her mouth. MacKennan felt the pull of her mouth as he looked down at her wide, expectant eyes and the sensation shot to his groin making his already hardened cock throb in need and anticipation.

'Christ, I can't wait much longer…' MacKennan muttered, withdrawing his thumb from the girl's mouth and tracing a line down her throat and neck with it before caressing her breast through the fine cotton of her crisply starched white blouse.

'Would you like me to do something for you Doctor?'

The girl reached forwards and began unbuttoning his white coat. MacKennan gazed down at her blood red fingernails as they worked calmly and skilfully, freeing each button then unfastening the belt of his trousers and slowly unzipping the material from behind which his erection pressed, seemingly as hard as an iron rod.

'Your boxer shorts are a bit wet,' the girl shook her head reprovingly.

MacKennan sighed but said nothing as his nurse lifted the

waistband away from his stomach and drew the shorts down to his thighs. MacKennan watched the girl, smiling with the sweet knowledge of what she was about to do as she gazed down at his tumescent cock. His organ, genetically enhanced at a private clinic that he had shares in, was longer and much thicker than even the most naturally well endowed male. The shiny purple tip filled the girl's palm as she caressed it, wiping the fresh seepage from the eye tip with her thumb as it welled and oozed thick, translucent pre-come fluid.

'Can't you wait Doctor and take your pleasure with her?'

The nurse glanced at the sleeping girl on the couch then she lightly trailed her fingertips down the length of his cock shaft, her fingernails skimming over the taut skin and making MacKennan catch his breath.

'Can't wait… just do it Zara… please just do it, there's a good girl.'

'Certainly Doctor, it's a pleasure to be of service.'

MacKennan held his breath for a moment as his nurse leant forwards in her chair and slowly took the head of his cock into her mouth. At the same time as her lips closed around the base of the cock head and her tongue flicked across the tip, the girl's hands closed around his scrotal sac, gathered his balls between them and gently tugged them down. MacKennan sighed with pleasure. The girl held his balls firmly with one hand and with the fingernails of her other hand she stroked his shaft. MacKennan gave a deep groan. The girl, sealing her lips tightly around the rim of his cock head sucked deeply and MacKennan's orgasm was triggered. Immediately she released the pressure on his balls and using both hands massaged them, forcing the man to ejaculate copiously and fully.

'Sorry Doctor, but there was just so much, I couldn't swallow it all quickly enough,' the girl gave a sheepish grin as she glanced down at the wet streaks across the front of her white blouse.

'You'd better go and make yourself more presentable, Zara.'

'Yes Doctor MacKennan.'

Alone with the sleeping Serena, MacKennan went back to the computer display screen to see how her dream was progressing.

* * *

Serena was woken by the sounds of dogs barking excitedly and climbing out of her bed she drew the curtain back to see a landscape whitened by an overnight fall of snow. In the stable yard below half a dozen hounds were excitedly gathered around two men who were leading horses from the stables. Serena immediately recognised one as Edward de Breville and instantly the memory of how he had treated her last night came flooding back and her cheeks blushed with shame to remember how wantonly she had submitted her naked body to him and how easily she had given in to his demands. Gingerly she touched her bare bottom and winced as her fingertips found her skin still a little tender from where he had whipped her with his riding crop.

Outside the man was using the same crop to turn his horse around and encourage it out of the yard; his dogs follow close at heel. The other rider had paused, had one leg lifted high, boot against saddle as he lifted back the saddle flap and adjusted the girth. The man glanced around him having tightened the saddle girth and chanced to see Serena looking down from her window upon him. Quick though she was to let the curtain drop as she ducked back into the room, Serena still had time to see the man grin as he saw her and she wondered if he knew what had befallen her last night at his associate's hands.

That first morning passed quickly for Serena who upon finding the Housekeeper was given a series of tasks that proved occupying but none too arduous. She learnt that Sir Hugh de Breville had brought his son, daughter and half a dozen friends to the hunting lodge just a few days ago and that they planned to stay for a fortnight. There were half a dozen servants to look after them including the old couple who stayed all year at the lodge to keep the house and estate in order during the family's absence.

After Serena had washed the fire hearths in the public rooms and scrubbed the fresh wine and cigar ash stains from the marble mantle-pieces with a mixture of fine ground coal dust and lemon juice, she had to sweep the corridors and clean the brass banister rail by which time it was gone midday. The servants ate lunch together in the kitchen, the leftover cold venison of the previous night with roasted potatoes and dripping gravy with bread. The butler, who had come with the family from their estate in Oxfordshire, was so serious a person that the other servants were afraid to talk much at the lunch table but the old lady who lived all the time at the lodge did at least make some conversation with Serena.

In the afternoon she was given a basket and told to go out and gather fallen sticks and fir-cones for the fires from a stand of pine tress that stood around a ruined farmhouse a quarter of a mile distant from the lodge. And so it was that Serena was found gathering these by Edward de Breville and his friend as they returned from their day's hunting.

'Well look what we have here Jamie, the new girl.'

'Good afternoon Master,' Serena smiled nervously as the two horsemen circled her. A hundred yards behind them their handful of hounds were following, all clearly tired from a day's hard hunting across the moor. Serena looked up at the horses, whose coats were damp with sweat from their efforts. De Breville's horse had bloodied a hoof; Serena guessed from failing to jump a stone wall cleanly and the other young man's mount looked thoroughly exhausted.

'My host tells me that you're a willing lass? Very devoted and keen to please.'

The man who was speaking dismounted and looked Serena up and down. Serena cast her eyes down and stood still not knowing quite what to say or do as the young man circled her.

'Tell you what Edward, I could do with a good hot bath when I get back. Would your servant here be willing to draw me a bath and give my back a good scrubbing? I feel quite stiff after today's ride. Quite stiff indeed!'

'I'm sure Serena will gladly do anything she can to help relieve your stiffness, Jamie. Won't you Serena?'

'Yes Master,' Serena answered shyly.

The two young men laughed, de Breville's companion resuming his mount and then as their hounds caught them up they set off back to the lodge, leaving Serena alone once again.

She took her time to fill her basket with fir-cones and twigs but there was no putting off forever the return to the lodge and in truth she was excited at what might lie in store for her. Now she had time to get over the shock of being whipped by her new master, she was left with the curious realisation that there had been something deeply arousing about the treatment that he had meted out to her and she had gone to bed afterwards, dreaming about what had happened and what might happen.

In the kitchen she encountered the butler counting out silver cutlery for the dinner who told her to go upstairs to Master Edward's bedroom immediately. Before she had to ask, the man went on to give her directions as to which room this was and so Serena hurried up the back servants' stairs. A timid knock at the door was met with a prompt 'Enter'and going into the bedroom she found Edward de Breville, sat in a deep leather armchair in the bay-window, a tumbler of amber liquid in one hand and a book in the other.

'Ah, Serena, Jamie wanted you. The other maid has run him a bath but he has asked you to attend to him.'

'But Master…'

'Come now girl, don't be shy,' said de Breville, discarding his book and standing. 'It's all part of the job. Not shy of seeing a man with nothing on, are you?'

Serena looked down nervously as the young man moved closer to her. Before she could find an answer he titled her chin up with one hand and smiled at her.

'Follow me,' he said and walked briskly from the room, Serena dutifully hurrying after him.

Leading Serena into another bedroom and shutting the door behind them then turning the key in the lock, de Breville gestured to her to go through another door, which led from the room. Dutifully Serena obeyed, casting one backward glance in time to see de Breville taking the key from the locked door and sliding it into his waistcoat pocket.

The bathroom was loud with the sound of water pouring in steamy billows from brass taps into a giant bath that stood on claw feet in the middle of the room. De Breville's friend was sat on the window ledge a glass of Champagne in hand with nothing more than a towel wrapped around his waist. Lifting a bottle from a silver bucket brimming with iced water, he replenished his glass and stood up.

'Damned grateful to you Edward.'

'Think nothing of it dear chap.'

Serena glanced apprehensively over her shoulder to see her Master leaning nonchalantly in the doorframe close behind her.

'Now then girl, when was the last time you had a good hot bath?' demanded de Breville's colleague.

'Me sir? I don't know sir,' Serena stammered.

'Well Serena,' de Breville edged Serena further into the bathroom then drew the door closed behind him, 'I think it's time you had a treat. Get your clothes off girl and in you go.'

'But Master…'

'No buts about it. This is your reward for last night girl. A hot bath is something no ordinary servant gets treated to. So let's be getting you out of these.'

As he spoke de Breville put aside his tumbler of whisky and pulled Serena's apron strings loose and discarding it proceeded to untie the laces of her blouse.

'Please Master, I don't…'

'Hush now girl, there's nothing to worry about it.'

As de Breville spoke the other young man joined his friend and began to unfasten Serena's skirt. Between them it took only a few moments before Serena 's blouse, skirt, shift, bodice and underwear had been removed and she stood trapped between the two men with not a stitch of clothing on. Her heart was hammering and mind racing but either because she knew the bedroom door was locked or because of some other reason, she made no attempt to escape.

'In the bath then girl and give yourself a good soaping,' de Breville encouraged.

Serena had very seldom enjoyed a bath and never before one so large or so deeply filled with deliciously hot water. She needed no encouragement to soap herself from head to toe and quickly forgot her shyness as the two young men stood watching her.

'Quite a sight isn't she?'

'How old are you girl?'

'Eighteen sir.'

'Stand up.'

Serena obeyed. The two men stood grinning at her. Her long, dark red hair hung around her face and across her shoulders in damp tendrils, some of which trailed across her breasts. Glancing down she saw her nipples were hard and as she stood obediently still, the soapy water dripping from her naked body she felt a fresh rush of excitement at what the two men might have planned for her.

'Right then, I think I might just join you.'

Discarding the towel, Edward's friend climbed into the vast bath and gestured Serena to sit back down beside him. Serena gazed mesmerised at the sight of his cock before it disappeared below the water as the man lowered himself into the bath beside her.

'Get the soap then girl and give me a good washing.'

'Make sure she does a good job Jamie,' de Breville laughed.

Starting with his shoulders and back, Serena rubbed the soap and then the sponge diligently over the man and when she had got down to his waist, he stood up and looked down at her with a grin. Serena slithered around in the bath until she was kneeling and then she resumed soaping him, this time starting at his ankles and working her way up his legs knowing just what was expected of her but deliberately making the man wait. When she proceeded to rub the soap over and around his rampant cock and to lather his balls he gave a satisfied groan and she felt his hand tighten in her hair.

'Now wash the suds off girl.'

Serena did as she was told. The cock glistened hard and shiny and she tried to imagine what it might feel like having it driven inside her. She was kneeling, gazing at it, almost hypnotised by the sight of it rearing before her as she realised that using the grasp he had upon her hair the man was gradually encouraging her face closer and closer to the erect organ.

'Now be a good girl and lick it clean.'

'But sir, I've...'

'Just do it girl!'

The grasp upon her hair pushed her face closer still. Serena cautiously gave the tip of the shaft an experimental lick with her tongue.

'Good girl, now don't stop there.'

Serena gave the shaft another lick and finding the experience not unpleasant and aware from the man's contented sighs, how much it was affecting him, she proceeded to bathe the shaft from base to tip with numerous enthusiastic licks of her tongue.

'Very good... very good...Christ, she's a natural Edward... that's it girl, keep at it. Now, put the whole of the end in your mouth and suck it nice and clean.'

When she did as the man instructed he gave a deep groan and then without warning she felt hot salty liquid splash against the back of her mouth and begin to trickle down her throat. Trying to pull her head away was, she found, impossible, two hands now cradling her head firmly against the man's organ.

'Just suck darling; suck and swallow, it won't last long,'

laughed de Breville obviously aware of what had just happened.

With no choice in the matter Serena did as her Master instructed and after a moment there was no more of the salty liquid coming from the man's cock and she felt his grasp upon her head relax a little.

'Well done Serena, now out of the bath and into the bedroom,' de Breville ordered.

Followed by the two men Serena did what was wanted of her, drawing the back of her hand across her lips after she'd licked away the last of the man's juices. The pungent taste was still in her mouth and she was looking longingly at the drinks they held. Guessing what she was thinking the naked young man, after taking another mouthful from the glass of Champagne he had picked up and brought with him, offered the glass to her with a knowing grin.

'Thank you sir,' Serena gave the man a coy smile and took first a small sip and then a larger one from the glass. Not being very used to alcohol the Champagne went quickly and pleasantly to her head and with a dismissive smile the man told her to finish it, adding that there was plenty more.

'Right then Serena, lie face down on the bed,' de Breville ordered.

Quickly finishing the contents of the glass, Serena did as she was instructed. The double bed was hung with drapes at the head and flanked at the both base and head by four thick poles of dark wood, carved into spirals. As she flopped down on the bed the two men moved to each side of it and pulling away the loose cushions that were piled about the bed head, produced red silk ropes that were already tied about the wooden posts.

'Give us your arms girl.'

Serena swallowed a nervous lump that rose in her throat and glanced at the bedroom door. De Breville reading her thoughts simply climbed quickly onto the bed and sat down astride her back, pinning her with his weight while his accomplice caught hold of her left arm.

'Now don't make a fuss Serena, we all know you like being treated like this.'

While de Breville spoke the other man drew her arm outstretched towards the corner of the bed and bound the rope repeatedly around her wrist.

'What are you going to do with me Master?' Serena asked as the naked young man set about binding her other arm in similar fashion so that she was left with her arms spread above her and drawn a little out to either side.

'What do you think dear girl? Just what do you think?' de Breville laughed, climbing off her back and stroking his hand across her bare skin.

'I think we'll do her legs as well Jamie.'

There was nothing Serena could do to stop them as one man held each leg in turn whilst the other bound a rope around her ankle and secured her legs so that she was left spreadeagled upon the bed and quite helpless.

'What a delightful sight.'

'Feeling excited Serena?'

Serena nodded and glanced over one shoulder to see de Breville coolly regarding her, a slender cane held in his hand.

'Don't worry Serena it won't bruise you as much as the riding crop did, although it might sting a little more.'

'Maybe you should gag her Edward?'

'Perhaps,' de Breville conceded, 'but as long as she doesn't cry out too loudly I don't mind leaving her ungagged. Some plaintive cries of distress and anguish are really rather pleasing to the ear I should say, wouldn't you Jamie?'

'Absolutely. Yes, feel free to express yourself girl, just don't make such a racket we disturb the others or we really will have to gag you. And then of course, you can't tell us when the pain gets too much can you? It would be such a pity if we didn't know when to stop. Such a pity…'

'So try not to cry too loudly Serena,' de Breville cautioned then without further pause he brought the cane down with a faint hiss against her exposed rump.

Thwack!

'Uhhh!'

Thwack!

The cane sliced down across her thigh just below her buttock, the stinging blow brought tears quickly to Serena's eyes and she gave a chocked cry of alarm at how intense the moment of pain was as the cane came into contact with her bare flesh.

'See, she really likes it… quite docile.'

Thwack!

The cane cut against her lower back and here where there was lest protective fat to pad her body the pain was more intense. Serena jerked her arms in alarm as the pain washed through her mind. Though just like the cropping the previous night, the experience excited her, the intensity of the pain was alarming.

Thwack!

'Please…'Serena shook her head; the strokes were coming in too quick a succession and were too intense. She already felt breathless and jerking and twisting her arms and legs to try to twist away from the next blow served only to underline for her just how helpless she was now they had bound both her legs as well as her arms.

Thwack!

The cane sliced across her thigh and she jerked her legs frantically as the shooting sensation of pain streaked through her tethered body.

'No more… please Master…too much…'

'Hush now girl, we've hardly begun. Relax…'

Soothing hands stroked her damp hair for a moment and then tightening their hold on her hair, drew her head back so they could see her face. Edward de Breville regarded her with the idle curiosity of a detached observer, as she looked wide-eyed with alarm at him. Panting hard, Serena looked imploringly at the young man so calmly observing her distress.

'Please... hurts... can't bear much more Master... sorry...'Serena tried to control her tears as she begged. De Breville nodded thoughtfully and smiled apologetically.

'Would you like a little rest Serena? We could find some other activity perhaps, if you would prefer?'

'Thank you Master!' Serena smiled gratefully and the hand released her hair allowing her face to sink back onto the pillows.

'The girl wants a little rest from the cane Jamie. You may as well bugger her now and then we'll resume the caning after.'

'No! Please!' Serena shook her head in alarm and disbelief and looked fearfully back over her shoulder.

'Be grateful girl that I have no intention of deflowering you just yet. Or would you rather that I did?' de Breville asked, his tone peremptory and icily cold.

'This isn't fair!' Serena blurted, dragging her arms against the ropes that held her helplessly spread and defenceless.

'Stop making such a fuss Serena!' de Breville ordered impatiently.

'No, you can't do this to me!' Serena shook her head, her voice rising in alarm as she felt the man climb onto the bed between her spread legs.

'Somebody help me please!' Serena cried out, twisting her limbs urgently against the ropes that held her down across the bed.

'Really, such a fuss the girl is making!' de Breville complained.

'Hush now, you'll disturb Edward's father's afternoon nap,' cautioned the other man as he clapped a hand across her mouth to stifle her cries.

'Nnnnhh!'

Serena shook her head in protest as a silk cravat was quickly forced into her mouth.

'NNNHH!'

'Come on Ed, she's thrashing her head like some hooked fish!'

'Hold her just a moment while I roll this one tight.'

'NNNHH!'

'Now then…'

A second cravat was drawn hard against her mouth and between her jaws, the rolled fabric serving to contain the first cravat within her mouth. Serena gave up shaking her head, knowing her efforts were now quite useless as she felt the cravat being knotted at her nape. Her silken gag was complete and to her dismay she knew that her muffled cries would certainly not penetrate the stout bedroom door and be heard beyond. The only people now who would hear her smothered cries were the two young men determined to enjoy her body.

Chapter Five

Doctor MacKennan exchanged a conspiratorial glance with his nurse as he regarded the unconscious girl lying on the couch. Under the pale green light, her smooth skin was bathed in a soft sheen of perspiration. The towelling robe she had been wearing hung open and redundant. Her dark red hair was tousled damply around her face and her slender neck was arched as she seemed to strain her body in her sleep, her breathing coming in urgent pants through her nostrils because her mouth was sealed with black tape. The girl's arms and legs slithered ineffectually across the couch padding, restrained at the ankles and wrists by broad cuffs of rubber. Simply but effectively fastened by Velcro, the cuffs were clipped to concealed rings at each couch corner and by this means Serena's arms were held above her head and her legs were kept spread.

'Looks like Miss Fairfax isn't so keen on experiencing being taken from behind,' commented MacKennan exchanging a wry smile with his nurse.

Serena had been happy to experience another taste of the whip but in order to bring her dream to the point she had reached had required her limbs being restrained and MacKennan making some manual over-rides to the unfolding dreamscape programme. Now, however unwilling the dreaming Serena might be to experience what lay ahead, there was effectively nothing she could do to stop what was about to befall her. Even the option of waking up and abandoning her dream had been denied her. The emothome in her blood had been increased a little and a small amount of voltrimal had been fed into her also. This muscle relaxant meant that her struggles to free herself were brought neatly under control. At best she could weakly slither her limbs across the couch and of course the rubber cuffs effectively restrained her anyway. She couldn't cry out because of the tape across her mouth and so Serena Fairfax lay helplessly under the Doctor's control, her mind trapped in the tethered body of her persona, Serena the servant girl. She had no choice but to meet her fate.

'Perhaps, we'll spin things out for a little while… after all, I think we can get her nicely addicted to the taste of the whip and then we'll gradually introduce her to some other experiences,' MacKennan decided.

'You could save the best for when she journeys into Lara's dreamscape, perhaps, Doctor?' the nurse suggested.

'Yes, that'll be a good idea, especially since I've warned her that she'll have no control over what happens to her in that dream. If she's headstrong enough to venture into the lion's den then she'll have to be prepared to take the consequences.'

MacKennan walked briskly back to the computer controls, leaving the sleeping Serena struggling weakly in her sleep against the cuffs that held her spread on the couch. Quickly keying in a series of prompts, MacKennan watched as on his visual display monitor Jamie, having soaped the girl's anus to soften the muscle, slipped his finger inside her, making the servant girl tethered across the bed, squirm even more.

Then at the suggestion of Edward de Breville, Jamie withdrew his finger from the girl's writhing body and began stroking her sex. Soon the servant girl was obviously well on the way to having an orgasm and once confident that he had her well aroused the young man climbed from the bed and stepped back so that his accomplice could deliver several blows with his cane against her rump. The girl shook her head vigorously and dragged her arms and legs against the ropes that held her spreadeagled upon the double bed. The two men grinned at each other and the naked one then climbed back onto the bed and resumed stroking her sex, commenting as he did so that she was well and truly wet now and obviously the caning was arousing her.

MacKennan leant back in his swivel chair and watched the monitor with considerable satisfaction and more than a degree of smugness as the Edwardian servant girl was brought to her first climax. The tender and naïve eighteen year old was well on the way now to becoming the devoted sex slave of her Master Edward de Breville, even if, as yet, she didn't know it herself.

'I'm going down to check on Jemma, if you could kindly just keep an eye on our client please nurse,' MacKennan announced.

'Certainly Doctor.'

Nurse Zara gave a rueful smile, guessing that the Doctor was once again in need of a fuck and poor Jemma was going to be on the receiving end of his monster cock once more.

'I have programmed Edward de Breville to leave the girl tied down on the bed to rest while he takes a bath himself. She should just sleep for a while now.'

'Should I remove the tape from her mouth or the cuffs, Doctor?'

'Oh, good heavens no, there's plenty more in store for Serena soon enough, so we may as well leave her gagged.'

'See you later Doctor.'

As MacKennan left the room his nurse reached forward and gently stroked the sleeping girl's breasts.

'Well, the Doctor is being rather kind with you so far, isn't he?' she said thoughtfully, licking her lips. 'He obviously has a soft spot for you. Still, his hard cock will invariably get the better of him and then…'

The nurse stroked her fingertips down the supine girl's body until they reached the thatch of dark hair between her legs. The sleeping girl sighed, her eyelashes fluttering. The nurse smiled maliciously and leant back in her chair.

'Soon, very soon you're going to taste such sweet pain… you poor little thing, if only you knew what lay in store for you.'

* * *

Taking the lift to the basement, MacKennan went first to the office to quickly check if any new orders for sex slaves had come in from his various clients and contacts amongst the barbarian nations. There were several enquiries and one purchase order, from one of his best clients, a despotic and sadistic ruler of a small and very backward central African nation, who titled himself the Emerald Tiger. The man had over the years bought numerous slave girls from MacKennan; always Alpha Class girls, the wealthier and more spoilt the better as far as he seemed to be concerned. He was not so much bothered by a slave's training or submissiveness as by her beauty. The last time he had ordered he had required three girls and amongst the three that MacKennan had sold him had been Lara Lustral, Serena Fairfax's friend.

Reading the e-mail from his client, MacKennan smiled to himself as he learnt that all three girls had been stolen from under the despot's nose and whisked away to be used as trophies for some big game hunters in a private game park. Of course the meaning of the game had long since changed and now the hunting of naked and defenceless girls was the game. The hunters, wealthy men from the advanced nations, would pay handsomely to go out into the bush and hunt the girls, using tranquilliser dart firing rifles.

So in furious revenge, the Emerald Tiger had launched a military strike against the man who had abducted his newly acquired slaves. Now, the despot was gleefully writing to tell MacKennan that he had not only taken control of the game park but he had recovered two of his lost slaves and forced the other man to flee for his life. The e-mail ended with a request for a replacement slave girl for the missing one.

MacKennan was left wondering which of the three he had not recovered and why? Had she been killed, had she escaped or had the park's former owner perhaps taken her when he'd fled? MacKennan guessed he'd never find out and in truth he wasn't that interested. The three girls he had sold the Emerald Tiger were all wealthy, spoilt Alpha girls: Lara had been perhaps the most stunning of the three. Well, perhaps it would be amusing to see if the Emerald Tiger still had possession of her and then he could sell Serena Fairfax to him and then at least the two girls would be reunited! Smiling at the irony of this possibility, MacKennan left the office and went in search of Jemma.

He found her resting in her bedroom cell, peacefully asleep. He summoned his two henchmen and the girl's sleep was abruptly ended as she was dragged out of the room before she was even fully awake.

'Doctor, please… what are you going to do to me? 'the girl begged as she was dragged down the corridor and into a room whose door was marked "D".

'Time for a little more discipline Jemma.'

MacKennan shut the door behind him and watched the two men as they took the naked girl across to a padded bench and pushed her face down over it so she was made to bend forwards from the waist. Pinned from behind by one man, the other took her slender, young wrists and slipped the rubber cuffs that lay fastened to straps on the bench around them.

'Please Doctor, don't be too rough with me… I'll do whatever you want,' promised the young girl as the straps were tightened and her arms were drawn to full stretch across the bench before her.

'Of course you will Jemma, of course you will…'

MacKennan smiled as he watched his men fasten straps around the girl's shapely thighs and drawing them tight from either side they spread the girls legs as widely as was possible.

He had abducted Jemma just five days ago but he had quickly bent her to his will. With as much ease in fact as his men had now bent her face down across the bench for his pleasure. The randy nineteen year old had quickly learnt to enjoy the rough treatment that was meted out to her in the basement. Her dreams had shown her inclination towards submissiveness and MacKennan had found her enjoyable enough to train although perhaps a little too willing. He liked it when they tried to fight him. He enjoyed watching them struggle physically and emotionally. How defiant Lara had been at first but in the end she became as slavishly devoted and submissive as the rest of the girls he'd abducted. Of course the skill lay in judging which were, deep down, naturally submissive. Whatever appearance they might outwardly show it was invariably a facade and once dreaming, their true natures were revealed. Jemma was certainly the most submissive girl he'd yet encountered.

'Has she been made to orgasm today?'

'Not yet Doctor, we were going to work on her this afternoon.'

Part of the treatment that MacKennan gave to his abducted girls was a conditioning programme that served to find what most aroused them and also coaxed from them their weaknesses and innermost desires. Of course, MacKennan already had a good idea of these because of the content of their dreams but by making the girls admit to him how they wanted to be treated he could exploit their sexually rapacious nature and so ensnare them all the more easily. Poor little Jemma had all too easily admitted that she liked being treated as roughly as she could bear and that she enjoyed getting off on the exquisite agony of having her clitoris and vulva clamped and weighted.

'Please Doctor… what are you going to do with me?' Jemma begged as, having strapped her thighs, the two men awaited their next instructions. MacKennan smiled as the girl craned her head back over her shoulder and looked so pathetically at him, her bright blue eyes wide with alarm and her blonde hair delightfully tousled around her young face.

'Fetch the clamps and weights.'

'No Doctor… please…no…'

The girl began sobbing uncontrollably and MacKennan grinned at her convincing performance. Perhaps in a way it was real. After all the pain she experienced would be unbearable for some girls. Perhaps a part of her really didn't want to be subjected to this torture. Then again…

MacKennan watched as his two dark suited male assistants set the tray of equipment beside the tethered girl and then, removing their suit jackets, they put on fine latex gloves. The girl looked anxiously over first one shoulder and then the other. MacKennan noticed her legs were quivering and her mouth trembling. She looked so vulnerable that his erect cock throbbed at the sight and he thought that merely watching what was happening to her might be enough to make him come.

'Please don't Doctor… the weights are too much… really!' Jemma shook her head despairingly as one of the men fastened a small clip onto one of the folds of her outer labia.

'No…let me go… please…'

A second clip was fastened to the matching lip of soft pink flesh and the clips were drawn back and taped against the inside of the girl's trembling young thighs. As a third clip was applied to one of her inner sex lips the girl shook her head urgently, biting down on her lip and sighing plaintively. MacKennan watched as another clip was fastened on her other inner sex lip and then tear shaped pieces of polished steel, each several inches in length were attached to the two clips that were tight around her inner labia. With the weights dangling between her spread legs, the delicate little sex lips were quickly distended and the girl was soon jerking her arms and legs frantically.

'Stop it! Please! Too much… please stop…'

MacKennan watched as Jemma struggled against the rubber cuffs and straps

that held her tight against the bench. The shiny weights swung freely between her thighs as she writhed and the glistening sex lips now seemed stretched to twice their natural size.

MacKennan walked around the bench so he could see the girl's face. Tears were coursing down her soft cheeks and her pretty mouth was contorted with the agony of what she was being made to experience. She looked up beseechingly at him and he smiled down at her.

'Poor little Jemma, is that really too much for you?' he asked sympathetically. The girl nodded urgently and MacKennan smiled apologetically as if appreciating her distress.

'Take the weights off and put on the next size up instead.'

'No!' cried the girl, 'Please! Don't!'

The order was quickly executed; the first pair of weights calmly removed and then another pair were fastened to the clamps. These were perhaps twenty five percent larger than the previous. The replacement shiny steel tears dangling freely between her tethered thighs, the girl's whole body seemed to strain and contort in an effort to extricate herself from the agony she was being subjected to. The rubber straps around her wrists and the straps around her thighs were utterly effective though and there was no escape for poor Jemma.

For perhaps five minutes she writhed and struggled, begged and sobbed and then, exhausted, she lay docilely, resigned to her fate and just whimpering plaintively. MacKennan fingered the girl's sex and found her very wet. Her clitoris was distended with arousal and at his touch she sighed and groaned. The weights alone had brought her almost to an orgasm, he reckoned. Tapping the weights to encourage them to swing drew a fevered moan from the tethered girl.

'Would you like me to make you come Jemma?'

'Yes, please Doctor… please…' the girl sighed.

MacKennan nodded to one of his men who without so much as a word of instruction knew what was wanted. MacKennan stroked his hand down the girl's bare back while the man unscrewed the lid of Gelphax gel. He then walked around the bench to the side that Jemma was facing and he looked down at her.

'Would you like it if I fucked you then, Jemma?'

The young girl nodded and smiling with satisfaction MacKennan proceeded to unfasten his trousers and draw his now achingly hard cock from his underpants. The expression on the girl's face was delightful; a mixture of nervous apprehension and lustful eagerness as she was visually reminded of the unnaturally large size of the cock that was about to be driven into her body.

'Take the weights and clamp off her *labia minora*,' MacKennan instructed as he walked back around the bench.

With the girl's outer labia still taped back against her thighs, MacKennan drove his cock into her exposed sex. In his aroused condition, her slick tightness triggered his orgasm after just half a dozen thrusts and in that time Jemma climaxed as well. MacKennan withdrew his cock and stroked his hand over the girl's trembling rump.

'Clamp her inner labia again and put the weights back. Put a little Gelphax on her clit so she comes again. Leave her tethered like that for the rest of the afternoon but reapply the Gelphax every hour to make her come. Let's see how many times she can be brought to orgasm.'

'No, please Doctor…don't…'

'Stop crying Jemma, there's a good girl,' MacKennan stroked the girl's hair then patted her rump. Allowing himself one last look at the distressed girl spreadeagled against the bench, he left the room and made his back upstairs. It was time to see how Serena was enjoying the delights of Edwardian England. Or more specifically how she was enjoying the delights of being servant to Edward de Breville.

* * *

Serena gazed despondently at her outstretched arms. Where she had struggled the silk ropes had now tightened against her wrists and her arms ached from being held outstretched for so long. And likewise how she wished she could move her legs other than just the few inches allowed by the ropes that bound her ankles. Whilst the double bed they had tied her upon was luxuriously comfortable compared with what she was used to, it was little compensation for being tied, limbs outstretched and made to endure the cruel caning they had subjected her to. Her bottom felt so tender now that the merest touch of a hand upon her reddened skin brought tears to her eyes. What a bastard her Master was! How she hated Edward de Breville, she told herself, but without that much conviction because, in truth, the way he had treated her had excited her greatly and even the pain he had given her tasted somehow bitter sweet. To her surprise and shame but also secret delight, the caning he had given her had brought her to a shuddering and heady rush of pleasure that had poured through her young body, suffusing her with a contented glow the like of which she had never before experienced.

Now she had been left while her Master bathed and Jamie, his friend, dressed himself. Thankfully they had removed the gag and Serena was given perhaps quarter of an hour to lie contemplating what might next lie in store for her, while the men otherwise occupied themselves.

'Feeling nicely rested, Miss Fairfax?'

Serena lifted her head at the sound of her Master's voice.

'Poor thing, you look a trifle sore. Jamie, keep an eye on her, I'll be back in a moment.'

Serena watched her Master leave the room, dressed now in a black dinner suit and smelling strongly of eau de cologne.

Presently the man returned a glass jar of something in hand and a satisfied smile upon his face. Serena watched him lock the door then sit down on the edge of the bed.

'Borrowed from my sister; she says it's very good for dry skin and such like.'

Serena watched as the man removed the lid and dipped his fingers into the creamy white contents.

'Now then Serena, don't say I don't look after you.'

Serena lay docilely as the man rubbed the cool, creamy mixture into her skin all over the tops of her thighs and her bottom where she had taken the majority of the cane strokes. The experience was far from unpleasant but when her Master's fingers began to dip and stroke well between her legs just below her sex it was all she could do to bite her lip and not cry out begging him to rub her sex in the same way. Evidently her sighs soon were obvious and without her having to beg him, Serena felt the man's fingers stroke closer around her sex and then, directly, they were upon the soft folds of her sex lips and she was all but moaning with the exquisite pleasure.

'You like that don't you, Serena?'

'Yes, Master,' Serena sighed.

The fingers slipped into her sex drawing a deep groan of gratitude from her.

'Would you like it Serena if I put my cock in you? Shall I fuck you now, quickly before dinner or shall I make you wait?'

Serena said nothing, unsure whether the man was actually addressing her or merely speaking his thoughts.

'Shame to rush such a pleasure,' said Jamie.

'Quite so Jamie, I suppose we had better untie her then so she can get on with her other duties.'

Dazed after her experiences, Serena stumbled from the bedroom, her clothes somewhat in a state of disarray and her embarrassment acute in the extreme because Edward had refused to give her knickers back and had ordered her to wear nothing under her skirt forthwith until he instructed otherwise. Back in her little room, Serena had splashed cold water on her face to try to lessen her blushing and had tidied her appearance. She had then hurried down the backstairs to the kitchen to help with the preparations for the dinner. None of the other servants so much as raised an eyebrow at her late appearance and even the butler seemed to have ignored the fact that she was late for work.

Present for dinner were Sir Hugh de Breville, Edward and Edward's younger sister, a young woman perhaps only a few years older than Serena but possessing great poise and elegance as well as much natural beauty. Seated with these family members were four guests of which only one, young Master Jamie, was familiar to Serena. There was another youngish man and an older man, perhaps in his fifties with a lady of similar age. These, Serena soon learnt were Lord and Lady Melbury and the young man, Thomas Rackthorn.

Evidently Sir Hugh came to Highmost Romanway every season to hunt but his wife remained at the Oxfordshire estate not caring for such a pursuit. The hunting lodge, Serena learnt had six principal bedrooms for the family and a further four attic bedrooms for the servants. There was also a cottage adjoining the stables where Adam the hounds man and his wife, Betty, the housekeeper, lived all year round. Whilst Serena, as chambermaid, the chef, butler and valet had bedrooms of their own, the stable boy had to sleep in the stable and the cook's assistant, another young girl of Serena's age, had to sleep on the kitchen floor.

The butler who remained throughout dinner in the dining room served the meal whilst Serena brought the food from the kitchen to the dining room. For this duty Serena had to wear a black cloth apron, lace edged, and was told by the butler under no circumstances to approach the table or to utter so much as a word. Until now, evidently this task had been carried out by another chambermaid who had lately left the family's service. Until Serena had been found as a replacement, the cook had been forced to ferry the food to the dining room and such a task she regarded well beneath her, so she was most pleased when Serena proved more than capable of this duty and Serena's reward was a piece of leftover sponge pudding which she gratefully ate after the pudding had been served and the de Breville's had withdrawn for brandies and cigars.

It was late in the evening and Serena was beginning to think that her Master would not want her again that day, when the summons came. She was in truth pleased to think that Master Edward de Breville desired her again already. She glanced in a hall mirror at her reflection before hurrying to the billiards room as ordered by the butler, without so much as the merest suggestion that this was hardly proper. Evidently the staff were quite familiar with the de Breville eccentricities. Smoothing her hands nervously down the front of her skirt before knocking, Serena wondered what was planned for her this time. Her sense of excitement had been kept bubbling in no small part due to the fact that she had no underwear beneath her skirt, as instructed and this made her feel deliciously wanton.

'Enter!'

Responding to the imperious answer to her timid knock, Serena let herself into the room. Edward and Jamie were not alone. To Serena's surprise, Edward's sister stood watching the young men as they played billiards.

'Ah, it's the Fairfax girl! Come in Serena and shut the door behind you,' Edward de Breville ordered.

There was a sharp crack as a white ball collided with one of the red ones that Serena saw dotted the baize. The red ball rolled briskly towards a corner pocket, but just missed its target and bounced instead against the cushion.

'Bad luck Jamie, my shot then. I think my dearest sister Miranda brings me luck,' said de Breville, cheerfully.

'Come here girl and let me have a proper look at you.'

Serena glanced apprehensively at the beautiful young woman who had just addressed her.

'Do as my dear sister, instructs,' de Breville ordered before playing his shot and successfully potting the very red ball his friend had failed to. Serena walked across to where Edward's sister stood. Her dress was dazzlingly expensive, a sequined creation with a plunging neckline that drew the eye to her generous cleavage, in the valley of which hung the several strands of a pearl necklace. Gesturing with one, expensively white-gloved hand, the young lady made Serena turn around so she could inspect her fully.

'Not bad, brother, she does have a certain something, one has to concede,' the girl said, her tone cool and almost disdainful. Serena swallowed a nervous lump that had risen in her throat as the young woman idly circled her.

'Bend over girl, put your hands on the table edge.'

Hesitantly, Serena did as she was told. Now the two young men had stopped playing their game of billiards and were watching the females in the room. Serena was more than a little surprised when her skirt was pulled up and her bare legs exposed by her Master's sister.

'She's got good legs, a bit too muscular perhaps, but then she works, so I suppose...'

Serena bit her lip to stifle a cry of surprise as she felt the other girl's gloved hands stroke up the inside of her thighs and then circle her buttocks.

'She still looks a little tender. Does that hurt girl?'

'A little Mistress,' Serena answered.

'Place your legs wider apart girl.'

Serena obeyed, excitement mounting in her as she saw a discarded white glove land on the green baize before her.

The young woman's fingers were delicate and confident. With less contact than Jamie had made she drew a swift, shuddering sigh from Serena just by touching her in a certain place that obviously she knew.

'You like that don't you?'

'Yes, Mistress,' Serena confessed, struggling to suppress another contented sigh as the woman's fingers stroked her so skilfully that she longed to thrust herself back against her teasing caress.

'Now, bend right over the table and put your arms above your head. Stretch your arms across to the side of the table where the boys are.'

Serena did as she was told and realised what was to happen next only too late.

Catching hold of her wrists, Jamie held her arms outstretched while his friend bound her wrists together with rope and then pulling the rope taut he knotted it to the far side of the billiard table.

'You're not afraid are you?' questioned the young Lady.

'A little Mistress...'Serena answered.

'I trust you won't be a silly girl and cry out now, will you?'

'No Mistress.'

'Jamie dear, lock the door, we don't really want to be

disturbed,' requested the young woman who stood behind Serena, her slender fingers now deeply immersed in Serena's aching sex. Serena squirmed at the invasive touch that was so unfamiliar.

'She's quite intact Edward and I dare say you'll find her pleasingly tight also. I would suggest we take the precaution of gagging her though the first time. However desperate she might be to have your cock inside her, the first time is likely to hurt her somewhat.'

Before she had finished speaking the young woman clapped her gloved hand across Serena's mouth and then withdrawing the fingers of her other hand from between her legs she covered Serena's mouth with both hands while Edward and Jamie came around the table to her side, silk cravats already in hand. All too aware of what was about to befall her, Serena shook her head vigorously, trying to voice her concerns but the female hands across her mouth smothered her protests and when the hands were eventually lifted from her mouth they were only replaced by folds of smothering silk that quickly submerged her tongue and filled her mouth.

Just as before, a second silk cravat was used lengthways between her parted jaws to complete the gag and then to make the gag even more effective Miranda de Breville used her own silk scarf, neatly folded, to completely cover Serena's mouth. With an ominous laugh of malicious satisfaction the young woman knotted the scarf firmly at Serena's nape.

'Right then brother dear, she's all yours to enjoy.'

'Nnnnhh…'

Serena could only just hear her own cries as she felt her Master move behind her. When she defensively closed her legs, a sharp blow against her thighs with a billiard cue swiftly encouraged her to part them again. Gazing at her outstretched arms and bound wrists, Serena told herself that she was quite helpless and therefore she was blameless for what was about to happen to her. She felt the man's cock nudge between her legs, find the lips of her sex and slide easily between them and into her body. The truth was she was wet with arousal and as she felt the tip of his shaft nudge a little way inside her and then partially withdrew she was secretly pleased that the gag so effectively muffled the sigh of pleasure that would otherwise have escaped her lips.

The man's hands tightened around her slender waist, there was a second's pause and then his cock was driven deeply inside her. Now Serena cried out, or at least tried to, in pain at first and then with exquisite pleasure as she experienced the man's cock pumping in and out of her. A wave of ecstasy rolled over her and she imagined herself fainting. She was still conscious though, gazing dreamily at her outstretched arms and bound wrists as the man continued to use her. After a short time her pussy was throbbing and Serena began to hope that the man would not continue to use her body so mercilessly hard for very much longer. Sure enough, with a satisfied groan, Edward came and Serena gave a sigh of relief as his cock was withdrawn from her tender young body. Gazing up breathless, thanks to the gag and what she had been subjected to, Serena saw her Master's sister looking down at her. Miranda de Breville smiled sweetly at her then turned her attention to her brother's friend.

'Your turn Jamie,' she announced with an effected degree of casualness.

Serena gazed up, her eyes wide with alarm at the prospect of receiving a repeat of what she had just been subjected to.

'My dear girl… is something the matter?'

Miranda de Breville stroked the tears from Serena's cheeks and then traced the taut edges of the silk gag that kept her silent.

'Come now Serena, you wouldn't want to deprive young Master Jamie of his turn would you?'

As Edward's sister was speaking the two men exchanged places and then Serena felt a second hard cock rammed into her tender pussy.

'Nnhhh!'

Vigorously Serena shook her head in objection although deep down she felt a heady rush of excitement as she now knew that she was powerless to refuse the second dose that was coming her way.

'Hush now girl… there's no point in struggling, it won't do you any good.'

Miranda de Breville smiled as she watched Serena jerking and twisting her outstretched arms against the ties around her wrists.

'Uuhh…'

Serena gazed up at the beautiful face of Miranda de Breville, slowly transformed now by a sneering smile into something quite malevolent.

* * *

'Perhaps its time to let her wake up?' MacKennan mused thoughtfully as he watched the sleeping Serena Fairfax, twisting and turning in her sleep as best she could given her arms and legs were drawn to the four corners of the padded couch and restrained by cuffs and straps.

'She's been dreaming for an hour and ten minutes now Doctor, shall I prepare her for surfacing?'

'Yes please Zara, usual procedure.'

MacKennan left the couch's side and went back to the monitor screens. Well, Serena certainly had given them good entertainment with her fantasy. He had not had to manually over ride her dream this time, she had of her own volition allowed herself to lose her virginity to her Master and even when she seemed to be in need of a respite for her tenderised pussy, she had then let herself be subjected to a fresh shafting by the other young man. Well, Serena Fairfax was certainly a natural submissive and it looked liked she knew it already. Of course, that just left one question: how much would she willingly take? It would be interesting, he decided, to allow her to venture into Lara's dreamscape: her lovely young body would certainly get more than enough attention at the hands of the evil Doctor.

'Her emothome level now is only four percent, Doctor, she should wake within five or ten minutes.'

'You've knotted her towelling robe differently to how she had it,' MacKennan commented, stood once more over the sleeping girl. The rubber cuffs had been removed along with the straps. The black tape that covered her lovely mouth was gone and once more the white towelling robe covered her sleeping body. His nurse quickly untied the belt of the robe and re-knotted it in an alternative fashion.

'Can you hear me, Serena?' MacKennan leant over his client and smiled as she murmured something. Her eyelashes flickered and then her eyes were open and she was looking up sleepily at him.

'How long have I been asleep?' Serena asked, expecting to be told hours and hours and surprised when she was given the answer that everything she had experienced had happened in little over an hour. Adjoining the dream room was the changing cubicle and shower and Serena spent a good ten minutes in the shower allowing the warm water to cascade over her while she replayed as much of her dream as she could remember. The memory of the caning and the sex was fresh and vivid but her body felt quite untouched, although oddly enough her wrists prickled faintly when she first stepped under the shower and as she stared at them she imagined she could almost feel the silk bonds that de Breville had bound her with. It had certainly been a remarkably vivid dream and she had felt so aroused when she woke that it demanded a lot of self restrain not to masturbate while she was in the shower. She would wait, she told herself and go out this evening to a club. She wanted to pick up a couple of young men and after a few drinks to release her inhibitions, whatever they got up to with her would be fine by her.

MacKennan was waiting for her in the leafy reception hall. As she approached he stood up and drew back her chair for her, before resuming his seat.

'A drink? Some refreshment?' the Doctor suggested, 'You will have dehydrated while sleeping, you should drink some water.'

'I will go straight home and have several large glasses, Doctor,' Serena assured him, thinking to herself that she now felt so excited that she was ready for a dry martini cocktail or two and for some decent male company. Did the Doctor have no idea of the effect that her dream would have had upon her?

'So what did you think Serena?' the Doctor enquired.

'It was an incredible experience; very vivid. It's a shame the memory will fade,' Serena said regretfully.

MacKennan smiled, the self-satisfied triumphant smile of a poker player about to reveal four aces.

'Would you care to take the recording of your dream back with you?' he asked, clearly amused as he watched Serena's face light up with unconcealed eagerness. Or course, she had forgotten! His computer recorded the client's dreams – everything she had dreamt was there to watch by her whenever she pleased!

'I'd nearly forgotten,' Serena admitted.

'Whilst it may not be as real as the dream felt, I am sure it should make interesting viewing.'

Damned right it would, Serena thought, and I bet you've sat and watched the whole thing! So not only did the Doctor get the chance to financially screw the young women who came to him, he got the chance to watch them getting screwed in their dreams. Every girl's secret fantasy would be free viewing for him! No wonder MacKennan seemed so content with his work, Serena thought.

'So are you still wishing to enter Lara's dreamscape?' MacKennan enquired.

'Definitely,' said Serena, thinking that it would be interesting just to find out what sort of sexual fantasy her friend had indulged in. If she found a clue as to where Lara had vanished, that would now be just a bonus.

'As I said, the Institute is heavily booked now for many

weeks, unless of course you could make an evening appointment with me? The Institute is really closed in the evenings but I could make an exception for you.'

'That would be brilliant, Doctor MacKennan. You just say when you want me and I'll come.'

'This evening?'

'I can hardly wait,' Serena smiled.

'Well, don't be disappointed if you find nothing that leads you to your friend Lara's whereabouts,' MacKennan cautioned.

'Well one way or another I'm determined to find out just what has happened to her,' Serena said adamantly.

'Yes, Lara Lustral…well, I wonder what did happened to her?' MacKennan mused.

Chapter Six

'That's too tight!' Lara begged, 'I can't breathe properly!'

The man laughed and ruffled her tousled, golden hair, which reached down to the broad belt he had just fastened below her ribcage.

'Oww... that hurts!' Lara complained as her arms were bent up behind her back and the clips on her wrist cuffs were fastened to the belt.

'Silence girl or you get gagged!'

Lara glowered at the man but bit her tongue and held herself in check. There was no point in making her situation any worse, she told herself.

It had been two days since they had fled by helicopter from the attack launched by the Emerald Tiger. Lara had been taken prisoner before even reaching the Palace of the Emerald Tiger, to whom MacKennan at the Dreamscape Institute had sold her. Having been abducted in transit she felt she had been on a roller-coaster adventure since the fateful day that she had first walked into the Dreamscape Institute. She had only just escaped capture by the soldiers of the Emerald Tiger when they launched a retaliatory raid because the man who now owned her had felt she was worth bringing with him as he was forced to make a breakneck dash for safety. His helicopter had whisked the two of them and the man's girlfriend from the clutches of the Emerald Tiger just in time.

The man had planned to fly them two hundred miles north and across the border into the relative safety of a neighbouring state. However, after covering only a couple of miles the helicopter was forced to make an emergency landing, an oil line having been ruptured by a bullet, one of many no doubt fired at them as they had made their escape. They had then marched on foot, north, as fast as they could manage. They had not got far before falling foul of local natives. The man had ruthlessly sold both girls to the savages to buy his own freedom.

For two days and nights Lara and the other girl had been mercilessly used by the native men until a patrol of soldiers wearing the cap emblem of an emerald green tiger had swept into the village and taken possession of both girls.

'You are the one we have been told to bring to His Highness,' the commander of the patrol announced as he finished clasping Lara's wrists to the belt so that her arms were held pinned against the small of her back. He looked her up and down and grinned. He was a tall and powerfully man, perhaps in his forties but very fit and held in obvious respect by not only the dozen soldiers he commanded but by the village natives as well.

'Are you sure it's not her you're after?' Lara glanced across to where the other girl was standing guarded by two soldiers.

'Oh no,' the man laughed, '"Bring me the girl with the golden mane like a lion,"; this is what his Highness the Emerald Tiger ordered. And that for certain is you!'

The man caught hold of her hair and using it like a leash drew her forwards.

'You are coming back to the Palace to please his Highness. The other girl is of no interest.'

'So what happens to her then?' Lara demanded sulkily, 'Don't tell me she gets to go free?'

'Free? Ha! No, my men can enjoy her and then we shall leave her with these tribesmen.'

'That's not fair!' the girl protested rushing towards where Lara and the officer stood. Before she had covered half a dozen steps though two soldiers intercepted her and Lara watched as the young woman was then dragged across to one of the patrol's two jeeps.

'So would you like to exchange places with her now?'

As the officer posed the question, Lara watched the girl being forced face down across the jeep's bonnet.

'Well?' prompted the officer.

Lara made no answer but stared as while two soldiers pinned the girl's arms down while a third proceeded to take her from behind.

'At least you can relax golden haired girl; no one will touch you now. You belong to his Highness and it is my duty to bring you untouched to his palace.'

'And then what will happen to me? I don't suppose I can look forward to a life of pampering and luxury can I?' suggested Lara scathingly.

'Wait and find out.'

The man gave an enigmatic grin and gestured for Lara to make her way across to the second jeep. When she hesitated he simply gave a tug on her hair and she was obliged to follow him. Passing the first jeep she glanced sideways at the other girl. Like Lara, she had a healthy appetite for sex but after the last couple of days held in the village and made to satisfy the men there continually, both girls were pretty exhausted. Held face down across the jeep's bonnet, the girl was now faced with the prospect of being used by a dozen soldiers. Little wonder she looked abjectly at Lara, as the officer led her past, one hand tight around her hair.

With the heat of the morning sun beating down on her bare skin, Lara had to sit in the jeep, the perspiration running down her slender arms and trickling in rivulets between her breasts while she had to watch the other girl being used by the soldiers. The commander of the patrol sat in the jeep next to Lara, content merely to watch the spectacle. The girl was given no rest between each man taking his turn with her and soon she gave up struggling as the soldiers took it in turns to use her. By the time her ordeal was over Lara felt shamefully aroused at what she had watched and a part of her wished that she'd been put in the other girl's place. Lara had learnt that being forced to sexually submit herself heightened her own pleasure even when she was subjected to such extreme punishment that the pain was as much as she could bear. Deep down she'd probably already been a natural submissive but when she had first gone to the Dreamscape Institute she'd gone to satisfy what she imagined was simply her sexually ravenous nature.

MacKennan had nurtured her penchant for sexual excess ruthlessly. She had come to his Dreamscape Institute eager to indulge in erotic dream fantasies. Quickly though, MacKennan had drawn her into a dream world where she had learned to love being forced to submit to whatever was demanded of her. Somehow MacKennan had manipulated her dreams and through them made her aware of her own natural submissiveness. In her dream world MacKennan had sexually tortured her and even though he had been directing her dream, she had actually got off on what he subjected her to. When he had then actually abducted her and she had been held prisoner in the basement of the Institute, it had been only a small step before she was made to realise that a part of her really wanted to be treated in this way.

She hated herself for what he had so skilfully drawn out of her but she was now hopelessly addicted to it. Her body and her mind now were keyed to respond to a subtle mixture of sexual pleasure and pain so that she craved the tormenting and longed for the pain of the whip or torturer's devices as much as she hungered for the sensation of having a cock rammed up her pussy.

She had wondered about MacKennan almost from the start; certainly from after the first session when she had gone home and replayed in her mind what she had dreamt and what she imagined she had actually felt. She had suspected then… but she had been aroused, too excited to really stop and consider what she might be letting herself in for. And of course once she returned to the Institute it was then too late, she was addicted and she was willing for MacKennan to do with her as he liked.

She had tried to tell her best friend, Serena, but she didn't know how to explain what was happening to her. And perhaps if she had confided in her, Serena would have been tempted to follow her. That would have been unfair on Serena; the girl was too young and too delicate to fall into MacKennan's hands. Admittedly Serena was as sexually wild as she was but she was only just a young woman. She had enjoyed an even more sheltered upbringing than Lara. Whilst Serena might like a bit of rough play, Lara could hardly imagine her friend revelling in the pain she had been forced to submit to at MacKennan's hands. And MacKennan knew just how to make her suffer! His training sessions had stood her in good stead for her new life as a sex slave out in the barbarian nations. She was accustomed now to more or less anything that was demanded of her. Of course she would struggle, scream and beg with her masters, but that was an instinctive response in a way. Or so she told herself. There were times when she wondered…

The journey back to the Palace of the Emerald Tiger took two days and showed her more of the country than she had seen so far. She learnt that they were in the far northwest and their journey would take them east and a little south. The country was divided north to south down the middle by a range of mountains; west of these there was arid scrubland but on the eastern side the countryside was forested and as they drove further east they descended from four thousand to a thousand feet and the forest turned to thick jungle. The road they followed was initially no more than a rough track, fit only for 4X4's until they emerged from the jungle into a land of fields and villages and after the first village the track became wider and better. Twenty miles on they reached a small town and they turned south onto a tarmac road. The surface was broken and cracked with weeds growing through but good enough still for the jeeps to belt along at forty or fifty miles an hour and the cool breeze against her skin was a pleasure for Lara after the stifling humidity of the jungle.

It was not until the two jeeps reached the Palace, that Lara became all too aware of her state of undress. In the wilds of the country, the natives wore little more than loincloths and the villagers not much more than beads and animal skins. Now Lara was faced with a sumptuous Palace and dozens of well attired people and as the jeeps drew to a halt she glanced down at herself and shook her head with shame at her appearance. The only material she had covering her was a broad belt of leather around her waist, to which at the small of her back her arms were pinned by wristcuffs also of leather. Admittedly she looked stunning, her slim body tanned, her legs toned, her breasts full and high and firm and her beautiful face framed by a mane of golden hair. Climbing from the jeep, she glanced around and telling herself to ignore the curious stares from courtiers and scurrying servants, she held her head high and followed the officer who had tracked her down and brought her as a trophy to his King.

The Palace had been built, Lara guessed some time back in the mid twentieth century at considerable expensive. It was reminiscent of a French 18th century chateau and looked totally incongruous in its African setting. Led by her hair once more, Lara was taken by the patrol's commander through a succession of state ballrooms and drawing rooms, some guarded by men in the colourful red and white uniforms and fez hats of the 19th century and others watched over by soldiers in green combat fatigues and caps with the ubiquitous green tiger motif. In a Library of dark panelled wood and countless shelves of mouldering books, half a dozen men in old fashioned dark suits sat in a circle, smoking a water pipe, sipping from tiny cups of pungent, black coffee and talking in hushed voices and the conspiratorial whispers of backstage politicians. Finally after the dark and dusty rooms, many of which were shuttered they emerged blinking into the dazzling light of a massive conservatory. From somewhere amongst the lush foliage came the sound of water trickling over stones and the humidity was such that the marble floor was damp under Lara's bare feet. The room was swelteringly hot and giddy from not having been fed well for days; Lara stumbled as the man jerked on her hair to make her follow him. Thankfully he caught her or else she would have fallen. With a light slap against both her cheeks to bring her to her senses, he caught hold of her by one arm and marched her forward.

Seated in a rattan chair, its high back fanned like a peacock sat the King of Pashkent, the Emerald Tiger. Wearing white cotton slacks and a white silk shirt, he had his legs extended, feet crossed and resting on a foot stool formed by the back of a crouching servant. Another servant, stood beside a table, its marble top supported by golden elephants, was strewn with bowls of fruit and luscious foods, crystal jugs of iced drinks and a silver three tiered cake stand, whose lavish cream cakes had long since melted and spread in a pool of strawberry juice, cream and chocolate that was trickling over the edge of the marble top and down the trunk of one of the golden elephants.

'So this is the third one?'

The Emerald Tiger smiled and gestured for Lara to take a step forward, which she did. She glanced sideways at the array of food and licking her lips, dragged the focus of her attention back to the man regarding her. He was younger than she had imagined and kinder looking and in a way Lara found this rather disconcerting. Standing behind the King were two armed guards, dressed in black body armour with visored, laser vision helmets, each had a modern laser gun and waist belt bristling with grenades and sundry doubtless violent accoutrements. A little way to one side stood a short, bald man, a European, in a creased white flannel suit and whose long, starched moustache and archaic reading glasses gave him the appearance of a character from a hundred years earlier when European nations had developed a penchant for ruling or at the least meddling in the affairs of African countries.

'Come closer girl,' the Emerald Tiger commanded.

Lara stepped forward, her heart beating a little quicker now. She was all too aware of the rising and falling of her breasts, her cleavage emphasised by the fact that her arms were drawn and held behind her back and so her chest was thrust forward somewhat. The man regarded her slowly, letting his gaze travel down her body, taking in her tangled mane of golden hair, her dark blue eyes, her deeply tanned skin.

'Turn around.'

Lara slowly turned. She knew her back was scratched from thorns and marked from recent whippings, her firm and rounded buttocks likewise she knew would still be showing faint red marks from punishment sessions she had been recently subjected to.

'Turn back and face me.'

Lara did as was asked, again glancing longingly at the display of food, so temptingly close and yet out of reach unless the man chanced to read her thoughts…

'How old are you?'

'Twenty six your Highness.'

The man nodded, raising an eyebrow and smiling. She guessed her deferential tone had pleased him and that he was surprised at how stunning she was. Her pert backside, firm breasts and slender waist could easily have been mistaken for those of an eighteen year-old. Her skin was flawlessly smooth and her muscle tone excellent. She looked awesomely fit and as one man had dryly commented on first seeing her naked, achingly fuckable.

'You came highly recommended by Doctor MacKennan. He said also that you have been well disciplined.'

'He spent a lot of time teaching me submission,' Lara answered.

The man smiled again and his gaze lingered on her sex. Shaved as she was, her pussy was shown, Lara felt to its best advantage. Her pubic lips were thick and full without being in the least soft or overly fleshy or distended. The inner lips of her vulva were already glistening with perspiration and arousal. When the Emerald Tiger slowly stood up, a knot tightened in her chest and her heart skipped a beat as her mind rushed through a dozen things that might be about to happen to her. She glanced at the armed guards and imagined herself being hauled away by them, her bare heels dragging across the marble tiles. What would the King do to her first? Her mind raced and butterflies of eager anticipation somersaulted in her stomach.

'I have had a long wait for your arrival. But I think my patience is now going to be amply rewarded.'

Lara held her breath as the man touched her, his fingertips slowly skimming over the swell of her right breast and down across her waist and lower. Lara struggled to keep still and to breathe normally as the man touched her pussy. She felt his thumb brush lightly against her clitoris and a piquant ache of arousal went through her body. His fingers stroked into the slickness between her lips and then he sank two fingers into her. Lara bit down on her lip but a sigh of pleasure still escaped her trembling mouth. The man looked into her eyes and smiling, he slowly twisted his fingers and bending them a little drew a plaintive, shuddering gasp from her.

'Keep still.'

Whether the order was directed a Lara or by it he meant "keep her still", the servant standing beside the table of food quickly stepped behind her and grasped her arms, just below the shoulders. With her wrists already fastened to the small of her back, Lara stood obediently still as the Emerald Tiger slowly withdrew his fingers and offered them to her to lick clean. With a longing glance at the food strewn marble table, Lara obediently took the man's fingers in her mouth and sucked on them, all too aware of the effect this would have on him but guessing that this was what he really wanted.

'Are you so very hungry?' he asked sympathetically.

Lara nodded timidly and managed a husky, "Yes". Her throat was achingly dry from the dust of the journey.

The Emerald Tiger dipped his fingers in the pool of cream and chocolate that had melted and spilled across the marble and gave them once again to Lara who sucked and licked them gratefully.

'Feed her, wash her and take her to the play room.'

Without another word the man turned away from her and resumed his seat. Before Lara could say or do anything the two servants took her by the arms and marched her from the conservatory.

Taken down a corridor of thick red carpet that was lit by chandeliers, the two servants brought Lara into a long, narrow room that was filled by a swimming pool. There were several dark skinned girls swimming and playing with a ball and immediately they halted their activities as the servants spoke to them in their native language. The girls, there were five of them, all no older than nineteen or twenty, Lara guessed, chatted back to the servants, laughing and nodding eagerly. Still wondering what they were all saying, Lara felt the men clasp hold of her arms again and march her quickly the last few steps towards the edge of the pool. Jerking her arms frantically as she realised what was going to happen, Lara twisted her tethered wrists urgently. But even as she struggled to free herself she was propelled over the edge, face first into the swimming pool.

Kicking frantically, she broke the surface and took a gasp of air as she struggled to keep her head above water. The girls were swimming towards her and only a few yards away now. Swallowing water and air by turn Lara turned onto her back and began to tread water. No sooner had she managed this though than a hand caught hold of her hair and pulled her backwards, her face going under the surface and water rushing up her nose.

Thrashing her legs Lara struggled to get her head back above the surface but to her dismay she realised the girl who had caught hold of her hair was actually deliberately pulling her head just below the surface. With her ears pounding and her head half under the water and then submerged completely by turns as she was pulled backwards through the water, all Lara could do was swim with her legs to try to keep up with the girl pulling her along. As her head broke the surface again she heard the girls chattering and laughing voices all around her. A soft young body slipped against hers, a hand caressed her breast, someone dived below her and arms closed around one of her thighs dragging her down below the surface again.

Her heart hammering now, Lara struggled to get back to

the surface again but before her head broke the surface for more than a second, numerous hands drew her back under the water. Someone caught hold of her ankles and now the girls' aim seemed to be simply to make her struggle to keep herself above the surface. Opening her eyes as she tussled with the numerous pairs of hands that were smothering her, she saw a grinning young face in the water watching her. The girl was quite naked and very slim and beautiful. She reached out with both arms and drew Lara into a caress. As she brought Lara into her embrace her lithe legs furled around Lara's waist and down they both sank, Lara thrashing and struggling to extricate herself, the other girl's face full of amusement and excitement.

Lara had no idea how long her torment lasted. The five girls took it in turns to keep her under the water and between turns they gave her just enough time to struggle back to the surface and gulp a little more air. They kept up the game until Lara was utterly exhausted and she had no strength left in her aching legs. By the time she felt herself being dragged out of the swimming pool she was so weak with exhaustion it was all she could to lift her head and focus her gaze on the five young girls as they danced around full of laughter and chattering. The cuffs about her wrists were unfastened and along with the waist belt removed. She was then dragged into a small pool of much warmer water and while two girls held her by the arms - not that she had the energy to struggle or resist what they did to her next – the others proceeded to soap and sponge her from head to toe.

Hauled out of the bath, Lara was laid face upwards on the tiled floor with two girls holding her arms still, and two others holding her ankles and keeping her legs drawn widely apart, the fifth girl lathered then shaved first one leg and then the other. With both legs shaved and washed down with cool water, the girl then lathered and shaved the stubble that had grown around Lara's sex since she had last been waxed there by her old owners. Cool water was then poured over her sex and with a towel her skin was patted dry. Lara lifted her head dreamily as fingers began to gently massage a cool creamy substance all over her sex. The girl who was doing this grinned when she saw Lara watching her and said something but it was utterly incomprehensible to Lara who lowered her head back against the tiles.

Exhausted after her escapade of the last few days Lara could easily have drifted asleep there and then but it was not to be. The five girls now hauled her to her feet and she was taken into an adjoining room where she was shown a table laid with food. Starting with fruit and finishing with sugared sweets Lara was allowed to eat as much as she wanted while the girls flopped down into sofas and took it in turns to brush each other's hair or to feed little delicacies to each other. While Lara ate she watched them. Besides eating and talking the girls petted and kissed each other and two, nestled on one sofa cosily together, even masturbated each other while the others watched.

After being allowed to eat and rest for an hour, it was time to be dressed. For all the girls this meant slipping on nothing more than bikinis and one of the five bothered only to wear bikini briefs and was content to cover her breasts with nothing more than a string of glittering beads than sparkled brilliantly against her dark skin. Lara was given a black silk thong to wear and a black leather collar, quite broad and soft but fastened closely at her nape and she had no trouble in guessing what might later get clipped to the large brass rings that were stitched to the collar at both front and back. One of the girls then gave Lara's hair a thorough comb and satisfied with her appearance they ushered her from the room by another door. Leaving three of their number behind, two girls led Lara by numerous corridors and turns and stairs until they came to a sliding door of modern carbon fibre that, when one of the girls touched it, simply glided open. With a nudge behind her shoulders, Lara was encouraged forward and before she knew it the door had slid shut behind her separating her from the two girls. Looking around the room, Lara knew at once its purpose and a knot of fear tightened in her stomach.

Facing her were two men, both tall, shaven headed and dressed only in

emerald green silk pantaloons, their powerfully muscled torsos bare and showing many scratches, some old and faint others more recent. Lara quickly guessed that these were scratch marks. Inflicted by nails of desperately flailing hands as some poor girl was subjected to one or another of the devices that the room contained. The two men grinned maliciously and advanced towards Lara with the unhurried pace of predators who know that there is no escape for their prey.

Chapter Seven

As soon as she was home Serena wasted no time in watching the video of her dream that the Doctor had given her. It was just like watching a film, only with her in the starring role and what was really weird was as each scene unfolded Serena found that she was able to remember what was about to happen just ahead of the event itself. She seemed to have envisaged the scenery of Dartmoor in 1905 very vividly and in remarkable detail considering that she had never even been there and certainly had no idea of what it would have looked like now or then, over a hundred years earlier.

Of course the way she was swiftly sexually dominated by the Edward de Breville was just what Serena would have wanted and even as she watched the man give her the first taste of his riding crop, Serena had her hand between her legs and was masturbating. Fast forwarding the film impatiently until she found the scene in the billiard room she began wondering more and more about what Lara might have dreamt and what it would be like to enter her friend's dream world. As on the screen before her, Serena the serving girl was tied down across the billiard table and gagged, Serena momentarily closed her eyes and gave a shuddering sigh as she fingered herself to a deliciously intense orgasm. Focusing again on the screen, her fingers still toying with her achingly erect clit, she watched as Serena the serving girl was shafted first by de Breville and then by his accomplice.

Serena returned to the Dreamscape Institute in the evening keyed to such a pitch of excitement that she was sure it could be read by anyone merely looking at her. After watching the video she had showered and she'd still been so aroused by the vivid scenes she'd witnessed that she masturbated again until she climaxed. Soaping herself clean she padded into her bedroom and with a large tumbler of iced vodka she slumped down and tried to rest for a couple of hours. This was impossible though and the only way to resist the urge to finger her pussy was to get dressed again. Choosing a short, tight skirt and a cashmere jumper to go over some of her favourite lace trimmed silk underwear, Serena nibbled at some lobster salad and drank a couple of glasses of chilled white Burgundy. All the time she was watching the clock, willing the time to move more swiftly.

She left for the Institute with time to spare and so had her chauffeur drive her a long way there choosing a route that was new to her. Her life in the city, she reflected was so dull, small wonder she was attracted to the Dreamscape Institute. There was just no frisson of danger or any unplanned excitement: she had everything her own way and it bored her. Deep down, below the civilized twenty-first century young woman she guessed a part of her was the primitive cave girl conditioned to be grabbed by her hair by a passing caveman and dragged into his lair and forced to submit to him. She remembered the scene in the video of her dream and how the men had tied her hands, leaving her arms outstretched and bound so that she was helpless while they proceeded to take it in turns to use her body. Of course she'd always enjoyed dominant men but even they hadn't been really rough with her; afraid no doubt that if they even bruised her delicate skin she might report them and they'd land up in jail. Only in her dream at the Institute had she found herself really dominated and it had been a deliciously heady thrill. Now, even better than going back to her own dream, she was going to have the chance to enter Lara's dream.

She found the main entrance of the Institute watched over by a dark suited

man who greeted her by her name and ushered her inside.

'Doctor MacKennan is awaiting you in the dream room, please follow me.'

The reception foyer was deserted now and the high, glass ceiling showed no illusion of a bright summer's day but merely the darkness of the night outside. In the quiet stillness, her high heels sounded loudly as she followed the man across the marble foyer and down the corridor that led to the dream room.

'Please do go in.'

The man smiled and stood aside for her. Disconcertingly, although it was evening and they were indoors, he wore dark sunglasses and along with his dark suit, he had more than a faint air of menace about him.

Inside the room, bathed in its now familiar green light, Doctor MacKennan and his nurse were stood waiting and both smiled as Serena entered, the nurse moving swiftly to take Serena's trench coat for her. Discarding the rain soaked item, Serena brushed her hands down the front of her short, fine wool skirt and drawing a few loose strands of her russet hair clear of her face, she smiled at the Doctor.

'It is very good of you to be so accommodating, Doctor.'

'Miss Fairfax, the pleasure is all mine.'

MacKennan gestured for her to go through to the changing room and Serena nodded, feeling oddly that there was a different atmosphere to the place than there had been during the day. But of course, the place was really closed, MacKennan had opened just for her and there was nothing more to it than this, Serena told herself as she stepped into the changing room and pulled off her jumper. Quickly shedding her clothes she changed into the towelling robe provided and went back into the dream room and without having to be asked went and lay down on the couch.

'So you are quite happy to go into your friend's dreamscape?' MacKennan asked, while his nurse began applying wires to Serena's neck.

'Sure,' said Serena as positively as she could manage. For some reason she was suddenly having some second thoughts, but it was too late now to admit that to the Doctor. What could Lara have dreamt that could be so different to what she herself had dreamt?

'Right then Serena, just relax, close your eyes and let your breathing slow right down.'

Serena closed her eyes, the last thing she noted before she

did was her own reflection upon the glass covering of the green lights above her.

'So I'll be asleep for about an hour again, right?' she asked, keeping her eyes closed and self consciously trying to settle comfortably against the padding of the couch.

'Why do you ask?'

'I told my chauffeur to wait outside for me.'

'I'll get my assistant to tell him to go home and we'll arrange for you to be driven home. If your dream sequence goes into a fluid action phase, resurfacing is best delayed until a less critical period.'

'Okay… I guess I understand what you mean by that,' Serena answered, then she added, 'but the chances are I'll be asleep for about an hour?'

'Yes, but in your dream it may be longer.'

'I can't wait to find out what Lara dreamt.'

'Just relax… you're going to drift asleep. You don't need to think or worry about anything, I will programme the computer with Lara's dream and take you there.'

'Good…I'm ready when you are…'

'Let yourself fall asleep then.'

The instruction was irrelevant; Serena felt a wave of drowsiness wash over her and she knew they had administered the emothome that would make her unconscious.

* * *

There was a little moonlight by which Serena could just make out some shadows and outlines which told her that she was in a thickly forested landscape and that she was standing in a hollow and all around her there rose dark slopes thickly covered with large pine trees. The only sound was the wind in the trees and the creaking of swaying branches high above her. Serena shivered, a mixture of both nerves and the cold. She was dressed not in the clothes that she had come in to the Dreamscape Institute but something quite different. Instead of elegant stilettos she wore heavy walking boots the style of which she imagined was adopted only by those idiotic members of society that actually liked to go tramping over the few remaining bits of wild countryside that could be found in the far north of Scotland. Instead of her skirt she was wearing black Lycra shorts and instead of her fine cashmere sweater she had on a dark red T-shirt that emphasised her generous cleavage and slender waist.

Tight around her waist was a broad belt from which hung a massive pistol in a holster and several pouches attached to the belt felt heavy with what she suddenly guessed must be replacement ammunition for the gun. My God, Serena thought, as she realised that the dreamworld she'd entered was already suggesting far more violence than she really imagined she had the stomach for. Momentarily she wished she was back in the Dreamscape Institute and then a disturbing though hit her. The Dreamscape Institute! She could remember that and she was aware that right now she was dreaming! She had managed to recall some of her dream as a servant girl in Edwardian England but at the time she had been the person of her dreams and quite unaware that she was dreaming. Now though she was fully conscious of the fact that she was inside Lara's dreamscape. But where was that and where was Lara?

Cautiously she advanced through the trees, she had imagined Lara would have conjured some erotic fantasy world for herself, hardly this! After not more than a dozen steps, edging around a broad pine tree Serena suddenly realised what her friend had been choosing to dream. Facing her was the opening to a tunnel entrance, carved into the rock, where a grassy slope came down to the basin of ground thick with leaves and broken branches in which Serena stood. Serena stared at the tunnel entrance and at the small object left balanced on a rock beside the gaping door of darkness.

The tunnel was low and dark, the stone walls cool and damp. Water trickled down from the roof, gathering in pools. The air was heavy with the smell of decaying vegetation. Serena was crouched facing the entrance. She looked down at the object so deliberately left on the rock beside the tunnel entrance and glancing nervously first behind her, she picked up the tiny mobile phone, whose luminous green facia had caught her eye. The text that the screen displayed read: *"Property of Lara, do not touch."*

Serena quickly stood up and took several steps back from the ominous blackness of the tunnel entrance. So her crazy friend had dreamt that she was the tomb raiding heroine that her mother had named her after! How could she be so stupid? Serena shook her head in disbelief and looked around her, shivering again as she scanned the encircling trees and darkness. For several long minutes Serena stood agonising at her choice and finally she determined that she would go into the tunnel in search of her friend.

The tunnel ran straight, sloped downwards and was utterly dark. Serena stumbled along, her fingertips trailing the wall. Another few steps and then she'd turn back, she kept telling herself. Glancing over her shoulder the entrance was lost to sight and the air was warm and close and a feeling of panic began to threaten to overtake her. Certain she couldn't stomach exploring any further, Serena gave a gasp of surprise when she came to an abrupt dead end. But what had stopped her was not rock but wood. Smooth wood and as she explored its surface in the darkness with her hands, her fingers brushed the cold metal of a circular handle. It took both hands to turn it and she had to lean her shoulder against the door to make it open.

The hall facing her was perhaps eighty feet square, the high ceiling supported by a dozen giant stone pillars. A shaft of moonlight spilt pale light down into the centre of the hall, revealing a long wooden table set with high-backed ornate chairs and silver candelabra. A thick layer of dust lay across everything but the dusty floor was criss-crossed by numerous sets of footprints. Serena stood motionless, breathing fast with fear as she strained for any sound. There were faded tapestries hung on the walls and double doors on the far wall that stood ajar. Half way along the left wall there was another door, which was closed. On each wall there was an iron candelabra which contained guttering candles that threw a pale orange light across sections of the vast room. Very cautiously Serena stepped into the hall and instinctively she realised that she had already drawn the gun from its holster and had it brandished before her, one finger brushing the edge of the trigger.

She was two-thirds of the way across the hall when from behind one of the pillars stepped a man. The first thing Serena took in about him was the gun he was aiming at her and quick as a flash she jerked herself sideways to the cover of another broad stone pillar. Flashes of the film of Lara Croft the Tomb Raider came back to her; her friend Lara had made her sit and watch it several times, plainly fascinated by the film's bizarre world and the adventure loving heroine. She stared at the gun she was grasping and realised that now she was going to have to use it. She guessed that to find Lara she would have to battle her friend's enemies and now she wondered just what had happened to her friend.

The sound of someone moving jerked her thoughts back to the moment and it suddenly dawned on her that someone else was creeping towards her from the very direction that she'd entered the hall. Well, even if she wanted to make a run for it, she'd have a fight on her hands now! A shadowy figure darted between two pillars and Serena raised her gun and squeezed the trigger. The shot hit the pillar the man had disappeared behind and sent a cloud of stone dust into the air. The gun leapt high in the air with the force of the shot, jerking Serena's arm upwards and pushing her almost off balance. There was the sound of boot steps close behind her and Serena spun around but before she sighted her opponent she felt the sharp pain of something hitting her in the chest just above her left breast.

Glancing down she saw a tiny, feathered dart protruding through her T-shirt. She saw the man who'd fired at her and instinctively she returned fire. Keeping her finger squeezed down on the trigger the gun erupted into a burst of fire that sent her enemy hurling himself into cover. Serena ran to another pillar, guessing that if she stayed put she'd be surrounded, but as she ran she stumbled and her legs felt achingly wobbly. Slumping against the new pillar she glanced down at the tiny almost harmless looking dart embedded in her T-shirt and quickly she flicked it out with one hand as she felt a giddiness sweeping over her.

Turning, she stumbled back towards the door, determined now to retreat but before she'd covered half the distance she felt a sharp prick as another dart embedded itself in her back between her shoulder blades. She reached behind her with her left hand and quickly flicked the dart away. Another hissed past her face and she turned to fire but her enemies were nowhere to be seen. Only as she turned back for the door again did she glimpse some movement from the corner of her eye. Before she could aim and fire another dart struck her bare thigh and though she quickly removed it her legs began buckling under her. She fired blindly, stumbled, giddiness rushing to overtake her then reaching the door managed to grab hold of the handle to stop herself from falling but she was already too weak to go any further.

Slowly she slid down the door and sank to the floor, her legs buckling under her, her ears buzzing and her eyelids shutting despite her efforts to keep them open. The last thing she remembered before she lost consciousness was the feeling of a gloved hand tightening a grasp upon her hair and lifting her head.

'Very pretty… the Doctor will be pleased!'

* * *

'Feeling nicely rested?'

Serena blinked away the drowsiness that still hung over her and focused on the man watching her. When she tried to rub her face with her hand she realised she couldn't move her arm and glancing sideways she saw that both her arms were held strapped to a wooden pole. There were four canvas straps riveted at intervals to the pole and these were bound and buckled tightly around her wrists and biceps so that her arms were held outstretched to either side of her. The pole was itself fixed to another and together they formed a cross. To her dismay Serena now realised that there was another strap tight against her chest below her breasts and yet another strap around her hips so that her whole body was effectively pinned against the cross.

Serena shook her head despondently as her senses slowly focused and she realised that more alarming still she had been stripped completely naked and her legs were spread and tied with further straps around her ankles and thighs against two poles that were bolted at forty five degree angles from the floor to the central. Her feet barely touching the stone floor, her whole body weight was held suspended and more or less supported by the ten canvas straps that held her spread-eagled.

'So how do you feel after your little sleep? Nicely rested? Ready to play some games with us?'

The man smiled, a sadistic grin and though the face was that of Doctor MacKennan from the Dreamscape Institute, Serena knew she wasn't in the Institute and the man facing her was certainly not the Doctor that she had come to know.

Flanking the evil looking Doctor were two blonde girls, who looked to be no more than nineteen or twenty. They each wore high black leather boots and short black leather skirts. Each wore a tight black leather bustier and while one wore elbow length black gloves, the other wore delicate white lace mittens that left her long fingers exposed. The girl wearing the long black gloves was brandishing a slender black rod, thinner than a finger but a metre long. Catching hold of the other end with her free hand she flexed the rod until it curved into a bow.

'The carbon fibre cane; twenty first century successor to the good old- fashioned whip. It may help you to answer the

Doctor's questions,' the girl threatened, grinning wickedly as she sliced the air experimentally with the cane.

' So you can start by telling me who you are,' the man demanded, his tone peremptory and icy.

'My name's Serena Fairfax.'

'And what has brought you here?'

'I'm looking for a friend,' Serena replied.

The man smiled and nodded, plainly pleased with her response.

'Who?'

'Lara.'

'Well, that's hardly a surprise. And how badly do you want to find your friend?' the man asked.

'So she's here then?' asked Serena.

The man gave a dismissive laugh.

'Well, that's for you to find out, isn't it? So tell me my dear, do you share your friend's penchant for pain?'

'I don't know what you mean,' Serena stammered nervously, her throat tightening with fear.

The man gave the merest nod and immediately the girl with the cane flicked her wrist and Serena felt a burning sensation lick across the bare skin of her outstretched left arm.

'Uhh!'

A pale red line appeared immediately across the soft skin of her exposed underarm then slowly faded as Serena was left to feel the sensation wash through her. She shook her head in disbelief and gazed despondently at the girl with the cane who was now grinning broadly, her icy cold blue eyes sparkling with mischief. The girl stepped a little closer and Serena felt the tip of the cane stroke across her ribs and brush against the swell of her breasts.

'Pain and pleasure, skilfully mixed... such a potent combination.'

As the girl spoke she drew the fingers of one hand slowly up the soft inside of Serena's thigh and then lightly stroked across her exposed sex, drawing an involuntary gasp of pleasure from Serena.

'Just too good, isn't it...'cooed the girl, her fingers delving a little way into Serena's pussy and then before Serena knew what had happened the girl had taken a step backwards and flicked the cane so its tip struck under Serena's right breast with such a stinging blow that it made Serena's whole body jerk against the canvas straps that held her spread-eagle.

'Uhh!'

'Nice?'

The girl stepped closer again and catching hold of Serena's jaw with one hand she held her trembling mouth still while she quickly kissed her, her eyes sparkling with malicious mischief as she then withdrew a step and the cane flashed through the air and struck Serena across her left breast.

'UHH!'

The girl smiled with satisfaction and flicked the cane so its tip bit against Serena's right thigh.

'Please... stop...'Serena begged, tears pricking her eyes as she jerked her tightly bound arms and legs ineffectually against the restraining straps.

Hiss!Twack!

The cane struck again this time on the soft inside of Serena's thigh, tears now filling her eyes; she bit her lip in agonised frustration as she twisted her tethered body helplessly in a frantic attempt to escape the torment to which she was being subjected.

'How are we feeling darling?'

The other girl, the one in the lace mittens stepped forward and gently pressing her body against Serena's she stroked her fingertips slowly down her trembling form until her hand was resting between her spread-eagled legs and her long sensual fingertips were stroking and caressing Serena's pussy. Serena sighed, shaking her head in dismay as she felt her arousal grow from the skilful female touch.

'Does this excite you? If I touch you like this...'

Serena moaned feverishly as the girl slowly slipped a finger inside her pussy and very slowly circled her clitoris with it.

'You're going to come to love submitting yourself to us, aren't you?'

'No, no...'Serena shook her head in denial.

The girl laughed as she then drew a plaintive sigh from her victim as her thumb now rubbed against Serena's clit.

'Please... no...'Serena sighed, closing her eyes as too her shame she found herself being propelled swiftly to an orgasm.

'Relax... just let yourself go.... there, now come for me baby...'

Serena gave a plaintive whimper as she knew that just a few more seconds of the girl's skilful touch would make her come.

'Now just a little more pain to mix with the pleasure...'

The girl teasing her moved her body aside without letting her hand lose contact with Serena's pussy and even as she dreamily opened her eyes again the other girl brought the cane slicing down against her right breast.

THWACK!

Pain shot from her breast to her head. Serena jerked her body frantically in response as she saw the girl aim a similar blow at her other breast. There was no escape though, she was held spreadeagled by the ten straps about her lithe arms, slender legs and struggling body. Down came the slim rod against her other breast and a similar pain lanced through her body, leaving both her breasts stinging terribly. Tears came flowing from her pretty hazel eyes, as she knew that this torment could go on longer than she could possibly bear it.

'Please! Stop! Please...'she sobbed, shaking her head desperately and casting a pleading look at the man stood behind the two girls and watching her suffering and torment.

'Shall I kiss it better?'

The girl with the lace mittens smiled apologetically and gently caressing her aching breast with one hand she lightly licked her tongue tip against Serena's nipple.

'Uhhh... mmm...'

Serena felt the girl's lips suck more forcefully, coaxing her erection to a piquant tightness and then just as Serena was willing her to once again sink her fingers into her aching pussy the girl stepped aside, laughing softly.

THWACK!

Serena cried out in pain as the cane sliced down stingingly against her other breast.

'Please stop… can't take anymore…'Serena sobbed.

With a throaty laugh one of the girls stroked Serena's perspiration soaked face, smoothing her tousled russet hair clear of her face then lightly kissing her fully on her trembling lips. The girl looked into Serena's eyes and smiled – a smile of such insincere apology that Serena jerked her arms against the straps, her anger driving her futilely for a moment to try to hit the girl. The girls laughed scornfully and the one with the carbon fibre cane flexed it thoughtfully before delivering another stinging blow.

THWACK!

The cane struck across her belly, knocking the wind from her. For a second she hung her head forwards, gasping for breath, her eyes closed. Then a hand grasped her by the hair and lifted her head so she was made to watch the next blow as it was delivered. Straight across both her breasts the cane sliced.

THWACK!

'UHH! No! Can't take any more!' Serena begged, fresh tears pricking her wide eyes and running down her cheeks. The girl holding her by her hair laughed softly and with her other hand caressed Serena's aching left breast.

'Please! Hurts… let me go… stop…'

'Hush now darling… there's plenty more to come and we know you're enjoying it really, aren't you?'

Serena groaned helplessly as the girl released her breast, slipped her hand between her spread legs and stroked Serena's swollen clitoris with her thumb.

'There now, doesn't that feel good…'?

Fingers slipped inside Serena's pussy making her sigh. She was achingly aroused and close to coming now. She gazed at her tormentors as she was brought to the brink of her climax and then as if sensing her condition, the girl with the cane delivered another sharp blow.

THWACK!

The piquant dart of pain was too much and with a loud groan, Serena came, her tethered body jerking frantically against the restraining straps as her climax shook her body. Even before her orgasm had subsided though the cane struck again, a jolt of pain needling through her right breast and plunging somehow straight to her groin bringing a second wave to her climax

'Uhhh.... Please...'

Whether Serena was begging them to stop or to keep up the delicious punishment she didn't even know.

The girl leaning close to her and still fingering her aching sex, laughed softly and sank to her knees, her hands resting against Serena's thighs as her mouth settled between Serena's spread legs. At the first touch of her tongue against her sex, Serena couldn't but help give a groan of deep pleasure.

The crouching girl's tongue licked slowly and deeply into the folds of her vulva and Serena moaned feverishly.

THWACK!

The pain of the cane cutting against her chest intensified the pleasure she was experiencing and suddenly, secretly, to her shame Serena longed for another similar blow against her other aching breast. The pain was now so blended with the feelings of being aroused that it was all one and the same: pain, pleasure... just as long as it didn't stop, she wanted it to continue now until she climaxed again!

THWACK!

'Yes! Uhh... yes...!'she panted, struggling against the straps that held her helplessly as she realised that this too was adding to her fevered state of arousal.

'That's enough...'the man ordered. 'She's ready. Collar

her!'

Lara shook her head in protest as she realised that she was being deprived of her chance to have what had promised to be the most intense orgasm.

'No… please…'

'Hush now baby, you'll like the feel of it once it's on.'

The blonde girl smiled mischievously as she slipped the cane into her thigh high boot and advanced upon Serena. As she stroked her face with one hand, the fingernails of her other hand furrowing deeply into Serena's hair, the girl who had been kneeling between her legs stood up and wiped the back of her hand slowly across her lips.

'The bitch is aching for it. She's a complete natural.'

'Now, keep still,' the blonde girl ordered.

The soft fingers twisted and clenched their hold upon her hair, forcing her head still as the other girl now moved behind the wooden frame that Serena was tethered to and slipped a broad leather collar around her throat.

'No…'

Serena tried to shake her head in objection but the girl tightened her hold and with her other hand she placed one cautioning fingertip against her trembling lips.

'Hush now darling, the real fun has hardly begun. Just let us look after you. You're going to experience things you've never even fantasised of in your darkest dreams!'

The leather was snug around her neck and buckled fast. The girl who had fastened the collar remained stood behind her, her breath warm against Serena's neck. Serena trembled nervously as the girl's hands caressed her bare shoulders then skimmed over her skin until she was caressing her breasts.

'Uhhh….so sore…please, don't whip me anymore…'

'Right, rope her collar to the pole so she can't move her head,' the man instructed, 'then get the electrodes ready. It's time for this little girl to find out just what sort of shocking treatment we've got in store for her!'

'Keep still darling…'

'Please, what's going to happen to me...?'

Serena felt her head being drawn firmly back against the pole as a fine rope was fed through a D-ring on the wide leather collar they'd fastened around her throat and then secured tightly around the pole behind her head.

'So Serena, are you wondering what happened to your friend? Would you like to see Lara?' the man asked, advancing to close in front of her and stroking his hand slowly across the soft skin of one of her outstretched arms.

'Yes... what have you done with her?'

'Done with her?' the man smiled and his hand trailed down her ribs.

'Oh, I did quite a lot with her... just like I'm going to do with you. You're just like her, except she took longer to learn her submissive nature. I think you're a quick learner, aren't you?'

The man moved his hand to the swell of Serena's right breast and she felt his thumb and finger toy with her nipple, coaxing the flesh until it was achingly firm.

'You have lovely breasts Serena... so tempting... they invite attention, just like you, your whole lovely young body. You like getting attention don't you? You crave all the stimulation you can get don't you?'

'No... not like this... please... let me go.'

The man laughed scornfully and squeezed her trapped nipple more firmly.

'Uhhh... stop... please...'Serena shook her head, biting down on her lip and looking wide eyed at the man as he continued to torment her aching nipple.

'Come on Serena, you can admit to me that a little pain goes a long way in the pleasure stakes...you want it don't you?' the man coaxed.

Serena nodded shamefully, tears pricking her eyes before she screwed them shut, too ashamed to meet the man's gaze as she was forced to confess her true feelings.

'Good girl; you see that wasn't too painful to admit to, was it now?'

As the man spoke something cool brushed against her nipple which he had been toying with and glancing down as best the broad leather collar allowed, Serena watched with fascinated horror as one of the girls fastened a steel clamp against her erect nipple while the man supported the weight of her breast with his palm.

'What are you going to do?' Serena asked plaintively as she saw a fine plastic coated wire trail from the clamp that was now firmly secured against her nipple. When the man removed his hand from under her breast she felt the gentle tug of the clamp and the delicate wire trailing against her chest.

'I'm going to give you the stimulation you wanted so you can come. That's what you want, isn't it Serena? A deeply satisfying orgasm... you don't care now what happens to you, just as long as you come! Isn't that right?' The man laughed scornfully and Serena sighed, shaking her head in denial.

Without bothering to wait for an answer the man now teased her other nipple until it was coaxed into a state of full hardness and then a similar steel clamp was screwed firmly against the erection until the trapped flesh bulged, purple and swollen from the delicate jaws of steel. When Serena saw that the trailing wires led to a small black box that the man had drawn from the deep pocket of his white surgeon's coat, her breathing quickened in alarm.

'So tell me Serena, does anyone know that you've come here?'

Serena glanced at the little control box that the man now held.

'No. No one,' she answered, her throat dry with fear as she knew what treatment she was about to receive. She glanced sideways in both directions at her outstretched arms. The canvas straps were snug about her wrists and biceps and there was, she knew with stomach churning certainty, no escape. She glanced down at her spread and bound legs and then at the delicate wires dangling from the little clamps that held her nipples trapped and swollen. She lifted her head and looked beseechingly at the Doctor.

'I'll tell you anything you want, Doctor, really!'

The man smiled triumphantly and then apologetically.

'I know you will my dear little girl, but that won't stop you from experiencing this. After all, you've come all this way for a taste of this. Now it's time for you to savour what you've so long hungered for!'

Chapter Eight

The two henchmen of the Emerald Tiger closed upon Lara who retreated first against the door and finding it locked behind her then edged her back along the wall until she came to a corner. The men grinned and moved closer. Something told Lara that she was being watched; this hunt was being observed, doubtless by the Emerald Tiger himself. This room was clearly designed and equipped for one purpose only and having heard it referred to as 'the games room', and looking around at the equipment presented, Lara knew just what sort of games would lie in store for her as soon as these two men had caught her. Of course, trying to evade capture she guessed would be just another part of the game, the prelude to more interesting things. There was no escape for her, the only point of interest was just how long might she escape from the men's clutches and then how much of a struggle might she put up as she was prepared for the games that lay in store.

Sure enough, as Lara had rightly guessed, the Emerald Tiger was watching through one of his spy holes. This one was in point of fact in the ceiling and the wide angled little glass viewing eye, unobtrusively placed above a light which shone down but not up, gave him a perfect view of the whole room but remained hidden by the glare of the overhead light to anyone below chancing to look up. The Emerald Tiger smiled with satisfaction as the new girl, looking even more stunning now she had been washed and groomed, backed herself into a corner as his two men closed in open her.

Lara glanced from man to man as they closed in on her. They looked very complacent and doubtless had every reason to be, what defenceless young girl stood a chance against two powerful built men? Lara though had been through more than her fair share of rough and tumble since the day, long ago now it seemed, when she had first gone to the Dreamscape Institute. She had fondly imagined that a part of her was every bit the adventuring tough girl, Lara the Tomb Raider and her desire to dream herself as such a heroine had led her from one dark and erotic adventure into another even more desperate. Now she was here, the sex slave of some African despot, a play -thing for him, a sexual toy for his amusement. Well, if he was hoping that she'd obligingly struggle and try to resist what he had in store for her, then she wasn't going to disappoint! If she had learnt one thing as a sex slave it was to oblige her masters whims and fancies. Invariably she would be better treated for it.

So now, she guessed, the Emerald Tiger was hoping she'd fight like mad; if he hadn't wanted her to then she would have been delivered here with her hands bound at the very least. As the men now closed the last few feet around her, Lara remembered scenes from the film of her heroine she had so often watched and she ducked to one side, pirouetting to allow herself a sideways kick with one foot at the stomach of the closest man. To her delight and surprise her foot connected squarely with him but not as high as his stomach – and she felt her heel plough between his legs the man gave a choked groan as he doubled up and stumbled backwards. Lara, quick as a flash, darted past and into the centre of the room.

Unseen, high above her, the Emerald Tiger smiled and stroked his achingly hard cock. Not in sympathy for the man who was lurching back to his feet after crumpling to his knees, but in anticipation of thrusting his cock into the new girl once she had been subdued and well tortured.

Lara glanced around her at the various implements and devices that stood ready to be used upon her. There was a table top, velvet covered, arrayed with various instruments of correction and torment and from it she grabbed a whip. For a second the two men hesitated.

'What's the matter boys; no balls for a fight?' Lara taunted as she now really began to imagine herself the tough girl adventurer she dreamt of emulating.

The two men attacked simultaneously and although she managed to bring the whip hissing down against one, the second one lunged forward unimpeded and was upon her before she could do anything further. For a moment she struggled for possession of the whip but then it was shaken from her grasp. Each man caught hold of her by a wrist and drawing apart they quickly had her arms spread and all but ineffective as they dragged her towards a long, low, padded bench.

'Damn you! Get your hands off me!'

Struggling all the way Lara was dragged across to the bench. Hissing and spitting she was then pushed face downwards and although she knew that she no longer stood a chance she continued to struggle with as much determination as she could.

The bench was perhaps a foot or so wide and no more than four feet long and the padded leather top was fastened to two chrome poles each ending in a T-bar with roller feet at each end. A sort of executive footstool, thought Lara grimly as while one man held her shoulders firmly down against the padded leather the other man threw a strap over her back just below her shoulders and fetching the two ends under the bench top threaded them together.

'Bastards! This isn't fair…'

Lara threw what energy she had left into a last ditch attempt to extricate herself from her impending fate. Once they had her held by one strap the end, she knew, would come quickly and now she really was worrying over just what they had planned for her.

'No…damn it! No…'

For all her swearing and struggling there was no way she could stop them now they had the upper hand. Her chest pressed against the padded leather she felt the leather strap across her back being drawn tight and then the strap's buckle was fastened and she realised with dismay that she was all but trapped! Although her chest and face were held close against the bench the rest of her was free for what good it was and she continued to fight and struggle madly.

Below the padded top, very close to the ground in fact, a

steel bar ran from front to back joining and bracing the legs of the stool. As one man remained holding her down the other now bound a rope around Lara's wrists and when she tried to lift her hands she realised that the bar was between her arms and now they were effectively held down.

For a brief moment Lara was allowed to kick wildly with her unfettered legs then powerful hands grasped her calves, held them together and other hands wound a rope around her ankles and bound them tightly to each other. Lara swore and cursed as her legs were then pushed forward against her body. With her chest held down against the bench by the strap across her back below her shoulders, when the men pushed her legs up against her body the effect was to force her backside high into the air and her knees were driven up onto the little bench where her stomach had rested. With another push her knees were edged higher to where her ribcage had been and now with her knees nearly brushing her breasts, Lara felt with dismay a belt being fastened around her calves so that her legs were immobilised in the position into which they had forced her.

Although she was now quite firmly securely upon the bench there was more to come. A strap was drawn around her thighs and pulled tight and fastened and then a rope was drawn around her arms above her elbows and threaded in a figure of eight between her arms it was bound repeatedly and tightly so her arms were pulled closed together and held firmly bound together below the bench.

Glancing back over her shoulder Lara saw how her rump was now thrust high and her legs were neatly bound up against her chest. With the bench being only a few feet off the floor she knew that she had been left with her rear and her sex neatly presented at the perfect height for a man to use whilst standing and the thought of what lay ahead for her poured molten through her loins and made her pussy drip with fevered anticipation. Her heart hammering, panting wildly she awaited what lay in store for her, she was then treated to one final finishing touch. Her head held still by one pair of hands, another drew a blindfold of heavy black silk against her eyes and tied it tight at her nape.

Lara felt deliciously vulnerable, blindfolded and tethered thus upon the bench, her arse thrust high and when fingers drew aside the silk thong and touched her sex lips, they found her slick with arousal. She turned her head this way and that but all was darkness for her though she could smell a new smell – aftershave, something expensive and she guessed that the Emerald Tiger had come to inspect his new toy. Lara wriggled as the hand stroked her sex and she murmured appreciatively as the fingers stroked her vulva slowly before sinking into her pussy and making her sigh with the need to be fucked. Hands caressed her rounded arse, appreciating its firmness and smoothness and then the fingers once more delved into the moist folds of her sex. Lara groaned with her need and wriggled impatiently against the straps and ropes that held her down. There was soft laughter and then a voice:

'Give me a knife.'

Lara guessed for what the knife was intentioned and sure enough second later she heard the blade slicing through the silk thong that she wore. The material slipped from her and then the silk, wet and musky with her juices was pressed against her lips. Obediently she opened her mouth and the fabric was insinuated into her mouth.

'Uhhh…'

She shook her head a little as a silk gag was then drawn across mouth between her parted jaws and tied at her nape.

'Fetch the tusk.'

Lara now in her world of darkness, her senses sharpened, was made to wait for what seemed many minutes before cool droplets of some slick oil were dribbled between the mounds of her arse against the crater of her rectum. When fingers rubbed the oil into her anus, probing her there to the first and then second knuckle, Lara groaned through the gag and pulled experimentally against the straps and ropes that tethered her.

They held her snugly and while she could wriggle her arse as much as she pleased, she could not extricate herself and even as she struggled experimentally, something hard and cool was pressed against and then driven into her anus making her writhe with alarm as she felt its girth widen quickly, forcing her sphincters to distend.

The Emerald Tiger gestured to his men that enough of the tusk was inserted and now he watched, very satisfied so far with proceedings, as crushed berries were tipped into the hollow ended elephant's tusk. The juice of the bright red berries would drive the girl mad with arousal and she would throb and burn with a need to be shafted soon enough. The berry juice was potently effective and the tusk served to administer it most efficiently. With plenty of berries now filling her rear, the tusk was withdrawn and slid into her sex. More berries were tumbled into the tusk and a wooden spoon was then stirred around inside the tusk to encourage the contents to spill downwards into the tethered girl's sex. Soon enough the girl was groaning through her gag and tossing her head from side to side, her arms and legs jerking and straining at the straps that held her immobile.

Lara groaned feverishly through the-saliva soaked gag, begging them to fuck her. She was achingly close to coming and just needed a cock embedded in her to bring her to orgasm. Please... she implored, unable to see the men standing around her but well aware that they were there, watching her suffering. Fuck me... please fuck me, she begged. The aching, the arousal, the sweet burning in her sex and rectum was agonising and driving her mad... she couldn't bear it any longer...

'Is something the matter?'

The sarcastic voice was that of the Emerald Tiger, the smiling young man in the white trousers and shirt she had been brought before in the conservatory. Lara could clearly imagine him stood there, right besides her, smiling at her distress. She groaned through the gag, begging him to fuck her but her pleading was made all but unintelligible thanks to the silk filling her mouth.

'She's desperate for it,' observed the Emerald Tiger, and Lara felt his hand stroke her back, from her shoulders where the strap held her down along to her curving rump which was thrust so high and now ached so much she couldn't bear it any longer. She felt the man's hand curve over her swell and then pat her.

'She can't come though, not without some more stimulation, so we'll leave her like this for a while. Give her half an hour, by then the effect of the berries will have worn off. Then we'll get her all worked up again, only by a different means.''Nuuuhhh!'The hand patted her rump affectionately.'I'm sorry my dear, did you imagine I would pander to your needs and fuck you? No, you will be left to ache for a while and then you'll be made to ache again in some different way. Eventually you may get to watch me fuck another of my slaves, but for you there will be no gratification… just torment and pain.''Nuhh…'Lara sighed abjectly through the gag.The man laughed and teased her by rubbing his thumb agonisingly close to her aching sex. Lara jerked and struggled against the restraints but it was hopeless. She felt hands stroking her hair and drawing the lustrous, golden strands clear of both her ears, then before she knew it, something was being inserted in both her ears at the same time. Lara shook her head in objection as best she could but hands were restraining her head and too late she realised that her ears had been plugged and now as well as blindfolded she was plunged into a world of sound deprivation. She jerked her arms and legs against the straps and ropes to demonstrate her frustration and objection. There was no response though, no one touched her, and she heard no voices. She turned her head this way and that straining for some sound but whatever they had insinuated into her ears it was utterly effective. Now she had absolutely no way of knowing what was about to befall her and the awareness of her vulnerability made her achingly aroused and combined with the potency of the berry juice they had forced into her sex and arse, she was frantically close to having an orgasm. If only someone would touch her, stroke her, whip her, punish her… anything just to make her come! Lara shook her head and groaned feverishly through the gag. This was so unfair… she'd rather be fucked senseless repeatedly than be left to suffer like this! Please fuck me! She begged, unable to even hear own muffled begging, except in her fevered mind.The Emerald Tiger stood and smiled at the girl's obvious distress. Like all these European Alpha females, she was utterly, shamelessly driven by an insatiable sexual hunger. Desperate for sexual gratification, she would submit to anything, even tormenting pain, as long as it brought her to her climax, that was what she, they, craved. Well, this one he would make wait… he would subject her to plenty before he finally took her and satisfied her. By the time he had finished with her she would be the most devoted slave girl… she would willingly do anything for him and because he would be in control of her so totally, she would worship him. She was so driven by her sexual craving that he knew he could use her weakness to subdue her; tame her and bend her to his will. For the Emerald Tiger though the need to have a satisfying orgasm was just as paramount as for Lara. But while the she would remain frustrated, he could satisfy himself easily…No sooner had he clicked his fingers than the young blonde was led into the games room. The two soldiers had her grasped firmly by the arms – not that she could have offered much resistance tied and drugged as she was – and hauled her across to a bench, upon which they forced her face down. The Emerald Tiger watched as the soldiers moved to the far end of the bench and each grasping the girl by a wrist they pulled her arms outstretched, forcing her to bend at waist across the bench. Discarding his trousers, the despot moved to behind the young girl and stroked her soft legs, encouraging them to part a little. Glancing over at his new acquisition he saw the berry juice was having its desired effect: gurgling into the silk gag and tossing her head this way and that, the golden haired girl was writhing and struggling frantically to free herself. All she could achieve though for so much effort was pathetic. So well bound and tethered was her delicious young body that there was no way she could ever hope to extricate herself from the bench.

The Emerald Tiger smiled and parting the girl's sex lips with the fingers of one hand he eased his throbbing cock into her body. The girl moaned, though sedated, she was conscious enough to appreciate what was happening to her and when he withdrew a little then rammed his cock back into her to the hilt, her head lifted from the table as she gave a long sigh. The Emerald Tiger caught hold of her blonde hair with one hand and drew her head back so he could glimpse her expression.

'Is that good?' he demanded.

The girl nodded affirmatively and sighed with pleasure. The Emerald Tiger released her hair and grasping her around the hips with both hands withdrew his cock and plunged it back into her. The girl gave a carnal moan and abruptly the sadistic monarch withdrew his cock and stepped back.

'The bitch is enjoying herself too much! Take her back to her cell but bind her hands behind her back so she can't play with herself!'

Turning his attention back to the new girl as the blonde was dragged from the room he smiled thoughtfully as he pondered all that he could subject her to. He would see just how well trained she really was! There were devices of torment and torture that would have her begging him soon enough. But he would take his time with her… long and agonising would be her suffering. He stroked his cock, which twitched and throbbed now with the urgent need to come.

'Ungag her!'

While his instructions for Lara were quickly carried out he wandered across to the table of instruments and picked up a simple ring gag. While his henchmen forced it upon the girl he stood watching, stroking his cock as he regarded her jaws being coaxed apart and the hardened circle of plastic being insinuated between her teeth, so that once the strap was fastened behind her head, her mouth was held open by the gag so that whilst she might wag her tongue there was no way she could close her jaws. Controlling her head by a firm grasp on her hair with both hands, the Emerald Tiger drove his cock into her mouth and gazing down smiled as he felt her struggle in his hands, the heat from her mouth and the slickness of her tongue coaxing him to his orgasm even though the girl might have wished it otherwise. There is nothing you can do to prevent this or anything else that I fancy submitting you to, he mused, as his cock began to throb madly and he tightened his hold on the girl's head coaxing her closer against him so that the tumescent head of his cock pressed against the back of her throat. This is just the beginning dear girl, merely a taste of what lies in store. He felt the girl struggle in his hands like a hooked fish. He grinned, savouring the feel of her mouth around his cock. Her perfect white teeth were forced into an accommodating circle by the ring-gag and as his cock erupted he tightened his hold on her hair, holding her head close against him so his shaft remained deep inside her mouth.

CHAPTER NINE

Serena sighed, opening her eyes and blinking as she adjusted to the brightness of the fluorescent green light after the more shadowy environment of her dream. She slowly drew a deep breath and then closed her eyes again. The dream world was gone though and although she could clearly remember being tethered to a pole and subjected to some exquisitely painful torture, the details were already eluding her.

'How do you feel, Serena?'

Glancing up at the white-coated man standing over her, she smiled reassuringly and nodded. MacKennan bore more than a passing resemblance to the evil Doctor in her dream and this Serena found disturbing. Had she or Lara invited him into their dreamworld or had he somehow entered by his own choosing. Already her mind was rushing, thinking not about the enjoyment she'd drawn from the dream but about Lara's disappearance and how it might be connected with the Dreamscape Institute.

'Would you like to just lie there and rest for a while?'

'No Doctor MacKennan, I'm fine. I was just trying to remember bits of the dream.'

She looked searchingly at him as she sat upright on the couch. Did he know what she'd dreamt? Presumably he'd watched the dream on one of the monitor screens. The thought was at first embarrassing but then amusing. She was sure she was no different to his other female clients. It would be a safe bet to assume all their fantasy dreams revolved around sex. What Serena was now wondering was whether Lara like her had dreamt of being forced to submit herself sexually.

Under the shower and while dressing, the same questions kept going round in her head. In her own dreamscape she had been the submissive servant girl but in Lara's dreamworld had her friend meant to be like the tough heroine of the old film who never let any man get the better of her or had Lara deep down wanted to be like Serena and to allow herself to be dominated? As she was driven home she gazed down at the recording of her latest dream that the Doctor had given her. She couldn't wait to watch it; not just in case it offered her any clues but because she was already imagining herself curled up on her sofa, masturbating with a dildo as she watched the film of her alter ego.

Only when she watched the film through for the third time did she stop playing with herself and concentrate on looking for clues about Lara in the film. There were more than could have dared to hope for. Of course first of all there was the mobile phone left blatantly outside the tunnel entrance and obviously placed there so that anyone following Lara would find it. Had her friend left it there hoping Serena might find it? Who else knew that Lara fancied herself as the tomb-raider heroine? Serena began to imagine that perhaps Lara had guessed she would follow her. And if so, was the phone meant as a directional sign encouraging Serena to follow her friend or was it perhaps meant as a warning? She was allowing her imagination to carry her away, Serena admonished herself and padding barefoot through to her kitchen she poured herself a glass of chilled Chablis and gazed out of her kitchen window onto the night-shrouded city landscape.

Sipping her way through her second glass of wine she saw the other clues that she'd missed on the first two viewings. Lara had without any shadow of a doubt fallen foul of the evil doctor. In the room where Serena had been tied to the pole, there was a another pile of clothes and two guns, like the ones that she herself had been wearing and which were piled in the centre of the floor, lying discarded in a corner of the torture chamber. And then there was the evil Doctor's own admission that Lara had taken longer to learn her submissive nature than she had. So was that it then, Serena wondered? She recalled the last thing her friend had said to her: something along the lines that she knew what was coming to her but that it was no more than she deserved or wanted. Serena gazed at the last frame of the film of her dream, frozen on the screen before her, the light of the pause button on her remote control still flashing. She stared at the picture; herself, arms outstretched and legs spread and held tethered by ten canvas straps tight against her naked skin. A broad leather collar was snug about her neck and clipped to the pole, holding her head forcefully high. There were pale red lines across her breasts and thighs where the carbon fibre cane had hit her. There were shiny steel clips fastened to her nipples and from them trailed two fine wires that ended at a small black box the evil Doctor held. Serena silently cursed MacKennan; certain that he had deliberately chosen that moment to wake her. She stared at the frozen image on her screen for several more minutes and then reluctantly she switched it off. There was nothing for it – first thing in the morning she would have to call the Institute and arrange another session.

* * *

'Thank you for seeing me again so soon,' Serena smiled warmly at MacKennan as he crossed the Institutes foyer to where she was sitting. By good chance, he explained, another client had cancelled at the last moment and so he had been able to see Serena the day after she rang. As she followed MacKennan, Serena felt her pulse quicken and by the time she had been ushered into the room where she was to dream, her pussy was wet with arousal. Watching the film of her torture at the hands of the evil Doctor and his two female assistants, Serena could see the torment she was suffering but all she could really think about was how satisfying it had been when she had been brought to climax after climax by the skilful mixture of pleasure and pain meted out by her tormentors. Even without the pretext of continuing her search for her missing friend, Serena wouldn't have needed an excuse to return to the Institute for another dream session.

'I hope you find your next dream sequence as satisfying as the last,' MacKennan smiled as Serena lay down on the couch and the nurse proceeded to prepare her.

'And you're certain my dream will resume where it left off, Doctor?' Serena asked.

'Yes, that I can promise you, but from then on, well…'

Serena tried not to smile too much and closed her eyes. She knew that the wires connected to the nipple clamps presaged just one thing; more excruciating pain. As if the cane wasn't enough now the evil Doctor was going to release an electric current into her breasts. Serena was shamelessly eager to experience what it would be like. She knew such practices went on at sex clubs devoted to S&M and whilst she'd been too self-conscious to explore such places, she now had the chance to try out such torture on herself and without actually hurting herself because, after all, it was only a dream…

* * *

Serena gazed despondently at the evil Doctor as he idly fingered the little black box that he held in his palm and from which trailed the fine wires that were connected to the steel clamps that bit with such bitter sweet pain upon her aroused and aching nipples. Standing watching her distress were the man's two female servants, menacing dark reflections of the two young nurses that MacKennan of the Dreamscape Institute employed. While they wore uniforms of crisp white and angelic smiles, these two girls now surveying her suffering were uniformed in black, which contrasted starkly with their platinum blonde hair and frosty blue eyes.

Watching her impending torment also were two of the Doctor's male henchmen. These were the two who had ambushed Serena. Each was a genetically enhanced fighting machine against which no one, Serena realised with dismay, stood much of chance. The men looked menacing in the extreme, nearly seven feet tall and as powerfully built as any gym fanatic or body builder she'd ever seen, their strength was awesomely apparent. Their arousal was also all too evident: pressing against the fabric of their khaki combat shorts were erections of massive proportions.

‘Impressive aren’t they my dear?’ said the evil Doctor, evidently reading Serena’s thoughts.

‘They look…’Serena stammered, ‘Unnaturally…’

‘Unnaturally powerful?’ the man suggested.

‘Yes…’Serena admitted, her throat under the leather collar constricting with fear.

‘Genetic modification;’ explained the Doctor, ‘I have bred and produced these excellent specimens.’

Serena gazed at the two men who she now imagined more as brutish monsters and whose genetic enhancement she realised had created men who looked to be hung like bulls judging by the size of what pressed against the fabric of their shorts.

‘Don’t worry my dear,’ MacKennan smiled sadistically, ‘you won’t have too long to wait before I allow my guards to have the pleasure of making your acquaintance.’

‘You have to be kidding! They’re animals not men!’ Serena looked wide-eyed with alarm at the two men stood leering at her. Hung spread-eagled upon the wooden cross she knew she had no control over what might happen to her and the sight of the men’s arousal poured molten through her own loins.

‘So did you ever dream such stimulating pleasure would lie in store for you my dear Serena?’

‘You can’t do this to me!’ Serena protested, gazing frantically at her outstretched arms and the tightly bound canvas around her wrists and biceps.

‘But you have come here of your own volition dear girl. You must have known what you might find at the end of the tunnel.’

‘No! No, I’d no idea… please, let me go!’

The evil Doctor shook his head.

‘Too late to leave now Serena: you may as well embrace what is coming to you. After all, I’m sure you’ll find it rather stimulating.’

Serena saw the man move his thumb from the side to the

top of the little black box he held and even as he smiled she suddenly felt the first ripple of electricity pulse from her nipples through her breasts.

'Uhhh! Uhhh….'

'Refreshing isn't it, my dear?'

Unable to move her body more than fractionally and with her head held against the pole by the collar, all Serena could do was jerk and twitch her feet and clench and unclench her hands as the electricity flowed through her tethered body from her breasts.

'Nuuhh! No! Please… stop… it…enough…'she begged, tears streaming down her cheeks as the torment went on for what seemed like forever, though it was in truth only a few seconds. When it ended, Serena hung exhausted, her nipples aching madly, her breasts throbbing and her whole body trembling and bathed in perspiration.

The evil MacKennan smiled with satisfaction as he saw the condition the first taste of the electric treatment had left the girl in. By discharging the current into her nipples which were already aching from being clamped, the girl was neatly tenderised and all the more receptive to the shock. The current was stimulating without being too vicious to produce a pleasing response from a tethered victim

'Please… not again…no more…'Serena begged, wide eyed with fear now as the man stepped closer to inspect her. Her breasts were still throbbing from the shock that had been administered as he touched them, caressing her aching orbs and then lightly fingering the clamps that dangled from her swollen nipples. Serena groaned and struggled to bring her tears her under control.

'You enjoyed that my dear, didn't you?'

'No…no… please…'

She felt the man trail his hand down her body to where her spread thighs were held bound. When he stroked between her legs, his fingers exploring the delicate skin between her anus and her pussy, to her shame she sighed uncontrollably and the man laughed softly.

'I think you're ready to taste a little more stimulation aren't you?'

'No... can't take anymore, please don't...'

'Relax, I wouldn't subject you to anything I knew you wouldn't, deep down, enjoy.'

As the man spoke he removed the wires that dangled from the clamps fastened upon her nipples.

'Thank you... I couldn't have taken anymore, really,' Serena sighed as she saw that now nothing more than harmless clamps dangled from her throbbing nipples. Ignoring her, the man turned aside and addressed the two young girls.

'Bring some clamps and tape and two wired probes.'

'No!' Serena blurted in objection but the man only grinned sadistically as she struggled helplessly against the straps that held her outstretched while the two girls quickly and gleefully responded to the man's orders. First, as if to underline her helplessness, extra straps were fastened around her thighs, this time as high up her trembling legs as was possible. With her thighs pinned wide, Serena could only gaze down as best the collar permitted and watch as one girl proceeded to play with her pussy until she was lathered into a state of slick arousal.

'The wetness will help to conduct the electricity. Peg her outer lips.'

'No... please!' begged Serena but her pleading went ignored and soon she felt the hard coldness of metal against her pussy as long, curve handled, flat bladed tweezers were applied to her labia. With the serrated metal of the blades gripping her outer labia, the curved implements were then taped against the insides of her thighs and their handles taped together so that they retained a firm bite upon the delicate folds of flesh they had drawn apart.

'Very pretty... most revealing... feeling excited Serena, are we?'

MacKennan slowly brushed his thumb along the exposed

crease of moist, soft pinkness drawing an involuntary groan of sexual hunger from Serena. All she could do was gaze in fascinated horror as the man showed her what he had in store for her next. The tube, some six inches long and two inches wide was clear plastic but set into the plastic was a spiralling wire that coiled from the pointed tip to the flared base from which two metal insertions protruded.

'No... please... this isn't fair... this isn't my dream, I didn't know any of this would happen. Doctor, please don't ...'

'Gag her until we're ready, she's whinging like a spoilt little girl!'

'No! Stop it! NUHH!'

Serena gave a muffled cry of protest as a hand clapped across her mouth. While one girl silenced her with a hand across her mouth, the other went and fetched a gag, returning with a malicious smile on her pretty face as she held the device up for Serena to see.

All Serena could manage was a brief, choked cry as the hand was withdrawn and a rubber, phallus shaped gag was forced between her jaws. With the phallus filling her mouth and keeping her jaws apart the gag was drawn tight from behind her head and the broad pad of rubber to which the phallus was moulded, pressed against her mouth stifling any further objections she would have made.

Tears welling now in her wide eyes she moaned through the gag as the Doctor inserted the plastic tube into her sex. The broad leather collar snug around her throat prevented her from seeing it being actually slipped into her body but she felt it sliding into her pussy and she gave a muffled cry for help, as the appalling certainty of what she was going to suffer impressed itself upon her.

MacKennan smiled smugly and showed her a second identical tube.

'You're going to get so much excitement at one time that it could be enough to make a young girl quite dizzy!'

Serena tensed and groaned through the gag as the man's

thumb forced a passage into her anus.

'Come on darling… relax… what's wrong with a little pain mixed with so much pleasure?'

Serena felt the man's thumb twist and then withdraw and then slip into her again, this time, slick with something sticky and warm.

'Doesn't that feel good… now for something a little more substantial perhaps?'

'Nuuhh!'

Serena gave a gag-muffled groan of protest as she felt her rectum being filled by the tube. With its full six inches of length pushed into her she felt the flared base press against her anus.

'Tape them both girls so they don't slide out by accident.'

One of the black-clad girls produced a roll of adhesive tape and cutting a strip off smoothed it across the base of the tube protruding from Serena's rear passage. As Serena felt the tape being pressed against her skin she knew now that there was no chance she could possibly use her anal muscles to expel the device. More tape was then used to keep the other tube snugly inside her pussy and then Serena was cruelly shown the two sets of plastic coated wires, black and red that were then fastened to the metal insertions that protruded from the tubes.

'Now my darling Serena,' the man smiled as he clipped the other ends of the four wires to the little black box that he held, 'let me explain the game we're going to play.'

Serena stared wild-eyed as the man finished securing the wires to the box.

'I believe that you will find this deeply arousing. You will love the sensation that is produced from the electricity warming and exciting your pussy. Soon enough you'll be begging for more and all too soon you'll come, enjoying such an exquisite orgasm that you'll be well on the way to a delicious addiction to the stimulation of such bitter sweet pain that I can offer you. Don't you agree?'

'Nuhh!'

The man laughed scornfully.

'Pity to leave those nipple clamps redundant… fetch some weights, nothing too extreme, just a little something to enhance the moments ahead for Miss Fairfax.'

'Nnnnhh…'

With abject dismay, Serena watched as one of the girls quickly produced two small tear shaped weights of shining metal and proceeded to clip them onto the clamps that were so tight about her nipples that they showed purple and swollen between the steel jaws. With the weights fastened the girl stepped back and Serena was left for a moment to whimper plaintively as the pain from the weights pulling upon her aching nipples washed through her tethered body.

'So how about a friendly little wager my dear Serena?' The man stepped closer to her and glanced down at her trembling body. The aching now in her nipples was unbearable but worse in its way was the feeling of the two probes embedded in her helpless body. She knew what was about to happen and after the first taste of electric shock treatment she'd had she would have begged for anything else but more of that.

'Your friend Lara loved the taste of pain; it made her very randy, very appreciative of how I could pleasure her. I think you, since you've come here after her, are like your friend.'

Serena shook her head as best she could but with the collar roped tightly against the pole, her gesture of denial was rendered useless.

'I'll make a deal with you Serena; if this little session of stimulation doesn't give you the sweet orgasm you're desperate for, then I'll stop it and free you. However, if we all get to see just how much this turns you on, then to teach you not to lie I'll have to keep you here and really punish you until you're truly sorry.'

Serena shook her head in objection, jerking her arms desperately against that straps that restrained her.

'There's no point in struggling darling… while it makes

you look quite delightful, writhing so desperately, you'll never extricate yourself from those straps or the predicament in which you have now placed yourself!'

Taking a step back the man glanced down at the black box he held then looking at Serena he smiled – a smile so knowing of what he was about to inflict upon her that Serena's stomach churned and despite the numerous restraints that she knew tethered her with such ruthless efficiency, she struggled for a moment as she saw his thumb hovering above the switch on the control box he held.

'Take the gag off, 'the man ordered, then glancing back at his two brutish guards he laughed.

'If this makes her come: then you two can have her to yourselves for the rest of the night. I do trust you'll be able to keep our new guest suitably entertained?'

Serena stared at the two henchmen as they edged closer to enjoy the spectacle. For a brief second she was afforded a chance to reflect upon the situation she'd got herself into. How on earth was she going to get out of this dream if this got worse and she really couldn't take anymore? Would she be able to just wake up? She panted hard as the gag was removed from her mouth and knew there was no point in pleading any longer for the man not to torment her. Her eyes locked with his as his thumb touched the control.

'Uhhh!'

The jolt of electricity lasted for only a second or two but left Serena feeling dazed and breathless. Now the shock had finished she was left for a moment, tethered and helpless, to dazedly register how it had felt and how she was left feeling. She gazed at the man standing before her and she felt almost mesmerized by the little black box balanced in his palm and the potent effect it could have upon her. Her pussy ached, her rear passage throbbed and her legs felt helplessly weak now. The man brought his thumb down upon the button again.

'Uuhh!'

This time there was no abrupt end to the torment.

'No! Please... stop...'Serena begged, writhing frantically against the straps that held her against the cross as the electricity continued pouring into her shaking body, leaving her, when it stopped a few seconds later, sobbing and exhausted, her slender body bathed in perspiration and aching not just from the pain of the shock but from where she had struggled so madly against the straps that were bound around her delicate arms and legs.

'Now let's feel...'

The man stepped forward and fingered her throbbing sex around where the tube was plunged and held inside her. She was as he had predicted wet with arousal and to her shame, Serena knew it even before he touched her. The whole experience as humiliating, painful and frightening as it might be was also potently arousing and just before he had sent the second jolt of electricity into her, she had not just tensed knowing what was to happen but she had felt a keen, dark anticipation of how it would feel. Just as she was turned on by being treated a bit roughly by her sexual partners she had found herself even more excited by being rendered so totally helpless and forced to submit to the whims of the man into whose hands she had now fallen.

'Oh yes, you just can't help yourself can you Serena? The torment is just too exquisite. I do believe you're going to come for me quite quickly.'

'Please, no more...'

With an apologetic smile the man switched the current on again and this time it lasted even longer.

'Uhhh...UHHH! NO!' Serena cried, writhing and jerking helplessly against the tight straps.

'Does that feel a little too intense?'

The shock continued to pour through her, drowning her sex and filling her aching body unbearably. The pain was getting no worse but now Serena was all too aware of how it was cruelly stimulating her sex. Her pussy now throbbed with an aching need to come.

'No more… no…please…'Serena pleaded, a fainting giddiness overtaking her and her head lolling forward, her eyes closing. The evil Doctor was right, she realised with dismay, the torture of the electric current pouring through her sex and rectum was going to bring her to orgasm and there was nothing she could do to prevent it. Weakly she lifted her head and gazed at the two henchman watching her torment. She knew then with stomach churning certainty that she would be given to them next and the thought of them taking her body for their cruel pleasure made her ache even more with sexual longing.

'Uhhh! No….uhh… mmm…'

Writhing and moaning as the electric surge rippled through her pussy and into her rear, Serena could do no more than groan feverishly and struggle against the straps and restraints. By the time it was over her sex was achingly aroused and she was gasping breathlessly. She hung spread-eagled from the wooden frame, too dazed to even to speak while the man again examined her. The touch of his thumb against her clitoris though, so sensitive was it now, made her cry out.

'Feeling very tender there now? Desperate for a little more stimulation now are you?'

Serena gazed at the man, blinking back the tears that filled her eyes and her body trembling, she gave a weak nod in admission of the truth.

'Yes…'she answered breathlessly.

'Good girl.'

Another jolt of electricity ran through her body and this time it didn't stop.

'Time to come then Serena… there's a good girl.'

'Uhhhh…'

Serena groaned feverishly, twisting her wrists and writhing with her arms against the straps as she felt herself rushing achingly to a climax.

'Nearly there…'

Serena felt herself fainting, the sensation of the sustained electric shock now too intense for her body. Abruptly the pain stopped. A hand lifted her head up by the chin and focusing she saw the man scrutinising her. With his thumb he brushed away a fleck of blood from her mouth where she'd bitten down on her lip in her agony and ecstasy. Satisfied that she was still conscious he glanced down at her spread and tethered legs. When his thumb stroked against her throbbing sex, Serena groaned helplessly.

'Just a little more pain Serena and the pleasure you'll enjoy will have made it all worthwhile. You don't want me to stop this now do you?'

'No,' Serena answered breathlessly.

'A little more pain then?'

Serena nodded affirmatively.

Again the burning sensation filled her sex and spread into her aching body.

Serena gazed at the girls and men stood watching her and after another couple of seconds of the torment she was panting hard as her bound body strained against the straps and she was driven towards her orgasm. She saw the hungry, lascivious gaze of the two brutish henchmen and knew that if she came she would be turned over to them. The thought was too much and with a long, desperate moan her tethered body was convulsed by the most intense orgasm she'd ever experienced. Mercifully the electricity was stopped.

She would then easily have slid into unconsciousness but the man lifted her chin with one hand again and with his other hand he lightly flicked the weights clamped to her nipples, bringing a fresh jolt of pain to her exhausted body.

'Sorry my dear girl, there's no rest for you just yet. My men have waited so patiently and I know they're very keen to get to know you on better terms.'

'No…no…'Serena groaned weakly.

'Remove the probes, it's time for this sweet little girl to discover the joys of male genetic enhancement.'

'Please… no… can't bear anymore… stop…'

'You'll find my guards have great physical stamina Serena and with such delightful company as yours, they'll find plenty to amuse themselves. So shall we say that I'll see you again tomorrow morning?'

'Don't leave me with them! Please Doctor… no…'

Serena watched as the man turned on his heel and walked away.

The two female assistants having removed the probes from her aching body began unfastening the straps around her legs. With one last backward glance, the Doctor smiled with satisfaction as he saw her being dragged down by the arms from the cross. Too exhausted to offer any resistance, Serena was hauled across the stone floor by the two girls and dragged face down onto a waist high bench.

Glancing sideways Serena saw the Doctor walk out of the room then looking the other way she saw one of the two brutish guards unbutton his shorts and pull out his cock and then balls. As the Doctor had warned her, his henchmen had been genetically bred to be unnaturally powerful and not only was this man physically built like a bull he was hung like one as well. Serena stared disbelievingly at the massive erection and its scrotum filled with balls twice the size of any normal man's. Weakly she tried hauling herself from the bench but one of the girls pushed her back down. The other had gone to a table and now returned with four leather cuffs and grabbing hold of Serena's ankle she slipped one cuff around it and buckled it tight.

'There's no point in struggling you silly thing… you're not going anywhere,' one of the girls laughed as she held Serena still while her other ankle was dealt with in like fashion.

'Okay, now her wrists.'

'No! Let me go!'

Serena struggled to drag herself free from the girls but they were too determined and she was now too weak with exhaustion. As soon as her wrists were bound with a cuff on each the girls then forced her onto her back.

Now the two men joined the girls and while one of the men held her down by pinning her shoulders with both hands the other forced Serena's left leg to bend back upon itself until her thigh was pressing against her chest. While the man held her still one of the girls then caught hold of her left arm and pulled it up alongside her left leg allowing the other girl to use the bulldog clip dangling from her wrist cuff to fasten it against her ankle by clipping the two leather cuffs together. Struggle as she might after a brief moment Serena's right arm and leg had also been bound together in a similar fashion and now she was stranded on her back, her legs drawn up against either side of her chest with her arms outstretched and her wrists pinned against her ankles.

'Pull her down the table a bit.'

Serena felt as helpless as an upturned turtle as she was dragged until her arse was just at the end of the bench and lifting her head she saw with dismay the brutish guard with his cock at the ready standing waiting, a sadistic grin on his face. Had she met such a massively endowed man under normal circumstances she doubted that she would have risked letting him try to fuck her. The prospect of what was now going to happen to her made her stomach churn. Serena knew she had a tight little pussy and while she loved being filled, she knew there was a limit to what any girl could take.

'No! You can't do this to me!' she protested as loudly and determinedly as she could. Her protest though fell on stony ground.

The girls were standing to each side of the bench and each now took a hold on one of her thighs. Serena shook her head in despair as her legs were encouraged apart.

'Please… don't let them…'

Wide eyed with alarm, Serena glanced from girl to girl beseechingly but they only smiled with eager anticipation as the man standing between her spread legs stepped close against the end of the bench and Serena felt the hardness of his hand press down over her panting stomach to stop her wriggling.

'Let me go! This is crazy, he's too big… please!' Serena begged, struggling against the numerous hands that held her down. Craning her neck against the leather collar that was still buckled around her throat she glimpsed again the massive cock and the sight sent a shiver of nervous anticipation and terrible expectation through her helpless body. An insidious voice though at the back of her mind was now willing them to get on with it, eager to experience just how it would feel to be shafted by such a thing. Unable to believe that she was actually getting aroused at the prospect, Serena struggled all the more wildly as if to escape not just what was about to befall her but to escape from her own dark thoughts.

'Uhhh….uhhh…'

The thickness of the shaft as it penetrated her took her breath away and then as it relentlessly ploughed into her the sensation of her pussy being so filled as to make her cry was too much and Serena came, a shuddering climax that had her bucking against the hands that subdued her body.

'She likes it. Give it to her,' one of the girls encouraged.

The cock, only a little way embedded in her, withdrew and then was pushed back into her sex until half of the massive shaft was buried in her.

'UUUHHH!'

Serena threw herself forward, dragging her legs together with all her strength as the force of the assault upon her slender body by the monster organ brought tears to her eyes. The man stood holding her shoulders, momentarily lost control of her but with a ruthless swiftness he caught hold of her hair and dragged her head back down. Four determined female hands forced her thighs apart once more. The cock was pulled from her sex and then driven into her again to over half its length.

Serena now couldn't lift her head from the bench so tight was the hold upon her hair. Strain as she might she couldn't prevent the girls from keeping her thighs drawn apart. The cock eased from her aching pussy, ploughed back into her and the exquisite pain of another violent orgasm shook her.

'Please... enough... stop it...' Serena sobbed, too shattered now to struggle much. She felt the cock pull out and sink back into her and so intense was the sensation hard upon her climax that she felt herself fainting. A firm slap to both her cheeks in turn though brought her back to her senses just in time to feel the cock ram into her again.

'No...uhhh...please...'she begged, gazing up imploringly at the man who stood looking down at her face, his fingers tightly meshed into her long hair.

The man grinned maliciously, plainly amused at her distress and with his free hand stroked the tears from her cheeks. Serena gave a plaintive cry as the cock was driven into her again, pulled out as far as the tumescent head and then forced back into her aching pussy.

Though the penetration was deeper than any she'd experienced little more than half the massive shaft was penetrating her, not that Serena was aware of this fact. The sensation though was enough to make her come again, every thrust inside her was bringing her to a climax and shamefully Serena knew that deep down a part of her was getting deliciously intoxicated by what she was being subjected to.

'Please... really...can't bear it... stop, please...'she sobbed hoarsely but her protest now was instinctive and the successive orgasms she'd enjoyed were compensation enough for the pain mixed with the pleasure she was being given.

The shafting continued relentlessly.

'The bitch was really tight to start... sweet little thing she is. How's she doing?' called the man from the far end of the bench as he sank his cock into her yet again. The man pinning Serena's head smiled and his hand that had been brushing her tears from her cheeks now slid, palm down across her mouth.

'The randy little tart's loving it! Aren't you?'

The man smiled as he looked down at Serena, his hand tight across her pretty mouth and smothering her attempt to answer him or cry out.

'Give it to her a bit harder. She's up for it.'

Serena felt the man fucking her quicken his rhythm and now his cock ploughed even deeper into her.

'Nnnnhhh!'

Serena gave a muffled cry as the intensity of the deep penetration sent stars shooting to her brain.

'Is that good darlin'? Too good eh?'

The cock was unbearably deep now and Serena struggled frantically, managing only to drag her thighs a few inches closer together before the girls pulled them apart again, laughing at her distress. She shook her head desperately but there was no extricating herself from the hand that gagged her. The man tightened his grasp upon her hair and leaned over the table closer to her.

'This is just the start… once we've had you this way, we're going to flip you over and you're other little hole is going to get a taste of cock as well!'

'Nnnhh!'

* * *

Doctor MacKennan exchanged glances with his nurse. Under the pale green lights of the dreamscape couch the petite red headed girl tossed her head from side to side, moaning faintly, her slender arms and legs slithering a little upon the padding of the couch, which was shiny with moisture. The girl's naked body was bathed in perspiration. Her towelling robe had been removed. Rubber cuffs around her ankles held her legs apart a little and drawn to the corners of the bottom of the couch. Her delicate arms were bent back above her head and rubber cuffs about her fine wrists kept her arms pinned thus. Though plainly disturbed enough in her sleep to have woken under normal circumstances, Serena Fairfax was quite unable to because of the amount of emothome that had been administered to her.

'I think we had better increase the votrimal a bit more nurse.'

MacKennan watched his sleeping victim unconsciously

pulling weakly with her arms against the restraints. His nurse adjusted the dial regulating the flow of muscle relaxant being intravenously administered to her and almost immediately they could see her struggling diminish.

'Something tells me that Miss Fairfax hadn't anticipated quite such an adventure… still, she'll get used to it all, given time, I'm sure.'

As if in objection or denial to what he said the sleeping girl gave a muffled sigh of distress. MacKennan leant over the couch and stroked the girl's face, smoothing his thumb around the edges of the adhesive tape that covered her mouth.

'Wishing you could wake up my dear?'

MacKennan glanced down to the recumbent girl's spread legs. The end of a large dildo could just be seen protruding from her sex and its faint hum was just audible.

MacKennan walked back across the control panels of the dreamscape computer and leaning back in his swivel chair regarded the main computer visual display screen. The first guard was still shafting her mercilessly, driving his massive cock now repeatedly into her right to the hilt. MacKennan glanced to one of the side screens that displayed the client's mental state and he laughed quietly as he read the contents. The screen was full of adjectives of pleasure and pain but even as he watched more of the latter were quickly being substituted for the former. Poor little Serena was beginning to find this fucking a bit too much for her. Along with her brain's responses to what she was being subjected to were her unfulfilled wishes and now just one sentence was duplicating itself again and again down the luminous display in bold capitals: PLEASE STOP! Of course the purpose of displaying the client's mental response to their dream situation was, theoretically, so that they could be woken if they really wished. Curiously, whilst Serena was seemingly begging for her ordeal to end, she was making no attempt to be woken, suggesting that a part of her was now emotionally too attached to her suffering at the hands of the sadistic Doctor.

MacKennan swivelled his chair so he could reach the keyboard that he used to issue instructions into the computer programming. He had already typed in a series of commands and now he ran the cursor down to one that read: "First guard ejaculates". The timing schedule told him there was less than a minute now left before this command was implemented. Glancing back to the main screen he marvelled at how vivid and lifelike the dreamworld seemed to be.

This particular dreamscape had been created by this particular girl's friend; Lara Lustral. She had blended her own fantasy world with that of her namesake heroine from twenty-seven years earlier, the tomb raiding tough girl with the magnificent cleavage: an endowment that that Lara of 2027 shared with her namesake. Miss Lustral like many of the other spoilt rich alpha class girls who had come to the Institute for a dream adventure had ended up getting more than she had bargained for. MacKennan had used her sexual cravings exposed in her dreams to manipulate and then trap her. He had forced her to admit to and then to embrace her sexual submissiveness. He had then abducted her and holding her prisoner in the Institute's secret basement, he had by hard discipline turned her into a willing sex slave who he had sold abroad. Well, MacKennan mused, it wouldn't be long before the lovely Serena was down in his basement prison and undergoing similar training. Then when suitably prepared, she would be sold into slavery just like her friend had been.

On the screen before him, the brutish guard was still giving the helpless Serena a shafting that she wouldn't forget in a long while, though there was only now five seconds to go before he'd orgasm and stop. MacKennan saw the cursor on his screen was still flashing on the command for the guard to ejaculate and with a sadistic smile he calmly pressed the delete button. With the instruction removed on the screen the assault on the girl continued.

MacKennan leant back in his chair, idly stroking his aching cock through his trousers while he watched Serena on the screen being shafted relentlessly. Her dark hazel eyes were wide with alarm and moist with tears and clearly showed her excruciating torment.

'Don't you think she's really had enough Doctor?'

MacKennan looked across to where his nurse was sitting next to the sleeping girl.

'It's just a dream,' MacKennan replied, smiling.

Chapter Ten

Lara's cell at the Palace was high in one of the towers that afforded her a tremendous view of the exotic landscape that surrounded the Emerald Tiger's seat of power. The Palace gardens extended for perhaps a mile in every direction; formal English rose gardens, lawns, avenues of lush green hedges, an Italian sunken garden with fountain, numerous enormous hot houses of glass; all bounded by a high stone wall topped with razor wire. Beyond were fields of maize and rice, banana plantations, villages and gently rising hills, thick with bamboo forest, their peaks swathed in a steamy mist.

As prison quarters went, where she was now was quite the most comfortable she had experienced. Her room was spacious and airy; the wood panelled floor was strewn with rugs, one a tiger skin the other two brightly coloured woven fabrics. The walls had once been papered in a floral design but the paper had peeled off in the steamy heat in places and now bare plaster showed over much of the wall surfaces. One of the two windows opened onto a tiny balcony where Lara sometimes sat once the sun was going down and the daytime heat had diminished. Below her the gardens, popular with courtiers by day were deserted in the evening as thick clouds of mosquitoes came out. Curiously these never seemed to rise above the fourth floor of the Palace and so perched as she was a couple of floors higher, Lara could sit on her balcony and enjoy the cool evening air.

For three days and nights now she had been held at the Palace and in truth she had quite settled into her role as sex slave to his Highness the Emerald Tiger. It seemed a long time ago already that she had been the property of the safari park owner and his mistress's sex toy. How she had suffered at their hands! Sometimes pleasurably and at other times not! MacKennan at the Dreamscape Institute had been right, she was a natural submissive, though she had found his way of making her learn this truth far from easy to accept. The days she had spent captive in the basement of the Institute had been the toughest she'd been put through in their way. Firstly because everything he subjected her to was new to her and secondly because he had pushed her to the limits of her emotional and physical endurance. The bastard certainly knew how to play rough!

Lara rolled onto her back and gazed up at the ceiling of her room. Lifting her arms she stared at her wrists. There were no marks on her skin but the memory of the cuffs she was so often made to wear was vividly clear. She had slept in late again, naked as usual under her mosquito net and now, just from the temperature of the air she guessed it was already mid-morning. Slipping out from under the muslin netting she padded bare foot through to her shower room. Sometimes there was no water at other times it was muddy brown. This morning there was water in abundance but sadly only cold. Shivering, soaked but washed, she dripped her way back to the window where she stood bathed in the heat of the sun and quickly her body warmed and dried without her having to even think about bothering with a towel. A sharp knock at her door made her jump and look around for some clothing. They had given her some, although it was designed to please her master rather than suit her own needs.

'Can you wait a minute please?' she called.

When the King wanted her, there was no warning, guards would simply sweep into her room and drag her down to the games room or wherever instructed. When someone knocked it was either a servant with food or the young local girl whose duties included oiling and massaging Lara on a daily basis. Evidently the Emerald Tiger appreciated that as his property, Lara was to be well maintained and she had quickly learnt to thank her lucky stars that he was not interested in beating or whipping her in any way that would mark her skin. Perhaps he was a merciless cruel tyrant but as far as Lara was concerned, his treatment of her was so far better than that which she had experienced at the hands of her previous owners.

'Come in.'

When the door was unlocked from the outside and the servant entered, Lara had slipped on a black G-string from the handful of items of clothing she'd been given. The others were a short Lycra skirt of emerald green – a ubiquitous colour in the Palace repertoire – a black latex mini dress, a leather collar and matching wrist cuffs and a soft rubber blindfold.

'It's time for your exercise.'

The man looked Lara up and down, he had not seen her before and after allowing his eyes to feast on her near naked body for several seconds, a tell tale bulge began to show at the crotch of his trousers. Lara nodded and asked if he could wait for just a second. He was new to her: dressed and behaving neither like a servant or official. He was European, his skin tanned but his sun bleached hair fair and closely cropped. Perhaps in his twenties or early thirties he looked fit and was dressed in khaki trousers, stout boots, a loose fitting polo shirt and in one hand he held a pair of sunglasses.

'Let me just have a drink.'

Lara gulped down what was left of her bottle of mineral water, she knew the servant girl would bring a fresh one today and in the heat water was what she craved most. She expected the man to demonstrate some impatience with her but he seemed relaxed and unconcerned by her slowness to follow him.

'Exercise? Just what sort of exercise?' Lara asked as she slipped on the only footwear she had been given, precariously high-heeled court shoes that effectively hobbled her as well as any ankle cuff and chain might. When she picked up her wrist cuffs and looked questioningly at the man he gave the merest affirmative nod. Dutifully Lara slipped one leather cuff around her right wrist and held her arm out for the man to fasten the buckle.

'His Highness wants to keep you fit, that's my job. He has merely issued certain guidelines,' the man answered ambiguously as he proceeded to fasten the second cuff about her other wrist.

'So who are you then?' Lara asked, turning around so that the man could clip the cuffs together behind her.

'I am his Majesty's personal instructor. You can call me sir, unless we are in company and then you will address me as "The Puma". Understood?'

The man attempted to announce this with as much brevity as he could and Lara did her best not to smirk. If the Emerald Tiger had one obvious flaw it was his penchant for giving his chief servants, government ministers and army generals alike, ridiculous titles. Smiling to herself, Lara dutifully followed the man from her room, her arms held behind her the only obvious sign, apart from her lack of clothing save her G-string, to indicate that she was a prisoner and not some courtesan girl, of which there were many at the Palace.

Six flights of steps later, perilous in stiletto heels especially with her hands bound behind her, Lara was down in the main halls of the Palace and amongst the bustling servants and courtiers, visitors and businessmen. The sight of a white girl, naked save for a G-string, her slender arms bound behind her back, drew plenty of glances but Lara knew better than to show any sign of protest or to attempt to talk with anyone or even indulge in lingering eye contact. She belonged to the Emerald Tiger and was his property alone.

The instructor led her outside through a set of side doors that opened on a terrace, deserted except for four men in suits sitting and talking business over iced tea. At the far end of the terrace a soldier stood gazing down into the gardens, a machine gun slung over one shoulder, he was in the combat green fatigues and beret of the King's Guards. Serena had learnt that these men were one of his three most trusted, best paid and loyal units. His Guards, his Commandoes and his Tiger Regiment formed the elite backbone of his army and the Palace itself was always protected by several hundred of the Guards.

'So what's the plan?' Serena asked the man leading her as

they drew alongside the table of four businessmen. For a moment their conversation faltered as she walked past, head held high, her stilettos striking loudly on the stone paving, she caught a few words as they resumed their conversation.

'Who's that, for Christ's sake?'

'The Emerald Tiger's plaything I do believe.'

'She looks like a girl I knew once in London.'

'Yeah, we believe you – don't tell us you shagged her as well!'

Lara turned her head and glanced back at the men and something quickened inside her chest as she suddenly recognised one of the men, whose gaze was still following her. He hadn't been lying; she'd met him in a nightclub and back at his place, a luxury apartment over looking the Thames, they had fucked. She'd lingered in his company for three days and nights then found someone else to amuse her as familiarity had given way to boredom.

'This way!'

Lara turned her attention back to the man leading her. He stood at the top of a flight of stone steps leading down onto one of the lawns. Just as she took her first step down though she heard a chair scrap behind her and then footsteps hurrying towards her.

'Excuse me! Please!'

Turning again she faced the man, who was a little breathless now and struggled to keep his eyes on her face and not let them be drawn to her sumptuous and naked body. She sensed the Instructor take a step back towards her and at the same time she glimpsed the Guard as he began walking towards them, his pace brisk and his machine gun already couched at his hip.

'Excuse me, but don't I perhaps know you?'

Lara, her heart hammering now, felt her voice catch in her throat. She could hear the boot steps of the Guard closing and then a hand from behind, the hand of the Instructor clasped hold of her wrist cuffs where her arms were held against the small of her back.

'No. You're mistaken. Sorry.'

As soon as she'd answered she quickly turned and descended the steps, lest her emotional expression betray her. She knew that the man had unwittingly had a close brush with death. If she'd acknowledged him both he and his colleagues would certainly have ended up as crocodile meat if the rumours about the Emerald Tiger's way of dealing with problems was to be believed.

The gymnasium was a recent purpose-built addition to the Palace in functional concrete and concealed behind a high hedge of Cypress trees. Although watched over by another of the King's Guard, the building was quite deserted. For two hours Lara was put through her paces, using weights, track running, performing press-ups and sit-ups and whatever else pleased the man who was instructing her. Finally, exhausted and bathed in sweat she was allowed to collapse onto the floor.

'Good, very good: you're a pretty fit bitch aren't you?' the man remarked.

'Well I haven't exactly had a lazy time of it in recent months!' Lara replied sarcastically.

'His Majesty is away on Royal business at the moment.'

As the man spoke he wandered across to the door by which they had entered and pulling the key from his pocket he slid it back in the door lock and turned it.

'So that's why I didn't have the pleasure of his company yesterday?' Lara said watching the man as he walked back across to where she was sat.

'You'll find that he'll have plenty of other calls on his time. And on those occasions you'll be shut up alone in your room and forced to amuse yourself.'

'Are you asking me if I like to masturbate?' Lara raised an eyebrow and got to her feet. Glancing at the man's crotch, she saw the telltale bulge of his erection and guessed just what he was driving at.

'And do you?'

'You could be playing with fire if his Highness found out that you'd been poking his personal property,' Lara licked her lips as she smiled impishly at the man.

Already a plan was formulating itself in her head. This man was obviously keen to get into her knickers and if she gave him that pleasure she could easily soon wrap him around her little finger. Then, under the threat of exposure, she could control him. Perhaps initially just to get herself favours but perhaps later for more... they might come a time when she needed serious help, help to escape perhaps. The brush with the London businessmen on the terrace had reminded her of who she really was and now she was questioning whether she belonged here. Did she really want to spend her best days as a sex slave? Or at any rate a sex slave stuck out here in the middle of nowhere? What if there was a coup or a war or something, without the protection of the King, she could really get thrown to the wolves. At least back in London she could mess around knowing that if she didn't like it she could run home and curl up again in the comfort and safety of her own luxurious home.

'What are you thinking?' the man asked, his hand reaching for her but hesitating to do more than lightly rest on her bare shoulder.

'How good a fuck you might be,' Lara answered smiling.

'Not a word to anyone.'

'Girl guide's honour,' Lara smiled wickedly.

The man moved his hand down from her shoulder and caressed her breast, his thumb sliding up under her nipple and toying with it.

'Bend over against that vaulting horse then.'

Lara did as he said, glancing behind her to see the man pull his cock from his trousers. He grinned at her and she smiled back coyly.

'Don't be too rough with me...will you?'

'Don't worry, I know how he treats you and I know what

you like.'

The man encouraged her feet a little further apart and Lara sighed encouragement as she felt his thumb feel up the crack of her arse.

'Not there… do you have to?' she asked petulantly, secretly smiling to herself at the thought of getting a nice hard anal shafting.

'You'll do what I want and enjoy it!' growled the man, 'Now spit on your hand!'

Lara knew what he was wanting so she gathered a mouthful of saliva before cupping her palm under her lips and opening her mouth. Reaching behind her she found his cock.

'Uhh, yes… good girl…'the man groaned.

Lara smiled as she furled her slick palm more firmly around his shaft.

'Please stick it in me now, I can't wait much longer,' she asked in her sweetest, most contrived, spoilt little girl tone of voice.

The man grasped both her buttocks a hand on each and coaxed them apart. She felt the head of his shaft press into her anus and then with a thrust he penetrated her, sinking his cock into her up to the hilt. Lara gave a deep groan of pleasure. This was the sort of physical instruction she could force herself to put up with every day, Lara sighed dreamily as she rested her head against the horse, her arms embracing the hard padded leather while her slender body remained thrust backwards, her arse feeling the delightful slapping of the man's balls against her skin every time he rammed his cock into her. The sensation was quite exquisite and if only he'd continue or pause to rub her clit, she knew that she'd quickly come. As it was, just as she guessed would happen, the man was intent on only pleasuring himself and after a few short moments he came. She felt his spunk jet inside her and she sighed with disappointment. Doubtless now he would want to stop and she'd be left frustrated.

'Christ, that was good, I needed that,' the man sighed, pulling his cock from her and slumping down on his back on an exercise mat.

'Could I tempt you to seconds?' Lara dropped down beside him and quickly began fondling his scrotal sac with the fingers of one hand.

'No, I don't think so.'

'All right then, if that's how you feel.'

Even as she spoke she was rolling his testicles between her fingers and lightly stroking under his sac where she knew all men were so sensitive.

'We should be getting back to the Palace,' the man said but already there was little conviction in his tone.

'Okay, if you think that's best.'

Lara lightly trapped the head of his cock between a finger and thumb and gently squeezed. She then drew one nail down the length of his shaft and smiled as she saw the semi flaccid shaft start to harden again.

'Christ you're a randy bitch all right aren't you?' the man sighed.

'I guess so. Now then, would you like to fuck me again?'

Lara furled her hand around his shaft and began to pump him with her hand while with the fingers of her other hand she stroked his scrotal sac.

'Get down on all fours then.'

The man caught hold of her hands and pulling them clipped the wrist cuffs together.

'What's that for?' Lara protested.

'Don't tell me you don't like to be bound?'

The man pulled her wrists back above her head, making her forehead drop with a slap against the exercise mat.

'Oww! What are you doing?'

'What do you think?' the man asked scornfully as he clipped the wrist cuffs to the D-ring at the rear of her collar, then grasping Lara by the waist he promptly thrust his cock into her sex, making her gasp at the force with which he took her. Lara moaned with pleasure as she felt his engorged cock begin shafting her once more.

'You horny bitch, you just love it don't you!'

CHAPTER ELEVEN

Slowly Serena felt herself surfacing from a deep sleep. She sighed and tried to stretch but somehow her arms wouldn't move and as she tried to twist her body sideways and curl her legs up she found that this was impossible. Forcing herself to focus her senses she blinked several times and as she saw the pale green light above her she remembered suddenly just where she was.

'Uhh, how long have I been asleep?' she asked dreamily, trying again to move her arms and now as her sleep fuddled brain slowly focused itself, she realised with alarm that her arms seemed to be pinned above her head.

'Doctor MacKennan?'

'Hello Serena, welcome back to the world of reality.'

Turning her head to the sound of the male voice she saw the white-coated Doctor looking down at her; a sympathetic smile on his face.

'I feel so sleepy… can't move my arms…' Serena tried twisting her head and craning to see above her but it was too much of an effort and she felt so lethargic!

'Just relax my dear Miss Fairfax, it's natural for you to feel like this after such a session. Can you remember much of it?' the Doctor asked, his tone smooth and professional but also more than faintly patronising.

Serena closed her eyes again for a moment and sank her head back against the couch. What could she remember? A forest at night, a tunnel, the ambush, then waking to find herself prisoner… and then her dream had ended but she'd come back to the Institute to let it carry on. She remembered being tied to the pole and tortured and then being held down by the evil girls whilst the brutish henchman of the sadistic Doctor had used her. She sighed and opening her eyes again tried to sit up but to her horror she found her arms were pinned above her head.

A shiver ran through her body as she lifted her head to look down at her body. She was naked, the white towelling robe was gone and as she stared in disbelief the truth of what she saw was hammered home to her: her ankles were bound with rubber cuffs from which ran cords that disappeared over the far edge of the couch.

'Christ! What the hell…'

Serena jerked her legs but immediately the straps became taut and she realised that she couldn't move her legs more than a few inches. With a feeling of panic rushing over her, she jerked her arms with as much force as she could manage but they wouldn't move down from above her head. Twisting her body frantically sideways she saw that her wrists were fastened with similar cuffs and her arms were being forcibly restrained above her head. The realisation that the Doctor had her at his mercy and that he knew just what she'd been dreaming poured through her, arousing her instantly. Imagining herself being subjected to sexual torment and torture was no longer just a dream. The thought burned through her, quickening her pulse and making her imagination race with a dozen fevered images of what she might now be subjected to.

'You bastard! What do you think you're doing? Let me go!' she swore, determined to at least give the appearance of indignant fury at what had befallen her whilst she'd been asleep.

'Come now, Miss Fairfax. Relax… there's nothing to worry about.'

'Doctor MacKennan, I don't know what you think you're doing but if you don't untie me immediately I'll report you to the Police and…'

The man's smile, sinister and cold, made Serena's protest falter then fail.

'And precisely how to you propose telling the Police what has happened to you?' the Doctor asked smugly as he watched her writhing and twisting ineffectually against the restraints that held her.

'Just what until I'm out of here!' Serena glowered, straining with all her energy to pull free from the wrist and ankle cuffs. The rubber bindings though were buckled tightly around her limbs and try as she might she quickly realised that she had no hope of extricating herself. A few moments later, exhausted and fuming, she sank back on the couch and glared at the man standing watching her.

'So what the hell do you think you're doing Doctor MacKennan?' Serena demanded angrily.

Without answering her he stepped close to the bench and allowed himself a lingering appreciation of her naked body. Serena was just about to blurt out a furious tirade when he placed his hand on her taut stomach and made her catch her breath. Smiling but saying nothing he moved his hand slowly down over her hip and onto her thigh. Instinctively Serena tried to draw her legs protectively together but the ankle cuffs held her legs spread and her breathing quickened as she realised she could do nothing to prevent him touching her body wherever he pleased. She was not surprised when his hand moved from her thigh to between her legs and she sighed, struggling to control her primal feelings as his fingers brushed lightly across her sex.

'Damn you… damn you…'she muttered, sighing as this thumb slid a little way into the soft crease of her sex and then moving slowly upwards came into contact with her clitoris.

'So did you enjoy your dream Serena? You seemed to be appreciating the attention afforded to you by the evil Doctor's guards.'

'No…'Serena sighed, closing eyes, arching her head back and sighing as the man's skilful touch swiftly aroused her. Somehow being tied down and helpless added to her state of arousal and she was shamefully aware of what she had dreamt.

'Is that good? May I slip my fingers a little way into your sex? Would you mind?'

The man's voice was as soft and persuasive as was his touch and all Serena could do was to sigh with pleasure as she felt his fingers slide into the wet folds of her vulva and then push deeper into her sex drawing a deep groan of pleasure from her.

'What are you going to do with me?' Serena asked plaintively.

She was now achingly aroused and all too aware of how easily he had demonstrated his control over her. She should have objected, she should have struggled more, she told herself reproachfully but without any conviction because she knew that she was a randy little girl, as more than one man had described her, and that MacKennan had quickly got the measure of her. Well, he knows my dreams, she thought, so there's no point in pretending otherwise. Serena gave a carnal grunt of pleasure as the thumb stroking her clitoris now began to rub forcefully against her swollen erection, quickly propelling her towards an orgasm.

'Mmmm...so good...yes...'

Confident, firm and fast, the man masturbated her, his thumb rubbing her clitoris until it throbbed and his fingers stroking and delving into her sex until she was arching her back and pushing with her hips against his hand.

'Are you going to come for me now, Serena?'

'Yes...oh yes...'

And she did, crying out loudly as her climax rocked her sweat-bathed body and she dragged with arms and legs against the restraints, which only served to heighten her fevered state and prolong her orgasm.

'Good girl, well done. See, you're enjoying being treated like this aren't you? Deep down it's just what you want; we both know that.'

The man soothed her brow and caressed her face sympathetically, smiling at her as she struggled to regain her breath and composure.

'So then Serena, you are my prisoner now to do with as I wish. That's not too terrible a prospect is it? After all I know just how you really like to be treated and I can offer you pretty much everything you've ever dreamt of experiencing.'

As he spoke the man stroked her breast, his fingers gliding over her skin, appreciating its fullness and weight as he experimentally lifted and cupped it. Kneading it gently he drew a moan of pleasure from her and all she could manage to do was to look up at him and wonder just what he would do to her next and how good it would feel.

'So what are you going to do with me?' Serena asked.

The man smiled and brushed her nipple with his thumb. Serena gazed at her breast in his hand as he brought her nipple to a piquant degree of firmness. Having rolled her little erection between finger and thumb he subjected it to a flew light flicks with one fingertip and each made her sigh and her nipple harden and ache that little bit more.

'Well, can you remember what you experienced in you dream, Serena?'

'Yes,' Serena nodded blushing as the memory of the brutish guards fucking her came back to her, so vivid that it seemed as if it had really happened.

'Did you enjoy it?' MacKennan asked.

Serena gazed up at the man and hesitated to answer, too ashamed to admit that she had in truth, deep down, enjoyed the experience.

'Did you? ' he prompted, rolling one of her nipples between his finger and thumb.

'Yes…'Serena admitted.

'Good, then you're going to enjoy how I intend looking after you.'

He nodded to the nurse sitting opposite him, the young woman produced a clamp and as Serena watched in disbelief, the device was fastened on her nipple. Serena gasped, dragging her arms helplessly against the straps that held her down.

'Let me go…stop it…let me go!'

The nurse, exchanging a satisfied glance with the Doctor, clipped a second clamp upon Serena's other nipple.

'Take them off…they hurt… please!' Serena begged, lifting her head and staring at her breasts whose nipples now protruded swollen and purple from the shiny steel clamps.

'How does that feel, Serena? A little sensitive? A touch delicate?'

'Uhh…'.

Serena couldn't but help cry out as the Doctor touched the exposed tip of her nipple and then lightly tapped the steel clamp. MacKennan smiled triumphantly and turned his attention from Serena's aching breasts to her face. Stroking her perspiration soaked hair clear of her soft cheeks he caressed her face before allowing his thumb to lingeringly brush along her trembling lower lip.

'Suck it, there's a good girl.'

Serena obeyed; too aroused now to think clearly or to appreciate what was happening to her or what she was doing. She had always deep down enjoyed dominant men and this man knew just how to control her. She was bound and helpless and so doing whatever he commanded was easy. Absolved of any guilt she was hardly caring of what happened to her next. Though her breasts throbbed with a dull aching pain from the nipple clamps, part of her craved more attention in the same vein so potent was the effect it had on her.

'Does that feel good?'

As MacKennan posed the question with one hand he caressed her pussy while with the other he toyed with one of her aching breasts.

'Uhhh… yes… yes…'Serena sighed, tossing her head from side to side.

'Suzi, fetch me a wired pussy probe. I think Miss Fairfax would like to come again and I know that a little electric shock treatment is just what she wants.'

'Oh God, no… you can't be serious…Doctor, please…'Serena sighed, trying to ignore the delicious state of arousal he had brought her to and to focus on what he was proposing.

'Relax Serena… we both know that from past experience you're going to enjoy this.'

'No, please… you can't…really…'Serena protested, half heartedly trying once again to pull free from the restraints that held her down on the couch.

MacKennan laughed softly and shook his head.

'My dear Serena, there's no escape and you are going to suffer everything you've dreamt of and more, so stop pretending to be so unhappy at the prospect. We know you enjoy getting treated like this, so stop being so coy.'

'This isn't fair…'Serena sighed as she lifted her head and watched as MacKennan fingered her pussy until it was slick and achingly aroused.

'Now, lie still, you're going to love this.'

'No… please…'

Serena gasped as something hard and long was slid easily into her moist sex. Craning her head she glimpsed a red and a black wire trailing from between her legs, across one thigh to where they were fastened to a small black box that lay on the little wheeled trolley that was beside the nurse. The girl grinned maliciously and stroked one of her long nailed fingers tauntingly across the controls of the box. Serena tensed but nothing happened, so light had the girl's touch been. Serena gazed mesmerized at the girl's hand, her blood red fingernail hovering over the dial and button on the little black box.

'Relax Serena, you're desperate for it, so just revel in it. Let nurse Suzi look after you,' MacKennan consoled her.

'But what happened before was a dream… you can't do this to me…please!'

'My dear girl, I can do whatever I please with you. You can't really stop me can you?'

The Doctor fingered the straps that were snug around Serena's wrists. She gazed up at him as he slowly circled the couch upon which she was tied down.

'The electric shock will be nice and mild. Just enough to make you writhe and beg us to stop, but not enough to really hurt you. Don't worry Serena, you can trust me to look after you…'

'No, I don't...uhh!'

Serena never finished her sentence. The charge of electricity shot like a dart through her sex, bringing her straight to an orgasm and leaving her too dazed to speak or respond for several long minutes after.

'I think she enjoyed that,' MacKennan said sarcastically as Serena lay groaning faintly after the shock had been administered. Serena felt him skim his fingers down her chest and along her thigh and then back up to her sex. Though the shock had lasted only a couple of seconds it had been utterly effective and Serena was more than un-nerved by the fact that it had made her come so easily. This man MacKennan obviously knew her better than she knew herself and he knew just how to produce the desired responses from her. The thought that he could so easily bring her to such an intense climax made her feel deliciously vulnerable and while part of her wished she was free from his clutches another part of her was revelling in the delicious torment he had just begun to subject her to.

'How do you feel now Serena? Would you like a rest? Perhaps a chance to dream?'

Serena looked nervously at the man as he stood over her. What would happen to her next if she was submerged back into Lara's dreamworld, she wondered? Then again what did he have planned next for her? Suddenly both worlds seemed disconcertingly similar.

'Well?' MacKennan prompted, 'as I see it you have three choices: Edwardian England, Lara's tomb raiding adventure or to continue to enjoy my company. Which, I wonder, would you prefer?'

Serena felt her heart hammering. She gazed down at her tethered body. Above the ripe swell of her breasts, her nipples stood erect and clamped, their swollen tips showing above the shiny steel of the jaws that were tight about the delicate flesh. She looked further down at her slender body, bathed now in sweat, her long legs forcibly spread, her stomach breathing hard. What was going to happen to her now, she wondered? Is this what had happened to her friend Lara?

She could feel the firmness of the device embedded in her pussy and she knew that another jolt of electricity was only a second away should MacKennan feel inclined. In her own dream of Edwardian England as servant girl to Edward de Breville, though starting as a virgin, she had already being deflowered. And in the tomb raiding adventure of Lara, she was now hostage to the sadistic alter-ego of MacKennan and having just been fucked by one of his brutish guards was about to get another genetically enhanced monster cock rammed into her aching body. The choices were sobering to say the least, thought Serena.

'Well?' MacKennan prompted.

'What's going to happen to me? What happened to Lara? What did you do with her?'

'So at least you are beginning to understand, or to at least surmise.' MacKennan smiled smugly at her and Serena glowered back.

'You bastard! Tell me what's happened to her!'

'Oh, Lara was pretty much like you – desperate for sexual satisfaction and deep down a submissive. She's now a slave to her desires, you might say. Just like you will be quite shortly.'

'You can't keep me here forever! What do you think will happen to you when I get out?' Serena snapped.

'My dear Serena, just like Lara, you'll never leave here – at least not in the way you imagine!'

'What do you mean? What did you do to her?'

'I sold Lara as a slave; a sex slave. She's now in Africa, doubtless enjoying her new life as a dutiful submissive. Perhaps I could sell you to the same buyer?' MacKennan gave a disparaging laugh and nodded to the nurse.

'Uhh!'

Serena gave a gasp of alarm and then a long, despairing groan as she was subjected to another searing jolt of electricity. The sensation aroused her pussy immediately and it took only a couple of seconds before Serena was gasping then crying out as another orgasm overtook her body.

'Had enough for the moment Serena? Would you like a little rest or shall we see if you can come for us again?'

Serena opened her eyes and gazed dazedly at the man stood over her. She was panting hard and now her whole body throbbed with a dull aching pain. The orgasm had been almost too intense to bear and she shook her head, feebly pulling with her arms and legs against the restraints that held her down.

'Time to take these off I think, if we leave them on much longer they may mark your skin and we don't want that, do we?'

Serena gave an appreciative sigh as she felt the clamps being opened and removed from her nipples.

'I imagine your lovely breasts must be feeling a little delicate now?'

'Uhhh...please...no...'Serena sighed, squirming then writhing as she felt the man toy with one of her nipples. The little erection of flesh was agonisingly delicate and she gazed up helplessly as the man caught it between his thumb and finger and gently toyed with it, squeezing it then flicking it with the back of one finger tip until Serena had tears rolling down her cheeks and she was whimpering plaintively.

'Please... stop...uhh...no...'

Serena tossed her head from side to side, twisting her arms and pulling weakly against the straps around her wrists, as the sensation of pain grew too intense.

'So Serena, would you like another chance to dream or would you rather have a taste of the real world that lies in wait for you?'

'You bastard, do whatever you want, I know I haven't got any say in the matter!' Serena snarled.

MacKennan smiled triumphantly.

'How right you are my dear.'

There was an agonising pause for Serena while the man contented himself with nothing more than regarding her tethered body while he idly stroked the generous swell of one of her breasts.

'So what are you going to do with me?' Serena demanded once again in a tone she hoped sounded defiant but which in truth betrayed her fear of what might be lying in store for her.

'I think we'll take you somewhere even more private than here and then you'll be afforded the pleasure of feeling just what a genetically enhanced cock can do for that tight little pussy of yours.'

'Please don't make me dream that again!'

'Who said anything about dream?' MacKennan laughed, 'My dear girl, from now on your sexual torment won't be a dream, it will be for real!'

'But... you can't mean...'Serena stammered.

'Oh, yes I can!' MacKennan laughed. 'Nurse, would you be so good as to show Miss Fairfax just what she can look forward to?'

The uniformed young woman rose from her chair and circled the couch where Serena lay tied down. Moving behind the Doctor, she unfastened the buttons on his long white coat and then unbuttoned the flies of his trousers. As Serena watched, the woman loosened the man's belt and released the waistband button then eased his trousers down over his thighs. Her long nailed fingers then slipped inside the waistband of his pants and pushed them down. The exposed cock was easily the largest Serena had ever seen. The shaft was as thick as a wrist and longer than anything Serena imagined could have been normal. The circumcised head, engorged with blood and the scrotal sac were massive, the balls just like those of the brutish guard in Serena's dream.

'Would you like to fuck her now, Doctor?'

As the nurse posed the question she caressed his cock, her talon-like fingernails skimming down the length of his shaft, which thickened and hardened even more in response to her touch.

'Not just yet, there's plenty more we can do with her before we give her the pleasure of accommodating my cock in her lovely pussy!'

'A bit more shock treatment then? 'the nurse suggested.

'Perhaps later, I think it's time now to take Miss Fairfax to the basement.'

'Shall I increase emothome then Doctor?'

'Yes, time to sleep Serena and when you wake you'll find yourself in somewhere perhaps even more stimulating than your dreamworld.'

'You can't get away with this MacKennan!' Serena hissed defiantly but already her heart was sinking. She glanced sideways in time to see the nurse administer more of the powerful sleeping drug and immediately she felt a wave of lethargy sweep over her.

'No... let me go...can't...'

Her eyelids grew heavy and the strength ebbed from her body. A blanket of darkness came up to meet her. Just before she slid into unconsciousness she heard the Doctor's voice again.

'Take her straight to Discipline. She doesn't need conditioning, the bitch is desperate for some good hard treatment, we don't need to worry about breaking her in.'

* * *

'Come on baby, wakey, wakey!'

The pain of having her hair pulled and her head jerked backwards, forced Serena back into a state of consciousness. The blue-eyed girl was watching her, her pretty face close before Serena's, her bow shaped mouth smiling. Tightening her hold on Serena's long red hair she drew her head further back.

'Uhhh...'

'Come on darling, time to wake up, time to play.'

With the palm of her free hand the girl gave Serena a stinging slap across the cheeks, bringing tears to her eyes.

She was lying face down on the floor of an almost bare,

windowless room. A man she had not seen before was regarding her, his features cold and impassive, his eyes inscrutable behind dark sunglasses. She could feel a broad collar snug around her neck and her arms were bound tightly together behind her back. The blue-eyed girl stood back, releasing her hold on Serena's hair and with the stiletto heel of her shoe she nudged Serena in the ribs.

'On your feet!'

Though Serena felt still too tired and weak she made an effort to obey the instruction and only when she had managed to stand did she see the rope dangling from the ceiling. Before she could take in what was happening to her the girl snatched hold of her collar with one hand and the rope with the other. A second later and the bulldog clip at the end of the rope had been clipped to a ring on the collar and Serena was now effectively leashed. The young girl grinned and wandered across to a small table from where she retrieved a long, plaited leather whip, the sight of which made Serena recoil. Before she had retreated a couple of yards though the rope became taut and she was brought to heel by the collar.

The girl circled her, grinning maliciously as Serena kept trying to edge away but the roped collar restricted her circle of movement to just a few paces. The girl glanced across to the man who nodded affirmatively, both smiling conspiratorially.

'Time to taste what it really feels like!'

The girl gave her wrist the merest flick and the whip cut across Serena's bare skin, so fast that it was a blur and Serena had no time to try to evade it. The leather against her skin felt like a burning hot tongue licking her and Serena gave a yelp of alarm as she jerked back.

'Don't… please…'

Like a pencil thin shadow the black leather whip sliced through the air and Serena gave a howl as it seared a line across her right thigh, its fine end wrapping around her leg in an embrace of pain.

'Uhhh!'

Thwack!

Against her back and across her tethered arms this time the whip burnt a fresh line of mind-jolting pain. Serena stumbled sideways jerking her arms frantically against the rope that tethered them together against her back.

'It would be better if her arms were above her head.'

'Wait a minute then.'

The man moved quickly to behind Serena and untied the rope that was binding her arms. Too exhausted and fearful to struggle, Serena held her wrists meekly together before her and allowed him to bind them then lifting her arms up he knotted the rope around the rope that ran down from the ceiling and was clipped to her collar. Glancing up Serena saw that there was a large hook secured to a plate of metal that was bolted to the ceiling and it was to this that the rope was secured. This room has been completely designed for just this purpose, Serena thought as the man finished knotting the rope and standing back left her with her arms extended above her. Before she had any more time to ponder where she had woken to find herself the girl brought the whip slicing down against her back.

Thwack!

'Owww!'

Serena twisted against the ropes that held her, instinctively trying to draw away from the source of the pain but quickly the rope tightened and the collar dragged her to a halt.

Thwack!

The whip burnt across her rump, bringing tears easily to her eyes and although she knew it was futile she was quickly begging again for the girl to stop.

'Please! No more… really, I can't…'

Thwack!

'Uhhh!'

Searing pain across her now achingly tender rear made her shake her head in dismay and recoil from the attack only to be dragged back by the collar and rope leash like a puppet being controlled by a puppet master so that she was just where the girl intended as the next blow was delivered.

How long the torment lasted, Serena had no idea. It was just like in her dreams but now the pain was real and before it was over she was begging and pleading with the girl to show her some mercy. Then, one minute she was cringing and howling as the whip stung and bit her helpless naked body and then without warning the girl had discarded the instrument of torture and was standing close behind her. She was close enough to wrap one hand around her waist to keep Serena still whilst with her free hand she stroked between her legs, coaxing Serena to part her thighs enough for her to play with her pussy. She was not surprised when told how aroused she was. She was hardly ashamed when as the other girl slipped her fingers into her sex she sighed appreciatively and leant back into her tormentor's embrace.

'Poor Serena, there now… just let me look after you.'

As the girl calmed her with soothing words so she skilfully masturbated Serena bringing her quickly to a state of hot arousal and urgent need.

'Does that feel good? Would you like me to make you come now?'

Serena was too intoxicated with the delicious feelings to answer coherently. The combination of tormenting pain and then this was too much for her and soon she was rocking and then bucking in the girl's embrace as she was coaxed to orgasm. Sighing and trembling though, just before Serena climaxed the girl abruptly stopped fingering her and stepped back. Turning around to look for the girl her gaze fell on MacKennan who had silently entered the room.

'She's ready for you.'

The girl grinned and blew Serena a sympathetic kiss in apology as the Doctor walked across to where Serena hung tethered and without preamble he calmly reached between her legs and sank three fingers of his right hand into her sex.

'Very accommodating. I bet you're desperate for it right now aren't you Miss Fairfax?' MacKennan grinned and withdrawing his fingers dragged his thumb across Serena's swollen clitoris coaxing an involuntary sigh of pleasure from her.

'Right then, untie her. Put her across the bench; I haven't got all night.'

The man and the girl unfastened Serena's wrists and unclipped the collar from the rope and between them they marched her across to a bench. Waist high and fitted with strategically placed canvas straps riveted to the top and sides, Serena was left in no doubt as to what was to happen to her next. Encouraged to bend at the waist face down across the bench, her arms were pulled to full stretch and then her wrists wrapped and buckled with straps. While the girl then crouched at her feet and coaxing her legs apart bound her ankles, the man drew a strap across her back just below her shoulders and pulling it tight then fastened it so that Serena was now unable to raise her body more than fractionally from the top of the bench. Before the girl had finished binding her spread legs the man was tightening then securing another strap that pressed firmly down upon Serena's back at the base of her spine. Glancing over her shoulder, Serena could see how neatly her arse was left thrust out invitingly and to her dismay her gaze then fell upon MacKennan.

The man had discarded his white surgeon's coat and had his trouser flies unbuttoned. His cock was already fully erect jutted from the opening of his boxer shorts. The sight brought a lump to her throat and a knot of fear tightened in her stomach. An insidious voice in her mind which she wished she could have denied or fought down told her that at last she was going to get the shafting she'd long dreamt of and more besides! As the man approached her spread and tethered legs she instinctively began to struggle but there were six stout straps pinning her down and at best she could do no more than squirm just a little as the man moved to behind her and stroked the exposed soft insides of her thighs teasingly.

'So Serena, it feels as if we've both waited a long while for this moment, wouldn't you say?'

The firm cockhead brushed between her legs and then she felt it touch the lips of her sex. Her vulva was slick with arousal and Serena sighed then groaned as she felt it nuzzle between her the lips of her sex then finding her opening, with one determined push, the man sank the bulbous head of his cock into her making her gasp breathlessly as she was forced to accept its unnaturally large girth.

'Uhhh...'

'Does that feel good Serena? A little too good perhaps?'

The man pushed his cock a further into her drawing another gasp from her then pulling back a little he paused, his hands caressing her rump and hips and soothing her trembling body.

'Aching for it aren't you Serena?'

Serena nodded in admission before she could stop herself and her reward was to feel the cock plough into her.

'Uhhh....please... no more...' Serena begged, dragging her arms against the straps that were bound tightly around her wrists as the sensation of the cock filling her grew more than she imagined she could bear and still it sank deeper into her sex.

'Come on Serena, just a little more...'

Teetering on the edge of a climax, Serena gave a desperate moan as the man withdrew his shaft except for the tumescent head then promptly sank it back into her. The sensation drove her over the edge and her orgasm was triggered.

'Dear me, Serena, there's no need to get so excited so soon, why, I've hardly begun!'

Serena felt the cock slide back out of her aching pussy and then it was driven back into her even before her climax had ebbed. The effect was to bring on a fresh wave of orgasm and Serena gave a plaintive cry as she felt the achingly thick cock force her pussy to accommodate it. As the shaft was driven into her deeper this time, she shook her head, pleading with

MacKennan.

'Too much... please...no...'she gasped, aware now that she'd not even experienced the full length of the man's cock inside her already aching pussy.

'Come now Serena, you don't really want me to stop, do you?'

The enormous cock was withdrawn from her sex until all she could feel was the massive, bulbous head lightly brushing the swollen folds of her vulva. MacKennan stroked his hands down her sides and then toyed with her tousled hair.

'Do you really want me to stop? Is that what you want?'

As he questioned her he gathered her long hair into a ponytail, which he then wrapped around one hand, holding it tightly then using it as a pull to draw her head back.

'Wouldn't you rather I carried on and fucked you senseless? You'd like to be shafted until you can't bear it any more, wouldn't you?'

'No...no...'Serena sighed, trying to shake her head but unable to because of the tight grip he had exerted upon her hair.

'Tell me the truth and I'll be good to you. You needn't be ashamed to admit it. You want me to fuck you don't you?'

'You're too big... I can't take it...really...'Serena answered with a choked sob as she felt the man's cock nudge against the wet folds of her pussy. She was aching for a cock inside her but she didn't dare admit that to him, his cock made her pussy feel like it was being stuffed so deeply it was unbearable.

'Then I'm afraid it's going to be more electric shock treatment and more whipping for you. Is that what you want?'

'No... please just let me go!' Serena sobbed.

'Are you sure that's what you want Serena? I do hope you're not telling lies. I think perhaps you're not being truthful with me?'

Serena said nothing but gazed abjectly at her outstretched and tethered arms. The truth was that she was deeply aroused by the way MacKennan was treating her but she was afraid to admit it lest he regard it as a licence to subject her to worse.

'Nurse, prepare five milligrams of truth serum. I think Miss Fairfax needs her real feelings coaxing from her.'

'No!'

Her objection though was irrelevant and a moment later the nurse was at her side with a needle and syringe and whilst Serena watched she administered the injection into her exposed arm.

'You'll feel no effects other than a mild drowsiness. Do you feel that yet Serena?'

Serena looked up at the man as he questioned her. She nodded and gazed at the man waiting for his next question.

'Good,' MacKennan smiled down at her sympathetically and eased the tightness of his hold upon her hair a fraction.

'Everything you've dreamt at the Institute, have you enjoyed those dreams?'

'Yes,' Serena admitted.

'And when you woke from the last dream and found yourself my prisoner, how did you feel?'

'Afraid but excited.'

'Good girl, 'MacKennan smiled sympathetically, 'and when the nurse administered the electric probes, did you enjoy how it felt?'

'Yes…'Serena nodded as best as the firm grasp on her hair allowed.

'And would you like it if I fucked you now?'

'Yes, Doctor.'

'Even if it feels as if my cock is too big for you and it hurts?'

'Yes…'

'Good girl, that's all we need to know. Now, tell me how this feels?'

Serena felt the thick head of the man's cock sink into her sex and she sighed.

'Nice… ohh, yes, so good…'

'And this?'

CHAPTER TWELVE

MacKennan watched the door to the cell slide open with no more sound than the faint hiss of gas from the door mechanism. Serena Fairfax lay sprawled fast asleep on her bed, evidently exhausted from her ordeal of the previous evening. She was, MacKennan reflected, stunningly sexy, her petite body perfectly shaped and begging for attention. She was lying face down and slightly on her side, curled into a loose curve across the bed. One slender arm was drawn defensively around her head, her long red hair spilled across the pillow. Her soft, sensual lips were parted fractionally and as she slept her long eyelashes flickered faintly. Her pert and generous breasts were now softly squashed under her, as she slept, her slender legs drawn close together.

Zara and Suzi moved silently into the room with practised ease. MacKennan gazed at them, reflecting that he had never seen their bodies so vulnerably naked. Still, he had no shortage of naked young girls to enjoy, Serena Fairfax being the most recent acquisition; he would spend several days pleasuring himself with her luscious body before he sold her for a handsome price. His two nurses moved confidently across to the sleeping girl. Zara the older of the two, twenty-two years old was a little taller than her work colleague and whilst from the rear she presented a technically more pleasing sight, her legs being just a little longer and her rump a little more generous, MacKennan was at present more drawn to Suzi, perhaps because she delighted in giving him the most satisfying blow-jobs he'd experienced or maybe because she had a better cleavage and always kept her blouse undone enough to afford him a tantalising glimpse of her tits. Every time MacKennan tortured one of his client's breasts, he'd fantasise briefly about Suzi suffering the same fate. The little tart seemed to enjoy seeing the girls suffer too and she was keener to give them hard treatment that Zara. Yes, mused MacKennan, Suzi could be a right little bitch given half the

The shaft pushed deeply into her sex making her gasp and than give a plaintive cry as she felt uncomfortably stuffed by the thickness and depth of the penetration.

'You don't mind a little pain with such exquisite pleasure, do you?'

'No...'

Serena heard her own reply and as she gazed at her outstretched and tethered arms she could scarcely believe what was really happening to her. He was right, she'd wanted this sort of treatment all along, she thought, sighing plaintively as the man's enormous cock was once more driven into her sex making her tethered body instinctively struggle against the straps that held her down, helpless across the bench.

MacKennan settled into a steady rhythm of shafting her, his massive cock ploughing into her tight little sex hole with a relentless and brutal force that on each thrust took the breath from her. Serena writhed and twisted desperately against the straps but there was no escape though, no respite and this time it was for real. Gazing tearfully she saw the nurse watching and then the girl reached out and caressed both Serena's cheeks, smiling with sympathy at her ordeal.

'I can't take any more...please make him stop... please...'begged Serena huskily, her voice ragged and plaintive with her torment.

The girl stroked Serena's tousled hair clear of her face and then drew her thumb across Serena's trembling lips.

'But you're enjoying it really aren't you?' the girl suggested.

Tears in her eyes, Serena gave a nod of admission and the girl smiled triumphantly.

'What did she say?' MacKennan demanded, tightening his grip on Serena's waist before ramming his cock once more back into her sex.

'She said, she's loving it,' the girl answered, her eyes sparkling with cruel amusement.

Serena gave a despairing sigh and shook her head as the sensation of the cock forcing her pussy acutely wide became too intense.

'Is that getting a little too much for your little pussy?' teased the girl, her tone full of insincere concern. 'I know what you want, let me look after you.'

For a moment the nurse turned away from her and Serena was left to focus on the sensation of the man's massive cock pumping in and out of her now aching pussy.

When the girl turned her attention back to Serena, she couldn't see what she had in her hand until her palm was pressing against her mouth. When the girl withdrew her hand Serena was left with her mouth sealed by a broad strip of adhesive tape.

The young nurse smiled with satisfaction at Serena's helplessness as she looked balefully at her. Tears coursed down Serena's cheeks as the thick cock repeatedly pounded into her achingly tender sex. Just as long as this current shafting didn't last too long, she could cope, she told herself.

'Doesn't it feel good, knowing that you're going to be looked after like this now every day/'the young girl laughed softly, stoking Serena's perspiration soaked hair clear of her anguished face as the merciless shafting continued relentlessly. Serena sighed through the gag and gazed at her tethered arms. Then with a gag muffled groan, she came. Mercifully, a moment later, she felt the cock inside her erupt and for several seconds remain embedded in her until it was spent and then at last withdrawn.

'Most satisfying,' MacKennan moved around the bench until he was afforded a view of Serena's face. He grinned when he saw her expression. She blinked away her tears and gazed at the man looking down at her. His cock was still erect, milky come slowly oozing from the hole in the bulbous purple head.

'Welcome to the basement of the Institute, Serena. Few girls have seen down here and none have ever left it on their own terms. You'll be my prisoner here until I've finished with you and then you'll be exported just like Lara and the others.'

Serena saw the man and his young female accompl exchange conspiratorial glances.

'Would you like seconds, Doctor?' the nurse asked, smili knowingly.

The man grinned and nodded.

'Yes, why not? I trust Miss Fairfax that you've n objections?'

Serena gazed forlornly, her heart sinking as she watche the young girl calmly kneel before the man and caressing hi now semi-flaccid cock take the bulbous head in her mouth MacKennan gave a satisfied smile and looked down at Serena.

'Give us a couple of minutes Serena and you'll be able to get another shafting. Would you like that?'

Her reply was effectively reduced to nothing more than an incoherent groan by the tape across her mouth. The man smiled sympathetically at her.

'I take it that's a "Yes, please,"' he laughed sadistically.

chance and clearly displayed a penchant for playing the sadist with very little encouragement.

Bending over the bed, Suzi now afforded him a brief glimpse of the tops of her thighs as her tight white skirt rode up her legs. There was flash of red G-string disappearing into the canyon of her arse as she reached out further over the bed and slipped a looped cord around the sleeping Serena's left wrist. Deftly drawing the girl's arm back from where it circled her head, Suzi pulled her arm behind her back and then looped another section of rope around Serena's other wrist.

MacKennan watched Serena begin to stir, but it was already far too late for her to defend herself against the fate that lay in store for her at the hands of his two young employees.

With one hand under her victim's chin, Zara turned Serena's face from the pillow and calmly inserted two small rubber cylinders into her nostrils. The cylinders were open at both ends but each was fitted with a tiny sponge soaked with a potent muscle relaxant. As Serena blinked and struggled to surface from her deep sleep, Zara was already smoothing a broad strip of adhesive tape across her mouth. As she gazed dazedly up at the two girls crouched over her, each breath she now took served to make her more and more helpless. For a brief moment she writhed and twisted as the two girls held her down and tightened then fastened the cord around her wrists. MacKennan grinned with satisfaction as he watched Zara and Suzi quickly and easily prepare the Fairfax girl for her short journey down the corridor to the room where she would be subjected to more discipline.

* * *

Serena gazed in dismay at the inside of the room as the door marked with a simple "D" slid shut behind them. The two girls carrying her by her bound arms marched her across to a low bench beside which was an ominous looking machine of gleaming steel, a massive rubber phallus mounted at one end on a long chrome pole.

Serena gave a muffled cry of objection as the girls pushed her chest first down onto the padded bench and the taller of the two girls then sat astride her back, pinning her down upon the bench and painfully crushing her bound arms between her own back and the girl's thighs.

Glancing weakly back over one shoulder, Serena watched as her right ankle was wrapped with a black tape that bound against itself so that the other girl was able to quickly and effortlessly bind Serena's ankle against a rear strut of the bench. Cutting the tape with a small pair of scissors she drew from a pocket of her white nurse's jacket, the girl then dealt with Serena's other ankle and in a moment her ankles were both bound and her legs were left drawn a little apart.

Serena stared up at the Doctor as he circled her, watching as the nurse now wrapped more tape around each of Serena's knees in turn and secured her legs at this point against the bench.

'Seeing how much you enjoyed getting fucked yesterday evening, I thought I would treat you to a session on my new machine. How long would you like Serena? Fifteen minutes perhaps? Longer, maybe?'

MacKennan smiled down at her as Serena felt the girls draw a long strap over her back close to the base of her spine and fasten it tight so she couldn't lift her lower body now from the bench. She gazed despondently around her; too weak to struggle thanks to the drug she was being forced to inhale as the girls now drew a second strap over her back across her shoulder blades.

'Well done girls. Right then, Zara, oil her up for a nice deep shafting session. Suzi, change the head on the fucking machine, I think Miss Fairfax deserves the second largest penetrator and set the timer for fifteen minutes.'

Serena groaned through the gag as one of the nurses taunted her, showing her the dildo-like device she removed from the machine and then the larger one she was going to replace it with. The thick rubber shaft the girl dangled for a moment before her face must have been eight or ten inches long and nearly as thick as the Doctor's genetically enhanced monster cock. Serena sighed as she realised that it would be just like yesterday's ordeal all over again only this time it would last for a full quarter of an hour.

'Now, just relax and enjoy this,' laughed the other young nurse as she fingered between Serena's spread legs and Serena felt a slick gel being stroked over the lips of her sex.

Serena closed her eyes as the girl applied more of the gel and used two fingers together to work it into her pussy.

'Nice and welcoming… and your clit's so swollen already I can see you're just aching for this aren't you?' teased the girl as she continued to finger Serena's pussy, sliding her fingers now deeply into her sex and then rubbing her clit with her thumb until Serena was beginning to struggle against the restraints as she felt the irresistible urge to come.

'Not yet darling… you'll have plenty of time to come once the penetrator's servicing you.'

'She's ready Doctor.'

'Good. Get the machine in place then, you know what to do. And you may as well take the nostril tubes from her, it'll be amusing to watch her struggle.'

'Shall we remove the gag as well?'

'Yes, she can scream all she likes down here, no-one will hear her.'

A moment later and Serena was able to breathe and speak normally again and then just as she felt the strength slowly returning to her tethered body she experienced the sensation of a broad rubber phallus sliding into her pussy.

'Please, Doctor MacKennan, don't….uhhh…'Serena gave a gasp of alarm as the phallus quickly withdrew then was rammed back into her to its full length.

'Uhh!'

The pistoning action of the machine was faster than any normal shafting Serena had enjoyed and combined with the size of the device, the effect quickly had Serena gasping and tossing her head from side to side as she was brought to a powerful climax. As her orgasm shook her tethered body the machine continued to fuck her and soon Serena was groaning then crying out as she felt herself being driven with relentless speed towards another climax.

The machine's piston thumped the phallus repeatedly into Serena's pussy, bringing tears to her eyes and making her writhe helplessly against the straps that held her down.

'No more... please that's enough...'Serena begged as one of the girls laughingly told her, after what seemed ages, that she was only half way through her ordeal. It had seemed much longer and already Serena's pussy throbbed from the hard shafting the machine was giving her.

'Please... stop...'Serena cried, shaking her head despondently, tears running down her cheeks.

'Come now Serena,' MacKennan said reprovingly, 'I had planned to give you a taste of the largest head we can fit to the penetrator once you'd got warmed up with this little introduction.'

'I can't take any more, really! PLEASE!' Serena sobbed as the mechanical shafting continued relentlessly.

'Just a few more minutes Serena, then we'll give the next size up a try, shall we?' MacKennan suggested.

'No... must rest... aching so much...'Serena sighed, now feeling so dazed she imagined she was going to pass out if the sensation of the device ramming into her pussy continued much longer.

MacKennan lifted her head by her tousled hair and looked down at her, grinning with satisfaction.

'Nearly finished... there now...'

The machine glided to a halt, leaving the phallus to slowly withdraw from Serena's sex and for Serena to gaze sorrowfully up at the man regarding her.

'If you'd like a little rest, you can have one if you're prepared to get those lovely lips of yours around my cock. Well?'

'Okay...yes, I'll do it,' Serena agreed, desperate for a respite.

'Right then, let's see how good you are at sucking cock!'

The man's massive organ was facing her now and as he looked down at her, grinning contemptuously, Serena gave the broad cock-head an experimental lick. The male taste was pungent and in response to her tongue flicking across it the whole organ twitched.

'Good girl, that's it, if you look after me nicely then I'll be kind to you.'

The man caressed her hair with both hands, encouraging her closer to his crotch and Serena responded, opening her mouth wide and just managing to get the head of the enormous shaft between her lips so that she could lap at it properly with her tongue. The man groaned appreciatively, stroking her hair while Serena furled her lips around the shaft and sucked deeply before allowing the cock to slide from her mouth so that she could concentrate on licking just the very tip repeatedly until MacKennan's sighs grew louder and she knew she was bringing him quickly and surely to his orgasm.

'Now, if you can swallow it all, you can have a rest.'

The hands caressing her neck slid up against the back of her head and Serena felt the man's fingers tighten into her hair, holding her head against his now excessively engorged organ, the head of which he had encouraged back into her mouth. Dutifully Serena sucked and licked, as her head was edged forwards still further and the shaft of the cock was pushed deeper into her mouth and she could feel the bulbous head in her throat.

'Uhhh..nhhh…'

Her mouth filled with the thick shaft of the man's cock Serena gazed up at the man but he merely smiled at her as she struggled to keep calm as she felt the cock threatening to choke her. Then suddenly the man came and Serena was gulping down mouthfuls of warm, salty semen.

'That's it, lap it all up, there's a good girl,' MacKennan encouraged.

As fast as she swallowed though she still couldn't gulp down the man's come quickly enough and soon semen was dribbling from her lips and the man was looking down at her with an admonishing expression on his face.

'Such a bad girl, you didn't do what you were told.'

Serena was too breathless to answer as the man pulled his cock from her mouth and the last spurts of come splashed against her cheeks.

'I told you that you had to drink it all up; now you're going to have to be punished!'

Serena gave a despondent sigh as the man stepped back and regarded her thoughtfully, a cruel glint filling his eyes.

'I think Miss Fairfax needs a lesson in what bad girls can expect before we resume her training. Set the penetrator to ten percent faster please Suzi and programme it for twenty minutes.'

'But my pussy's aching so much! Please, don't!' begged Serena, gazing imploringly at the man stood over her.

'Who said anything about your pussy getting a shafting? That's what good girls get to enjoy. No Serena, this time you're going to get butt-fucked. Zara, lubricate her rectum just enough for the penetrator to be inserted.'

'NO! PLEASE!' cried Serena.

Glancing at her tethered arms and feeling the straps tight against her back, the realisation that she couldn't escape what was going to happen to her made her tremble uncontrollably.

'This isn't fair, Doctor MacKenna, please...don't...'

Though tears filled her lovely wide eyes and ran down her pretty cheeks and she gazed imploringly at the man, he merely smiled smugly at her and shook his head reprovingly.

'My dear girl, you came to the Institute wanting some rough sexual treatment. Your dreams showed you craved it. Well now you're going to get it!'

'No, please!' cried Serena.

The man turned and walked away, calling back as he went.

'Start the punishment as soon as you're ready nurse and call me when it's finished. If she faints, revive her forcefully and start the whole session again from the beginning!'

A moment later and the man had gone from the room, leaving Serena in the hands of the two young girls. A nervous glance at both confirmed her worst fears; they were going to delight in tormenting her as much as possible. The thought even occurred to her that she might have been safer had the Doctor remained to supervise what punishment was now going to be metered out to her.

'Okay baby, it's punishment time,' laughed the taller of the two girls as she stalked around the tethered Serena, trailing her fingernails across her bare skin.

'Let's change the phallus head and put the largest size on, that should certainly bring tears to her pretty eyes!'

'No, you can't!' blurted Serena, casting a fearful glance around her as the two girls moved the machine back to behind her forcibly spread legs.

'Can't? We can do whatever we like! Who's going to stop us?' laughed the younger girl as she walked across to where Serena lay strapped down, an absolutely massive phallus in her hand. The sight made Serena shake her head in disbelief and she shouted to the Doctor for help, but the only response was a rush of laughter from the two girls.

'These rooms are all sound-proofed, you can scream and shout all you want!'

Serena jerked her arms and legs frantically but the tape held fast and the straps remained taut across her back.

'I can't take that in me… please, don't…'she begged, wide eyed with alarm as the younger girl crouched down beside the machine and unscrewing the phallus that had just been used on Serena, fitted the new one in its place one.

'Now then, a little lubrication, the Doctor said,' the older girl laughed as she smeared some slick gel against Serena's exposed anus and then worked it into her rectum with her thumb until she could slide her thumb in and out of the tight muscle.

'Now, let's see how you like this.'

'Uhhh... God...too big...'Serena gasped as she felt the rubber head of the phallus distending and then penetrating her anus.

'Good girl, not much more to go in,' soothed the taller girl.

Serena felt the shaft of the phallus slowly sinking into her arse, the sensation of it so excessively filling her making her gasp and writhe as inch after inch it was driven into her helpless body.

'No more... please, really can't take any more...'gasped Serena as the device continued to slide relentlessly deeper into her.

'Poor Serena, is that a trifle too much for your lovely little body?'taunted the younger girl, stroking Serena's perspiration soaked hair clear of her face and gazing into her anguished eyes, her own icy blue eyes, sparkling with cruel satisfaction at the torment Serena was being subjected to.

'We've set the penetrator on slow to start, just until you get used to feeling how deep it is.'

'And then we can speed things up a bit,'the younger laughed.

Serena shook her head and looked up imploringly at the girl. The device was now slowly withdrawing from her body, drawing a gasp from Serena.

'There, you liked that, didn't you?'

The phallus had withdrawn except for the bulbous head and was now once more sliding back into her arse, making Serena groan as she felt it filling her once more.

'Okay, Serena, ready now for a decent shafting?'

'Please don't make it go any faster... can't bear it...uhh...'

Even as she was begging the younger girl her accomplice adjusted the machine and the massive phallus began thumping in and out of her distended rectum at a mercilessly hard speed.

'Uhhh...no...can't take it... stop...'

Serena strained against the straps that held her down as the machine pistoned the phallus in and out of her body with brutal force.

'Well Serena, we hope you enjoy the next twenty minutes

as much as we're going to!'

The two girls stepped back and watched as Serena was left, gazing forlornly at her outstretched arms, her wrists bound tight against the bench as the machine punched the thick rubber phallus continuously in and out of her body, wrenching a gasp from her each time it was rammed into her rear. Serena closed her eyes as the punishment continued and she imagined that the machine was in fact one of the evil Doctor's henchmen from her dream and that the man was mercilessly shafting her arse while she was tied down over the bench. The intense sensation of the penetrator ramming the phallus repeatedly into her rear and the vividness of her imagination combined to arouse her so potently that her sighs turned to groans as she was driven to a climax that went on for several successive waves, washing over her tethered body and leaving her breathless.

'The bitch likes it, maybe we're being too gentle with her?'

'What shall we do with her then?'

'Fetch me a pair of pussy clamps, I'm going to weight her sex lips.'

'What and stop the machine?'

'Hell no! The bitch is going to get all she can take!'

'NO! You've got to stop!' cried Serena, when she heard what the girls planned to subject her to.

'And Suzi, you may as well bring a gag, 'cause she'll be screaming non-stop from now on and while it'll be fun to watch her, I don't want to go home with a headache.'

'This isn't fair! The Doctor said that…'

Serena's protest was cut short as the taller girl grasped her hair and jerked her head upwards.

'The Doctor said that your treatment was to be repeated if you fainted before twenty minutes was up and I got the impression that however many times you fainted we were to keep you here until you managed to last for a full twenty minutes.'

As she spoke the girl slid her hand palm down across

Serena's mouth, muffling her answer and then she edged her palm a little higher and Serena felt the girl's thumb and finger constricting then pinching closed her nostrils.

'Nnhhh…'

As she tried to thrash her head to extricate herself from the girl's grasp, her other hand tightened its hold on her hair and held her head forcibly still.

'Something the matter Serena?'

The blood hammering in her temples, Serena tried to twist herself free of the ruthless hold and momentarily she managed to shake her head free and breathe again through her nostrils.

'My, my, you are determined to struggle, aren't you?'

Once more the girl's finger and thumb squeezed Serena's nostrils closed and as the pounding of the phallus into her now aching arse continued, Serena felt a sudden dizziness overtaking her and the strength evaporating from her body.

The next thing she knew was the girl was kneeling before her, smiling sympathetically but the fingers of one hand were still buried in her long red hair and grasping her firmly. With her other hand she lightly slapped Serena across the cheeks until she came back fully to her senses.

'How are we feeling? A bit dazed? I think you must have fainted you poor thing, it must have been the intensity of the orgasm you had. Well, I'm afraid that means another twenty minutes of the penetrator,' the girl laughed softly.

'Not fair… please, let me go…'sighed Serena breathlessly.

The sensation of the phallus punching repeatedly and deeply into her arse continued and as she gazed blearily at the girl before her, the other nurse came alongside her and before Serena knew what was happening a broad strip of strong black tape had been applied across her mouth.

'Nnnhh!'

'What a lovely sight. Okay Suzi, let's get her pussy clamped and weighted.'

Serena felt the phallus slide slowly to a stop and withdraw from her aching body. Glancing weakly over her shoulder she saw the two girls roll the machine away from behind her so that they had a clear view of her exposed rear and a moment later Serena experienced the sharp bite of a clamp on one of her vulva lips. Groaning through the gag as her other sex lip was subjected to the same treatment, she had only a few seconds to get accustomed to the sensation of the clamps before weights had been clipped to them and the lips of her vulva were abruptly and painfully distended. The sensation was too much and gurgling through the gag, Serena came. To her shame she realised with dismay that the rougher the treatment being meted out to her the more sexually gratifying she found it!

'Right, get the penetrator back in her arse, set it for twenty minutes and switch it on!'

'UUHH!'

Once more the thick bulbous head of the rubber cock was forced into her rectum and the harsh shafting of her now achingly delicate rear was resumed. So sensitive was she there now that after a few minutes she was struggling against the straps that held her down as the sensation of being butt fucked grew too much for her. There was no escape though and the ramming in and out of the thick rubber cock went on relentlessly. Another five minutes dragged on and by then it was too much for her senses. Groaning and writhing against her restraints another climax overtook her. Now utterly breathless, Serena shook her head weakly as the penetrator continued ramming the massive phallus in and out of her aching rear. The sensation was overwhelming and combined with the feel of the tape gagging her mouth and the sensation of the weights dangling from her distended vulva, Serena came yet again and this time she was so breathless she fainted.

'Wakey, wakey Serena. Lots more to enjoy yet!'

A firm slap to her cheeks brought her back to a state of consciousness. Looking down at her the nurse laughed.

'Well, I guess as you fainted, that means we start the twenty minutes from the beginning again! Such a shame, if you'd only lasted another five minutes you'd have made it.'

Once more the machine was switched on and the artificial cock ploughed into her throbbing rear passage.

The shafting of her rear went on, hard and fast and with the sensation of the weights and being gagged and so helpless Serena was now hopelessly aroused and all too soon she came again. This time as her exhausted body writhed under the straps as she came, the taller nurse had merely to lightly pinch her nostrils for a brief moment and once more Serena fainted as she was breathlessly brought to a fresh climax.

'Poor Serena, I think this punishment is going to last quite a while for you. Still, you don't mind do you?'

Serena gazed up at the girl, her pleading made incoherent thanks to the tape across her pretty mouth and felt another rush of intoxicating arousal as she knew that the girl was determined to keep her strapped down and tormented for as long as possible.

Chapter Thirteen

MacKennan took a sip from his coffee and tapped into his computer his bank account details. Not the account for the Dreamscape but his secret account into which the funds came from the sale of girls. Last month had been particularly profitable since he'd sold three girls rather than the customary one. Until recently he had scrupulously avoided being greedy and contented himself in selling at most one girl a month. Already the Police had visited the Institute on several occasions to interview him in connection with the disappearance of a young woman who they had found out had been one of his clients. They had never become suspicious though that he might in some way be connected with the girls' disappearance. Of course he was careful, very careful. Even last month when he had sold three girls in one deal to the African Dictator, the Emerald Tiger, he had planned it all meticulously.

Now as he looked at his bank account he reflected how worthwhile it had been. The three girls had given him a very handsome return on the time he'd invested on them. Of course, he was dealing at the very top of the white slave market, a business that was rife these days. Plenty of girls were abducted and exported illegally but what set MacKennan's operation apart was three things: firstly they were all from very wealthy, spoilt backgrounds, which delighted their new masters. Secondly, they were physically the most beautiful girls imaginable. And thirdly in the time he held them in the basement at the Institute he conditioned them into embracing their new roles as sex slaves.

Having sold the sweet, young Jemma just the other day he was now left with only Serena Fairfax in the basement. His prisoner for two days and nights now, she was shaping up nicely. Serena in her dreams had shown all the usual traits of a natural submissive but unlike some, who found it hard to admit – like her friend Lara Lustral – Serena had quickly come to embrace the pain and pleasure that he administered to her in more or less equal measures and already she was getting addicted to the torment of the discipline he and his nurses were administering to her.

Leaving the office MacKennan went along the basement corridor to the room marked with a "D" and keying in his pass number he entered. It was just after ten in the morning and he knew that young Suzi had been in work an hour now as had Karl, one of his trusted henchmen. Suzi seemed to be getting more enthusiastic about her work each week. Her early hesitance when she'd participated in torturing one of the abducted clients had completely evaporated now. MacKennan was keen to see what she had accomplished so far this morning with Serena Fairfax.

The Discipline room was air-conditioned so that the heavy smell of female sweat, arousal and fear that tended to hang in the air could be removed. This morning when MacKennan stepped into the room he found Suzi had set the temperature to a balmy twenty-five degrees and she had stripped out of her white blouse and was standing in just her high heels, short white PVC skirt and nothing more than a skimpy half cup bra covering her magnificent tits. Instantly MacKennan felt his cock begin to harden.

'Morning Doctor, how are you this morning?'

Suzi smiled at him, turning her attention from Serena who was kneeling before her. MacKennan noticed the prisoner's lips and chin were shiny with wetness and as Suzi turned towards him, he noticed that the white material of her bra covering one breast was damp where her erect nipple pressed against the fabric.

'I'm feeling fine thanks, and you?'

'Just great,' the young nurse answered with a grin. She glanced back at the kneeling Serena Fairfax and MacKennan examined the prisoner more closely. Completely naked, there were rubber cuffs fastened around her wrists and these were clipped together drawing her hands together behind her slender back. Her slim neck was collared with a black leather collar, clipped to which was a short leash which he now saw Suzi was holding in her left hand. A soft black blindfold was fitted across Serena's upper face and her long red hair had been tied into a ponytail with a thin black leather cord which trailed tautly down her back and was knotted around the short clasp that held her wristcuffs together.

'I didn't think we'd have her this well trained so soon,' commented MacKennan, walking slowly in a circle around the kneeling Serena and glancing between the blindfolded girl and the generous cleavage of his nurse.

'She's getting to be most obedient,' replied Suzi, grinning as she reached to caress her own breast and as MacKennan watched she eased one tit up and out from the confining fabric of the bra and, bending forwards, pressing it against the face of the kneeling girl.

Dutifully, Serena found the offered nipple and began to lick and suck devotedly. MacKennan felt his cock thicken and fill his pants. His nurse had quite stunning tits, he reflected, and for a fleeting moment he imagined her tethered, arms outstretched, while he bound and pegged her breasts.

'You look thoughtful Doctor?' Suzi smiled at him, glancing up for a moment from watching the girl as she sucked eagerly on her now achingly erect nipple.

'I was thinking that I might spend an hour or two working on her.'

'We need to give her arse another day's rest I think, she was on the penetrator for nearly two hours the day before yesterday. She's loving having her pussy clamped now, so there's not much more left to initiate her to,' said Suzi.

MacKennan nodded thoughtfully. 'I was thinking I might just play with her for while.'

'Just for the fun of it?' suggested Suzi, lightly.

'Why not? What had you planned for her today?'

His young nurse took a step back and glanced down at her own swollen and slick nipple. Without taking her eyes from MacKennan she idly stroked her breast then toyed with her nipple.

'Would you like me to work on her breasts and you could watch us Doctor?' Suzi said, her voice slow and thoughtful.

MacKennan swallowed a lump that had risen in his throat and he nodded.

'That sounds good. Do it,' he said.

The young girl smiled knowingly and with a light pull on the leash ordered her prisoner to stand. MacKennan watched as she then led Serena Fairfax across to where two straps hung from the ceiling, the ends – steel bulldog clips – dangling about seven feet from the floor.

'Okay Serena, the Doctor has come to punish you. I'm going to unclip your wrists; I want you to lift your arms up above your head.'

MacKennan smiled as he watched the blindfolded girl obediently carry out the nurse's instructions. He gazed at Serena's breasts. Though smaller than Suzi's, Serena Fairfax still had a generous cleavage. Her tits were high and pert on her chest, their size emphasised by her slender waist and petite build. The areolas were a chocolate brown and large and the nipples thick and naturally erect.

As Suzi fastened the girl's wristcuffs to the two cords and then adjusted the length of the cords so that her arms were left drawn almost to full stretch above her and more than a little to each side, MacKennan felt his cock push against his pants, the head already sticky with pre-come fluid.

'Do her ankles as well please Suzi, I want her legs held spread.'

The nurse carried out his order willingly, fastening cuffs of supple black leather around Serena's ankles. Fastened to the floor were numerous clips on short high-tension rubber cords and Suzi confidently drew Serena's legs apart and clipped the anklecuffs to two of these so that the girl's legs were now held pleasingly spread.

MacKennan nodded his approval and walked up to within a few feet of his tethered victim.

The girl's breathing was quick and shallow. Blindfolded, he could see she was now straining for any telltale sound of what was happening around her. MacKennan grinned, he loved blindfolding them, it heightened their senses and emphasised their vulnerability. He admired the girl's breasts and tried to remember what treatment he had subjected them to so far. It was hard to remember, he had now tormented so many girls and given so much of the work to his nurses and henchmen he couldn't remember clearly.

'Has she had much work on her breasts?' he turned to Suzi as he stroked one hand over the swell of one of Serena's breasts and felt the blindfolded girl tremble.

'No. You clamped her breasts when she was woken after her final session of dreaming but then you ignored them and wired her pussy,' answered the nurse.

'Ah, yes, quite, I remember now,' MacKennan answered.

'Shall I get some clamps and weights then Doctor?' Suzi suggested.

MacKennan surveyed the tethered girl who dangled helplessly before him.

'Not yet, I think to start with I'll bind her breasts. It's time to make Miss Fairfax writhe. Bring some cord, I'll bind her myself.'

MacKennan caressed the spreadeagled girl's breast until she sighed and wriggled, her outstretched arms pulling against the cords.

'Time for a little torment Serena, you don't mind the pain though do you?'

The tethered girl shook her blindfolded head. MacKennan smiled and moving behind the naked girl so he could press himself against her warm body, he caressed her breasts with both hands, fondling her nipples until they hardened fully.

'What are you going to do to me?' asked Serena plaintively.

'I can't tell you that, it will spoil all the fun.'

MacKennan grinned and nodded to his nurse who without a word went and fetched a ball-gag.

'Now open wide, there's a good girl…'

'Uhhh…'

MacKennan watched as Suzi pushed the rubber sphere into the girl's mouth while he held her head still and then he fastened the gag's strap at her nape.

'There. Now we're ready.'

* * *

Serena shook her head to try to tell them the ball gag was too big but her protest provoked no response and now there was an unsettling silence in the room. She brushed her cheek experimentally against her outstretched arm but the blindfold was tight across her face and she couldn't move it enough to get so much as a sliver of light to appear. She concentrated on trying to keep her breathing calm and to await what lay in store for her. Panic would get her nowhere.

The air of the room was pleasantly warm against her bare skin but that was now the only pleasing thing about her situation. She was disconcerted by the Doctor's tone this morning, a certain impatience and coldness. She sensed he was determined to make her suffer perhaps even more than usual and she was well aware of how sadistic he could be and what fiendish equipment he had at his disposal. She had tried to embrace all the discipline he had meted out on her. There was no way she could escape it and in truth she had come to accept that a part of her was deeply aroused by the way he treated her.

So now, blindfolded and dangling by her outstretched arms, spreadeagled, she was as prepared as she could ever be for what was to happen to her next. The only thing that alarmed her was that he had seen fit to gag her as well as blindfold her and the ball-gag they had forced upon her was larger than the one previously used and as well as forcing her jaws acutely wide it made any form of communication utterly impossible.

The touch of something against her chest made her jerk herself backwards but immediately she came into contact with the hard frame of someone - the Doctor, she guessed, standing behind her. There was the cool feel of something thin and hard but supple wrapping itself around her left breast and then she felt it tightening around her it. Serena gasped then whimpered but no sound emerged from her mouth so effective was the gag. She felt the cord being bound repeatedly around her breast until she imagined that most of it must have been constricted and encased in the tight binding of the cord or rope or whatever they were subjecting her to. As she hung dangling from her outstretched arms, her bare feet just brushing the floor a second cord was bound around her right breast. Then while she was still struggling to get used to the tightness of the cords binding her breasts there came the piquant sting of something being fastened upon first one of her nipples and then the other. The figure behind her, keeping her still stepped away and once again she felt alone as she anxiously awaited what was to happen to her next. The clamps they'd fastened to her nipples whilst pegging her delicate flesh quite firmly, didn't really hurt and she realised too late why and for what they were intended.

The jolt of the electric shock through her breasts took her by surprise and made her cry out through the gag. Her scream though was reduced to little more than a faint muffled groan and as she hung suspended, bathed now in perspiration and trembling nervously, she realised how ruthlessly effective was the ball-gag that filled her mouth. There were a few seconds respite and then a second jolt was administered and Serena shook her head, dragging down on her arms as the sensation became swiftly, excruciating too intense. The effect was immediate and potent: the electric shock rippling through her tightly bound breasts made her ache with arousal.

'Does that feel good Serena?' the Doctor asked, 'Would you like some more treatment like that?'

Urgently she shook her head, panting hard through her nostrils. She had learnt to deny that she wanted to be treated like this but she guessed the Doctor knew all too well the effect such exquisite torture had on her. Being forced to submit to the man's whims and to be tied helplessly so that all she could do was writhe and squirm while being subjected to whatever sexual torment or torture he had chosen for her was potently exciting. The skilfully administered mixture of pain and pleasure the Doctor submitted her to had brought her to countless orgasms and for assuaging her sexual thirst so effectively she felt slavishly grateful and devoted already to the man who a part of her still hated.

Fingers touched between her spread legs, making her flinch then writhe as the moist lips of her sex were stroked and a thumb pushed its way up the deep fold of her sex before rubbing repeatedly against her clitoris.

'I think you might prefer to feel it here, wouldn't you?'

The Doctor didn't need an answer and of course Serena couldn't utter a word because of the ball gag that filled her mouth. The clasps were removed from her throbbing nipples and a moment later she felt their bite upon the outer lips of her vulva. The sensation itself was deliciously arousing enough but she knew there was more to come. A lot more…

A second later and her body was convulsed as a jolt of electricity rippled into her pussy. Knowing her now well, the Doctor administered the charge at just the amount Serena found bearable and the pain was humiliating exquisite. Her orgasm was rapid and intense but the treatment didn't stop. On and off every few seconds the electricity was applied and within a few moments Serena's pussy was so achingly aroused again that she hung, dangling from her outstretched arms knowing that another jolt of pain would make her come a second time. As if sensing her condition the Doctor made her wait. A minute dragged by and Serena's ragged breathing calmed a little. Then the clasps were removed from her pussy lips.

Blindfolded she had no way of knowing what was to happen next and the unexpected touch of something slippery being pushed against her anus caught her completely by surprise.

After the brutal session on the penetrator machine, her rear passage was feeling still more than a trifle delicate and the sensation of having a dildo pushed into her rear brought fresh tears to her fabric-covered eyes. Worse though was to come… the ripple of electricity delivered through the wired dildo made her howl with anguish. The ball-gag though muffled her protest and all she could was writhe and twist and the sensation of being shocked in her rear brought her swiftly to a heady climax.

By the time the dildo was removed Serena was hopelessly dazed and exhausted. Only the cords fastened to her outstretched wrists prevented her from collapsing to the floor. She shook her head weakly, the dildo was removed and she felt fingers exploring her still throbbing rear passage. She was certain that she really couldn't take much more but her tormentors had other ideas…

'There's no point in struggling Serena, you'll only tire yourself,' MacKennan admonished, Serena writhing urgently as a slender rubber phallus was forced deeply into her rear.

'Feeling a little sensitive there, are we?'

The young nurse's sarcastic question made Serena nod her head in urgent agreement.

'Okay Suzi, fill her up,' the Doctor ordered.

Serena gave a groan as she felt the device in her rear expand and she realised with dismay that the butt-plug was expanding inside her. Dragging her arms and legs against the restraints she writhed and twisted feverishly as the rubber plug, by means of a hose and air pump was forcibly expanded inside her rectum until the sensation was so intense Serena climaxed again, this time all but fainting.

'Come on Serena, there's plenty more to enjoy yet.'

A light slap to both her cheeks revived her enough to experience the sharp pull of her nipples being toyed with and pulled to harden them. Serena groaned through the gag as her cord-bound and aching breasts were lifted from her chest as her nipples were worked to two firm erections. Without any pause, clamps were then fastened to them, biting hard enough to bring more tears to her blindfolded eyes and for her to shake her head in vigorous protest even though she knew her objection was quite futile.

'Something the matter, Serena?' asked the Doctor mockingly.

The sensation of her nipples being clamped was agonising but combined with the feeling of the expanded butt-plug filling her rear, Serena was now breathing hard as she felt herself being brought to yet another climax.

'Is that a little too good, for you?'

The young girl's soft voice was close beside her and then her fingers were stroking Serena's inner thighs, tantalisingly close to her pussy, which now dripped with arousal juice.

'I think she wants to have another orgasm, Doctor,' the nurse said, matter of factly.

'Really, so soon? She's such a randy little bitch isn't she, she just never seems satisfied,' MacKennan commented.

'Shall I make her come then, Doctor?".

'I don't think there's any need to play with her, I'm sure if we just give her tits some more attention, that'll be quite enough to make her come.'

'They're looking rather swollen aren't they, don't you think we should take the cords off now?'

'Give them a squeeze and see how she responds,' MacKennan answered.

Serena felt the girl's hands closed around each of her cord-bound breasts making Serena struggle wildly and groan through the gag and toss her head from side to side.

'A trifle delicate I should say,' MacKennan commented dryly, 'remove the cords and clamps and give her a few strokes of the cane to bring the life back into her.'

'On her arse Doctor?' asked the girl as she began to unbind the cords that were constricting Serena's now aching breasts.

'No, not with a butt-plug in her, the sensation will make her come too easily. No, I think she can take a few light strokes on her tits, that'll refresh her nicely.'

Shaking her head in frantic protest, Serena tried to retreat from the sounds of the voice before her but the cords fastened to her wrist and ankle cuffs quickly became taut and then there came the stinging sensation of a slender cane striking across one of her breasts.

Thwack!

'I imagine that her breasts will be feeling very sensitive after the binding, don't make your blows too hard now nurse.'

'Of course I won't, Doctor.'

Thwack!

The cane sliced down against Serena's other breast making her jerk frantically against the cords that held her spreadeagled. She shook her head in vigorous protest, groaning through the gag as the cane struck her aching breasts again.

Thwack!

'I think that will do for now Nurse. Perhaps we'll ask her what she'd like next; un-gag her please nurse.'

'What about the blindfold, do you want it left on?'

'No, I think we may as well take it off.'

Serena heaved a sigh of relief when she heard the Doctor's words and a moment later she was able to flex her jaws once more and a moment after that the blindfold was removed. To her relief her breasts looked unmarked except for faint red lines where the cane had just struck her. Of the cord that had bound her tits there was no evidence, she gazed around her, reminding herself of her surroundings and then she hung her head and looked at her tethered body. How had she landed herself in such a mess, she wondered?

'How do you feel, Serena?' MacKennan asked, 'Doesn't this feel a trifle more vivid than your dreams?'

Serena gazed at the man and shook her head.

'No,' she sighed, 'this feels just as vivid but what's hard to believe is that I'm not dreaming right now. I can't believe this has happened to me.'

'Well, I can assure you this is no dream. Are you wondering yet what's going to happen next to you?'

'I'm sure you're going to take great delight in telling me,' Serena answered glancing sideways at her outstretched arms, the stout black cuffs buckled tightly around her wrists. Pulling her arms experimentally now she wasn't blindfolded she could see how she stood no chance of extricating herself from the bondage she'd been subjected to.

'Well my dear Serena, I have checked up on the whereabouts of your friend Lara and it just so happens the client of mine who bought her is in the market place for another purchase.'

'You smug bastard, you find this so amusing don't you?' Serena snarled, lurching forward towards the man grinning at her but immediately the cords restrained her bound to her ankles and wrists.

'It does please me to know that I can reunite you with your dear friend. She has pleased my client no end and as you have turned into a very model slave, I've high hopes for you too Serena.'

'Damn you MacKennan, do you really think you can go on get away with this twice!'

The Doctor gave a scathing laugh.

'My dear girl, I've got away with it dozens of times. Now enough of this idle chitchat: I rather fancy a fuck, would you care to oblige me?'

'Go to hell!' Serena swore defiantly.

The man laughed and shook his head reprovingly.

'Nurse, administer Miss Fairfax a sedative then get her strapped down ready for a shafting. Before I take use her though I want her tenderised so she can appreciate more fully what pleasure I can give her... I think fifteen minutes with the penetrator at a suitably high speed should suffice?'

'Certainly Doctor,' the nurse smiled sadistically and turning on her high heels strutted across to a table strewn with accoutrements.

'You bastard, MacKennan, do you have any idea of what it's like being on the receiving end of that machine!'

The Doctor laughed derisively and walking up to close in

front of Serena he caught hold of her hair and titled her head back, making her gasp.

'Of course I do Serena... and it's just what a randy little bitch like you deserves. You've dreamt of being treated like this, now I'm not going to disappoint you!'

Serena gasped as she felt the man's other hand close around her right breast and squeeze her still delicate swell of flesh.

'Once you're exported and spending all you time as a submissive slave you'll thank me for having prepared you so well.'

'Damn you MacKennan... you're crazy... you can't do this!' Serena gasped, writhing to escape the hold the man had on her but unable to prise herself free from the tight grasp he had on her hair.

'Insert the filters please Suzi, it's time for Miss Fairfax to be encouraged to relax.'

'Shall I remove the butt-plug, Doctor?' the nurse asked.

'No, leave it in but deflate it a little before inserting the penetrator. Once her pussy is filled though the you can enlarge the butt-plug again.'

'By how much, Doctor?'

'You'll know when to stop nurse, Miss Fairfax will be shaking her head frantically and her lovely slender arms and legs will be desperately struggling to extricate themselves from her restraints.'

Serena shook her head in protest as best as she was able as two cylinders were inserted into her nostrils and as she took her next breaths she immediately felt the chemical they were impregnated with rush to her head making her immediately drowsy.

'Please... you can fuck me, but don't use the machine on me again...too much... please, don't...'

By breathing through her mouth Serena managed to reduce the drowsiness that had threatened to overtake her but then as the Doctor held her head still, the nurse applied tape across her mouth, silencing her begging and immediately forcing her to inhale through the chemical soaked filters of the cylinders they'd inserted into her nostrils.

'Nnhh!'

'Just relax, there's a good girl… time to sleep and when you wake up it'll be time to enjoy a session on the penetrator, you like that don't you?'

'Nnhhh….'Serena sighed, shaking her head weakly as she felt her eyelids closing and a powerful lethargy sweeping through her weakly struggling body.

'Make sure you use the largest size head on the machine nurse and set it at the fastest speed. By the time I fuck her, I want Miss Fairfax to have already been shafted so vigorously that her lovely little pussy is well and truly tenderised.'

Chapter Fourteen

Serena was drugged enough to be unable to offer any resistance as she was unfastened from the cords that held her suspended from the ceiling and hauled across the room to the padded bench. She was still conscious enough though to be fully aware of what was happening to her and the knowledge of what lay in store made her pussy throb with expectancy. A part of her now was utterly addicted to the punishment being meted out upon her and despite the nervousness of experiencing the pain she'd be subjected to, she realised that she craved the torment more than she hated it.

MacKennan was right of course, she had come to his Institute fantasising about being roughly treated sexually and when she found herself his prisoner in the basement of the Institute, there had been a heady thrill at the thought of what she would be subjected to. Even so, now as she was forced face down across the padded, waist high bench, a surge of panic filled her and her body trembled at the thought of what lay in store. Serena shook her head, sobbing tears and writhing weakly as the cuffs around her wrists were clipped to rings secured on the opposite corners of the bench. The girl worked confidently, her task made easy by the potent chemical that Serena was forced to inhale.

'Nnnhh…'

Serena groaned through the tape that masked her mouth as she felt a strap tighten across her back.

'Come on darling, stop struggling…'

With what strength she had Serena was trying to prevent the girl from strapping her thighs to the legs of the bench. Her struggling though was ineffective and in no time her thighs were spread and snugly belted against the legs of the table.

'Feeling excited, are we?' taunted the girl, lightly fingering between her spread legs and making her squirm ineffectually.

'I think we can dispense with this now…'

The sticky tape was dragged from across her mouth, but

the potent little cylinders with the drug soaked filters were left inserted in Serena's nostrils so that she was made to inhale a little of the sedating muscle relaxant continually.

'Please… not the machine… too much…'Serena sighed, struggling ineffectually against the straps that held her waist down. She felt acutely vulnerable and when she glanced over her shoulder and saw the nurse wheeling the machine up to behind her spread legs, she felt a rush of panic that made her drag her arms and legs desperately but hopelessly against the restraints.

'Looking forward to it?' asked the nurse sarcastically as she slipped the tip of the machine's phallus between the folds of Serena's vulva and then switched the machine on to its lowest setting.

Even as Serena felt the butt-plug shrinking inside her arse she felt the thick rubber head of the dildo pushing forwards and into her pussy. The girl held her wriggling arse still as the device penetrated deeper into her making her gasp then cry out plaintively.

'Right then Miss Fairfax, it's time for your pussy to experience a nice hard shafting!'

'Uhhh…no…please, stop…please!'

The massive phallus thumped mercilessly hard and deep into her pussy, withdrew except for the thick, bulbous head and then promptly was rammed back into her.

'Too hard… can't take it… let me go!' Serena begged, tossing her head from side to side and dragging her arms and legs desperately against the restraints.

Thump! Thump! Thump!

The heavy rubber dildo pistoned back and forth, bringing fresh tears to her eyes and making her writhe so much that another strap was drawn across the small of her back and promptly pulled tight and fastened.

'Can't bear it… please…please let me go, too much…'Serena sobbed plaintively as the machine continued to ram the enormous shaft in and out of her now aching pussy.

‘Does that feel good Serena? You know I nearly forgot…’

The nurse laughed sadistically as Serena felt the butt-plug in her rear expand again. Combined with the sensation of the enormous phallus ploughing into her aching sex, Serena’s slender body was quickly writhing frantically under the excruciating sensation of the double assault on her.

Doctor MacKennan stood at the head of the bench staring down at her, his arms folded across his chest, a smug expression of satisfaction at her condition on his face.

‘Stop it… please…’Serena begged breathlessly, her wide eyes pleading with the man stood watching her torment.

‘Don’t expand the plug any more nurse, I think she’s stuffed quite enough. Let’s just let the penetrator just do the work now.’

‘Too… much… can’t bear it…’Serena gasped, breathlessly as the mechanised shafting of her throbbing pussy continued.

‘How long shall we leave her like this Doctor?’ the young nurse asked, idly stroking her fingernails down Serena’s writhing naked body.

‘Oh, not too long, just until the machine has warmed her up for me, then I’ll give her a proper shafting,’ MacKennan answered.

‘There are other possibilities Doctor…’the nurse smiled enigmatically and licked her lips thoughtfully as she circled the bench, her fingertips now gliding over Serena’s strapped thigh.

‘Just what did you have in mind Suzi?’ MacKennan asked.

‘Why don’t you just relax and watch Miss Fairfax while I look after you. Wouldn’t you like to just take it easy and let me make you feel good? I could slowly suck you while you watch her suffering. Wouldn’t it be fun just to leave the machine running?’

‘Okay then Suzi, you’ve talked me into it,’ MacKennan smiled cruelly.

‘No…please, Doctor…I can’t take much more…really…’Serena pleaded, her eyes wide with alarm as the nurse flicked the timer switch on the machine to continuous and the Doctor went and settled himself into a broad, black leather seat that was bolted to the floor in one corner of the room. The seat was of the same design as a gynaecologist might have except that dangling from the arms and legs of this seat were numerous straps evidently used for tying down some poor girl such as Serena. Now the Doctor merely slumped into the seat, pushing aside the leg rests and unfastening his trousers he pushed them and his pants down to his knees. While the merciless shafting of poor Serena's now agonisingly tender pussy continued, the young nurse Suzi crouched beside the Doctor's seat and smiling at the sight of his engorged cock, she licked her lips expectantly, glancing back over her shoulder to see Serena's anguished gaze.

'Please… Doctor… stop the machine… too hard… too deep…'Serena shook her head despondently, struggling weakly, thanks to the filters in her nostrils, against the straps that held her down over the bench.

'Stop complaining Serena, or we'll have to gag you,' MacKennan cautioned, leaning his head back and sighing with pleasure as his nurse caressed his heavy scrotum with the fingers of both hands.

'Your balls are so big Doctor I don't think I can get them in my mouth to suck, such a pity… maybe if I just lick here…'

MacKennan groaned with satisfaction, gazing dreamily across to watch Serena as the machine continued pounding her sex with the enormous rubber phallus.

'Please… make… it… stop!' Serena begged, her words coming breathlessly between each thump of the machine driven phallus ramming in and out of her sex.

'Nurse, you know it's very pleasing to watch her distress but her whinging is really spoiling this for me.'

'I'll attend to it Doctor.'

Serena gazed past her outstretched arms in dismay as the young nurse stood up, straightened her tight little skirt, then strode purposefully towards Serena.

'Why do you persist in being such a bad girl and disturbing the Doctor's rest time?' she admonished, looking down at Serena.

'Please... stop...hurts...so... much...'Serena gasped breathlessly, her body now slumped exhausted across the bench, the massive phallus still thumping in and out of her throbbing pussy. The sensation had brought her to a climax repeatedly but now her pussy felt so tenderised she really did wish that this punishment session had never even begun. The nurse shook her head reprovingly, crossed to a bench of equipment and returned to where Serena was strapped down, her naked body bathed in sweat, her long red hair tousled about her pretty, tear streaked, face.

'Okay then baby, open wide...'

Serena had no strength left in her body to object or resist as the young girl confidently prised open her mouth and insinuated a rubber ring gag between her jaws.

'There, does that feel nice?'

Without pause the girl drew the leather straps around Serena's head, the straps pressing firmly against her cheeks as the girl fastened them at her nape.

'Nnnhhh!'

Serena shook her head weakly in objection, gurgling incoherently in distress, as her jaws were now held wide.

'There, now you relax and enjoy yourself while I finish looking after the Doctor,' the girl grinned, then wiped some saliva delicately from Serena's lower lip as it spilt from her forcibly opened mouth. Turning on her high heels she then strode across to where the Doctor was seated without so much as a backward glance.

Serena gazed helplessly at her two tormentors as the girl knelt before the man and caressing his enormous organ with one hand, she delicately licked the tear of pre-come fluid that had oozed from the tip of his engorged cock-head. Very slowly the girl let her tongue tip lightly caress the bulbous purple head of the cock and then she began a leisurely descent with her tongue down the length of the shaft until Serena could see she was licking the man's enormous balls which she had cradled in one palm. All the time, as she watched, unable to tear her gaze away, Serena felt the mechanical penetrator pounding the rubber phallus repeatedly in and out of her throbbing sex. Unable to tear her gaze away from the sight of the girl servicing the man she gurgled helplessly through the ring-gag as the sensation of the machine shafting her brought her to another shuddering climax that had her writhing helplessly against the straps that held her down.

The merciless assault on her pussy continued and before the nurse had brought MacKennan to orgasm, Serena's exhausted, tethered body was convulsing against her restraints as she orgasmed yet again.

'The randy little bitch sounds as if she's enjoying herself,' MacKennan commented dreamily as he glanced down to watch his young nurse, who, having spent five minutes licking his cock now began to suck on the enormous head of the engorged organ.

'God, that's good... just keep that up Suzi, there's a good girl.'

The nurse was sucking deeply while with her hands she toyed with his balls, firmly squeezing and rolling them within the scrotal sac, then lightly dragging her fingernails against them.

'Yes...oh, yes, very good...'

Serena, the phallus still ramming relentlessly in and out of her pussy, gazed at the spectacle across the room as the shaft of the man's cock visibly throbbed then twitched vigorously. The girl, sensing his imminent ejaculation withdrew her lips from around the shaft head and tightening her grasp on his balls, pulled them firmly downwards away from his shaft to delay his orgasm.

'Uhhh...Suzi...'the man gasped.

'The Doctor mustn't come just yet...'

The young girl leaned back on her heels, surveying but

now not touching the man's genitals and the man gazed down at her slackly parted but smiling lips, his expression a mixture of impatient frustration and pleasure.

'Now Doctor, would you like me to make you come or would you perhaps like to ram you cock into Serena's nicely tenderised little pussy? 'the nurse asked, grinning smugly.

Serena saw the man look across to her and he smiled sadistically.

'Remove the penetrator Suzi; I'll give Miss Fairfax a nice quick fuck I think. She looks like she'd enjoy that!'

'Nnnuuhh!' Serena shook her head in dismay as the nurse crossed to where she was bent across the bench. The penetrator machine was switched off and the phallus withdrawn from her exhausted body.

'How are we feeling, Serena?' the Doctor was now standing grinning down at her, his enormous cock swaying before her, viscous fluid trickling from the tip of the engorged head.

'Don't worry girl, I'm sure this will be over soon enough,' MacKennan laughed, moving behind Serena's spread and tethered legs and stroking his hands over the quivering swell of her buttocks.

'I think we'll have this out,' the Doctor announced, deflating the butt-plug then prising it from Serena's aching rear.

'Now then Serena, you don't really mind if I give you a quick fuck, do you?'

'Wait just a moment Doctor,'said the nurse.

Serena glanced over her shoulder just in time to glimpse the young girl caress the man's massive organ with one hand. As she furled her fingers around the thickness of the shaft, a white cream oozed between her fingers.

'Now this will make things even better for you,' the girl laughed, rubbing her creamy fingers up and down the man's organ.

'What have you done, Suzi?' MacKennan demanded, grinning as he already had guessed just what the girl was up to.

'Just a little delay cream Doctor, it would be a pity for you to come too quickly and disappoint Miss Fairfax.'

'Nurse, you've put far too much cream on! Really!'

'I'll just rub it all in, there's nothing else we can do now Doctor. I'm sorry, you won't punish me will you?'

'Heaven's no, I'm sure Miss Fairfax has enough stamina to last for as long it'll take for me come, haven't you Serena?'

'Nnnhh!'

Serena groaned through the gag as the man's hand stroked between her spread legs and then his thumbs slid between the folds of her vulva and drawing his hands to either side he opened her sex.

'Uuuhhh…'

Serena lifted her head weakly, gulping air through her forcibly parted jaws, the rubber of the ball gag hard against her teeth, saliva trickling over her lower lip. She felt the man's enormous cock push up against opening of her pussy and then with one long deep thrust he penetrated her sex, making her drag her arms and legs against the straps and cuffs that held her down.

'Uuhh!'

'Is that good?'

The cock pulled back then was rammed into her again. Serena shook her head, gurgling incoherently that the sensation was too much for her. Ignoring her writhing body and gag-muffled protests, the man settled into shafting her at a pace that was nearly as fast as the machine and was certainly deeper.

'Nnnhh…'

Serena shook her head vigorously, certain she couldn't bear the sensation of the man's cock ramming so deeply into her a moment longer.

'What's wrong Serena? Feeling a little sensitive are we? Don't worry, I'm sure the Doctor won't be very much longer…'

Smiling reassuringly, the blonde girl walked away, leaving Serena to endure the continued pumping of the Doctor's excessively thick and long cock in and out of her aching sex. Serena would have struggled more but the sedative-impregnated filters were still in her nostrils making her muscles feel like jelly and all she could really do was gurgle incoherently through the gag begging the Doctor to stop, which plainly he had no intention of doing until it suited him.

The respite from the mercilessly hard shafting finally came some five minutes later. Breathless, Serena laid her face cheek down upon the bench, too exhausted from her ordeal to do anything more than sigh plaintively as the man pulled his cock from her stinging pussy.

'Most satisfying,' MacKennan commented, slumping down in the chair facing Serena.

'Did you both enjoy that then?' The nurse grasped a fistful of Serena's tousled hair, lifting her head.

'What shall we do with the bitch next?'

The blonde girl grinned with malicious satisfaction at Serena's condition and stroked her cheek where the flesh was distended by the rubber ring that forcibly held her jaws open.

'Do you think the bitch is ready for export?' the nurse turned her attention back to the Doctor, letting Serena's head slump back onto the bench.

'I think so, I e-mailed the Emerald Tiger yesterday and he's made me a very generous offer. It's just a question of arranging the transport now. I suppose I may as well get on with that this morning. Perhaps Suzi, I can leave Miss Fairfax in your capable hands?'

'Certainly Doctor; is there anything in particular you had in mind for her?'

'I think some finishing touches prior to sale, Suzi. Her pussy is quite delightful to shaft, pleasingly tight and she comes easily but her sex could look still more appealing. I should say that her pussy lips would benefit from being a little thicker and larger.'

'Some judicious steroid injections perhaps Doctor?'

'No, I was thinking weighting. We have a few days before

she's exported. I think two hours every morning, afternoon and evening in the chair with her vulva clamped and weighted should do the job nicely.'

'Nnnhh!' Serena cried out in protest but the gag reduced her cries of objected to nothing more than a muffled groan and went ignored.

'Anything else Doctor?'

'Well, I had wondered about her breasts,' MacKennan answered, 'I could make them bigger... perhaps it would be worth it.'

'But a course of suction tubes takes weeks and she could be sold and exported in a couple of days. Or had you thought of implant surgery?'

'No, I had thought of something else. I could dose her with tablets that trick her lactating glands into working as if she's pregnant.'

'So her tits would swell with milk, but wouldn't she then...'

'Need milking? Quite, 'the Doctor acknowledged, matter of factly. 'I'm sure the Emerald Tiger would be happy to oblige. It would give her a certain added appeal, don't you think?'

'Nnnhhh!' Serena shook her head in alarm as she was forced to listen to what was being planned for her.

'Of course, stopping the tablets would bring her back to normal, but if her owner preferred he could keep her with continuously swollen breasts.'

'He'd just have to remember to milk her every day.'

'One of life's little inconveniences...' MacKennan smiled at Serena who was balefully gazing at him. 'But a small price to pay for having such a delightfully slender girl displaying nice a pair of large tits. Of course, laser surgery and implants could do the same job but the added appeal of keeping her milk swollen is that the electric milking machines make the nipples wonderfully sensitive so that when it's playtime, she responds so much better to whatever one has in mind...'

'So when do you need to start dosing her?'

'Straightaway really. We may as well move her to the chair and get her strapped in. I'll dose her then leave her with you for you to clamp and weight her vulva. As we may only have a day or two, use the heaviest weights and just ignore her protests.'

'Nnnhh!'

'Stop looking so worried Serena, I'm sure you'll quickly get to enjoy the feel of your breasts distending,' MacKennan grinned.

'And your pussy lips distending too!' laughed the nurse.

'Before we unstrap her, remove those filters from her nostrils nurse and replace them with fresh ones. The more docile she is the easier it'll be.'

'Uuuhhh…'

Serena shook her head in objection as the tubes were withdrawn from her nose.

'Stop struggling you silly girl,' the nurse admonished as she insinuated the replacement tubes into Serena's nostrils.

'Cover her mouth with your hand for a moment so she has to take a good breath through her nose, that'll calm her down,' the Doctor ordered.

A moment later and Serena was too drugged to resist as she was hauled from the bench across to the modified gynaecologist's chair. While the Doctor easily held her still, the nurse lifted her legs and placed them in the two metal troughs that extended from the base of the chair for just such a purpose. MacKennan had fitted canvas straps to the chair legs and as Serena watched helplessly, the nurse drew one strap around Serena's right calf and buckled it tight.

'There's no point in struggling Serena, you're not going anywhere,' MacKennan held her still with hardly any effort as she writhed with what energy she could summon as the nurse strapped her left leg in a similar fashion.

'Well done Suzi, arms next I think,' MacKennan said, holding Serena firmly back in the chair with one hand while pinning her right arm with his free hand. Serena tried to resist what happened next but the young blonde girl easily held her left arm still along the length of the padded vinyl arm rest and looped a strap around her wrist and then pulled it tight. And a few seconds after that a second strap was binding her bicep firmly back against the padding of the chair.

'Nnnhhh…'

Serena gazed disconsolately as she watched them secure her other arm in a similar fashion and then a strap was drawn around her chest just below her breasts and tightened from behind the chair. Flicking a switch MacKennan made the chair tilt backwards and pressing another button the legs of the chair moved apart, dragging Serena's legs until they were widely spread.

'Excellent, now it's time for your first tablet Serena.'

With the ball gag removed and a ring gag applied and holding her jaws forcibly wide there was nothing Serena could do as a small tablet was tossed into her mouth and promptly encouraged down her throat with plenty of water.

'Right then, I'll leave her in your capable hands nurse!'

No sooner had the Doctor left the room than Suzi set to work, first fastening clamps to the outer lips of Serena's vulva and then clipping weights to them. Serena gazed at the girl, tears running down her cheeks as the pain from the weights distending her sex lips shot through her strapped down body.

'Don't worry Serena, two hours flies by when you're having fun!' the young nurse laughed as she watched Serena writhe helplessly against the straps that pinned her to the chair.

Chapter Fifteen

Lara strutted confidently into the Palace dining room, led by a servant. Once in the room the servant handed the leash, which was clipped to a collar about her neck, to another man who was guarding the door and he retired, closing the door behind him. The Emerald Tiger was seated with three other men, one of whom Lara recognised and knew to be the Head of the Pashkent Secret Police. Of the other two one was wearing the uniform of a Colonel and the third, a young European with short cropped blonde hair, was dressed in a safari suit and bore a black patch across one eye. All three men paused briefly to glance up and regard the naked girl who had been brought into the room then they resumed eating. The Emerald Tiger scarcely glanced up from his meal.

It had been nearly two weeks since Lara had last been summoned to the presence of the Emerald Tiger and since then most of her time had been spent with his personal fitness instructor, the Puma. The man had spent a great deal of time exercising with Lara and all of it Lara had found stimulating and most pleasurable. However the day after the Emerald Tiger had returned to his Palace, Lara found out his personal fitness instructor had disappeared. Several senior advisors, a government minister and some senior army officers also disappeared. For the next few days rumours flew around the Palace and finally about a week later the truth emerged. There had been a plot to overthrow the Emerald Tiger but before the coup could be effected, the Secret Police had foiled it, seizing those suspected of plotting the demise of the Emerald Tiger.

'Ah, my dear Lara,' the Emerald Tiger smiled, a smile could presage anything and invariably gave no indication as to his real mood or true feelings. Lara swallowed uncomfortably, shifted a little on her bare feet and glanced around the table for a clue as to what might be about to happen to her. The faces of the other men made her heart sink. The Head of the Secret Police seemed to be trying to suppress a malicious grin. This man, Amdoul Bakran, was one of the oldest and most powerful men in Pashkent and had a reputation for cruelty and ruthlessness that made his Monarch, the Emerald Tiger, seem like a saintly pacifist in comparison. Amdoul Bakran had a way of dealing with people who stepped out of line or whom he thought might be about to step of line. The result was always the same: the person would disappear. Occasionally part of them might re-emerge: usually it was a severed hand floating in a crocodile infested river.

'My dear Lara,' the Emerald Tiger beckoned her closer, 'I understand that you have been spending a lot of time lately in the company of the Puma?'

'Yes, your Highness, he told me that was your wish...'Lara smiled timidly, her heart hammering now as she began to suspect that the man's disappearance was now certainly at the hands of the corpulent Head of the Secret Police who whilst sucking on a lamb bone was gazing lasciviously at her. The fat slob had doubtless suspected that the Puma involved in some way with the planned coup. Either that or, and this was more likely, Amdoul Bakran had found out what the Puma and Lara had been getting up to in his Majesty's absence and Bakran had decided to use the rumoured coup as a way of getting rid of the Puma, so that he might be given Lara as a thank you present.

'Did he indeed tell you that,' commented the Emerald Tiger, dryly. Dabbing at his lips with his napkin he then picked up a glass of water and took several small sips before resuming what he was saying.

'The Puma was one of a number of people who we have found out were plotting against me. He'll not be giving you any more fitness instruction. Now, as a thank you for my trusted servant's service, I am giving you to the Head of the Secret Police. As of now, you are the property of Amdoul Bakran. Another girl who is arriving here this afternoon will take your place. I believe you know her; her name is Serena. An old friends of yours perhaps?'

'I don't believe it!' Lara exclaimed, 'Serena? The stupid idiot, she should have stayed away from the Institute and that bastard MacKennan!'

Lara took a step forward but a jerk on the leash fastened to her collar brought her obediently back to heel.

'Amdoul, the girl is yours. Enjoy her, you deserve the reward for your hard work,' the Emerald Tiger stood up, signalling that the lunch was at a close, even though the other men were still eating. All though, quickly stood and bowed. After wiping the back of his arm across his greasy mouth, Bakran thanked his Majesty for the present and no sooner had the Emerald Tiger left the room did he snatch hold of the leash and march Lara from the room and the Palace.

It took them just under an hour to make the journey back to the fortified house that served as Bakran's closest home to the Palace. The journey was made by bullet proof limousine but was not a comfortable journey for Lara as she was bound hand and foot and tossed onto the back seat of the car where she was forced to lie lengthways and across her new owner's lap. Amdoul wasted no time, once the car had left the Palace, in pulling down his trousers and impaling Lara on his engorged cock.

'Tell me girl, does that feel good? I bet you're looking forward to being my slave aren't you? His Majesty intimated that you love being whipped and beaten and treated harshly, well, you'll not be disappointed!'

'I knew you had your eye on me for ages!' Lara cursed, writhing ineffectually as with each bump on the road the man's cock was thrust deeper into her sex.

'Of course, I did, just as every man in the Palace did, only I have been rewarded with taking possession of you and now you're mine to enjoy!'

The man brought his palm down hard on Lara's bare rump making her give a yell of pain that only provoked a laugh and another sharp slap upon her exposed rear.

'And I bet the Puma probably didn't even have anything to

do with the plot?' Lara suggested cynically. She knew she was going to be in for a rough time at this man's hands but at least in consolation he had a decently large cock and seemed eager enough to ram it into her at the earliest opportunity!

'Oh the plot, yes!' Amdoul laughed derisively, 'there was no plot only a collection of men who all were loyal but who all disliked me intensely. They're all out of the way now and so when the plot to assassinate his Majesty does happen there'll be very few people left to protect him!'

'You bastard! You mean…uhh…'

Lara never finished her sentence. A powerful hand snatched hold of the collar about her neck and jerked her head up so she was face to face with the sweating grin and gleaming eyes of Amdoul Bakran.

'My dear girl, you'll not have too long to wait before your new master is made the first President of the newly formed Democratic Republic of Pashkent. His Majesty's days are nearly at an end!'

The man's laughter filled the car as it swung off the road and up a guarded private drive and arrived outside an imposing house ringed by lawns and high hedges and encircled by a barbed wire fence, fifteen feet high and patrolled by armed police with the most ferocious looking dogs straining on chain leashes that Lara had ever seen.

'Welcome to your new home Lara. I have prepared a room especially for you. I do hope you find it to your taste!'

Led by the collar and leash, Lara was taken into the house and upstairs. Whilst her ankles had been untied, her hands remained bound behind her back. The room that she was led into was large and sunny, though the windows, she was soon to discover were bullet proof plate glass and securely locked. The only fresh air that came into the room was from the air conditioning and although at first glance the room looked like any well-appointed bedroom, Lara had yet to discover just what lay stored behind numerous locked wardrobe doors. Freeing her hands, the man gestured for her to explore her new home.

'There is a bathroom through there and through the other door you will find your own living room and beyond that a sun terrace. If you had imagined I was bringing you to some dungeon, then I must disappoint you. That said, once you are settled in and refreshed, we can play some games together that I'm sure you'll enjoy.'

'But what…'

Lara gave a sigh, never having the chance to finish her question as the man left the room, shutting and locking the door behind him. As she wandered around the suite of rooms familiarising herself with them, she idly unfastened the collar that was around her neck and discarded it, so that she was now left with nothing touching her skin. No leather, no rope, no cord, no restraint. Somehow she doubted that it was a condition that she'd enjoy for very long… she suspected that all too soon her new master would want to see her subjected to some new torment that had been devised for her suffering and his amusement. Lara shrugged off this thought though, she'd been punished enough to know that whatever lay in store which might make her howl with anguish, it would also satisfy her sexual craving. But then her thoughts turned to her friend Serena who the Emerald Tiger had revealed was to become his next victim. Lara wondered how Serena had fared at MacKennan's hands and whether she would be able to adapt to her new life as a sex slave as easily as Lara had.

Her thoughts turned briefly back her life back in England before she'd first walked into the Dreamscape Institute. She gazed out of the plate glass window at the jungle-clad hills that rose, swathed in steamy mist away on the horizon. Idly she stroked her neck where the collar had been and then she glanced down at her breasts, her nipples were just brushing the glass of the window and she could feel the warmth from the sun penetrating them pleasantly. Caressing one breast with a hand she cupped its generous weight and then turning around so her back was resting against the window she trapped and squeezed her nipple between her fingers. It wasn't the same as when your own hands were pinned and someone else was doing it, Lara reflected. She hoped she wouldn't have too long to wait before her new master turned his attention to tormenting her. Just as long as he wasn't too harsh with her…after all, every girl had a limit as to how much pain she could suffer.

* * *

The Emerald Tiger watched as the new girl was brought into the games room. Blindfolded, she was oblivious to her surroundings but even so she was struggling desperately against the two men who dragged her across the room kicking and screaming. The girl was quite short and very slim, her skin olive brown and her complexion flawless. Her russet hair fell tousled around her pretty face and down over her smooth shoulders. The girl's sensual bow-shaped lips were distorted, her mouth forced wide to accommodate a black rubber ball gag whose slender leather strap was tightly drawn across her cheeks. Held by both arms by his two henchmen, the girl was writhing and twisting but her wrists were buckled with black leather cuffs and these were fastened together by a few inches of plastic coated wire, each end of which finished at a clip that was attached to a steel ring stitched securely to each wrist-cuff. In a similar way the girl was hobbled: a short length of wire trailing between ankle-cuffs of matching black leather. The Emerald Tiger stood smiling as he watched the two men hold the girl still in the centre of the room whilst his two eunuchs proceeded to strap her against a cross. Against four men the girl stood no chance and in a few moments despite her protests she was bound spreadeagled and the two men who had brought her were dismissed with a cursory nod from his Majesty.

Alone with his new victim and his two trusted eunuch henchmen the Emerald Tiger circled the new girl, admiring her beauty and inhaling the pleasing aroma of female sweat and fear. Of course blindfolded and gagged the girl had no way to see or to communicate and her mind would be racing with dark imaginings of what might be about to befall her. The cross to which she was fastened was made from hardwood polished and oiled to a mirror-like finish. There were numerous leather straps screwed to the wooden beams and now four of these were already tied and buckled firmly around the girl's lithe limbs. The Emerald Tiger fingered one of the straps that was tight around her right thigh, just above her knee. The leather had been drawn fully once completely around her limb before being fastened and with a matching strap securing her other leg, her shapely thighs were now held securely against the wooden cross but her legs were pinned well apart. The girl trembled as she felt the man's touch and her arms twisted ineffectually against the straps that pinned her biceps firmly back against the cross.

Without a word the Emerald Tiger pointed to the girl's wrists and ankles and silently his two henchmen swiftly fed leather cords through the steel rings fastened to her wrist and ankle cuffs and bound them repeatedly around the wooden poles so that the girl was now pinned in four more places. The Emerald Tiger ran his hand over the tethered girl, stroking down from her slender neck, over her generous breasts and down her taut stomach until he reached her shaven sex: the luscious lips of which were shiny and slick with arousal. Sliding a thumb into her moist folds he drew a gag-muffled groan from the girl. He then brushed his wet thumb across one of her tits and her whole bodied convulsed as much as the restraints permitted. Once more he slowly rubbed her nipple with his thumb and this time pale milky fluid rose from the swollen tip and trickled across his thumb.

'I don't suppose you've been milked since leaving the Institute, have you my dear?' the Emerald Tiger asked sympathetically, smiling sadistically as he caressed each tit with a hand, gently squeezing the swollen orbs of flesh.

The tethered girl shook her head vigorously, gurgling

incoherently through the gag.

Applying more pressure upon her breasts with his hands the Emerald Tiger watched as the girl's arms and legs twisted urgently against the straps that held her bound.

'Poor thing, you must be in quite a state of distress…'

A little viscous fluid trickled from the girl's distended nipples and ran down over the swell of her breasts.

'I have matters to attend to so I shall have to leave you for a while. I promise though that when I come back I shall look after you properly. In the meantime I will leave you in the care of my men.'

The Emerald Tiger nodded with satisfaction and walked from the room, pausing briefly in the doorway.

'Don't touch her nipples; I don't want her spilling any milk yet. She'll last a few more hours, summon me when it's obvious she can't hold out any longer.'

The girl gave a muffled cry of despair, shaking her head in protest at what she'd just heard.

The Emerald Tiger smiled with satisfaction; the English Doctor had told him that she'd developed a penchant for electric stimulation and so he had got a milking machine specially modified just for the English bitch. Each splash of milk spilling into the plastic tubes that would be suctioned onto her tits had fine copper wires inside. With each spurt of milk the girl should get a nice little electric shock through her nipples in return. As impatient as he was to watch the effect it would have on her he knew that the longer he made her wait the more tender her breasts would be and then when she was eventually milked the more milk she would give and so the longer the torment would be for her.

* * *

For Serena the next few hours were a torment more than she imagined she could bear. Not just because of the continuous ache from her swollen breasts but because the two henchmen left to watch over her decided to make her suffer even more.

Strapped to the cross there was nothing she could do stop them and even though they removed her blindfold and gag, she knew there was no point in screaming for help as none would be forthcoming. All she could was beg them to stop the torment and of course they had no intention of giving her any reprieve.

'Uhhh.... no....can't... take...anymore...'

Serena shook her head desperately, jerking and twisting her bound arms as one of the men once more dipped his fingers into the little bowl of crush red berries and scooping up a little juice he then drew his fingers up underneath and between Serena's forcibly spread legs. She felt his fingers brush against the crater of her anus and then against the distended lips of her sex. Immediately the aching sensation intensified once more.

'No...uhhh...stop it...'

Shaking her head, tears running down her cheeks, she whimpered plaintively as the heat of arousal was intensified once again in her body. She gazed down at her tethered legs, and then sideways at her outstretched and bound arms. The sensation got more and more intense, making her groan and writhe as she was driven towards another climax. How many times in the last hour had they made her come? She had lost count. Her body felt exhausted and her poor breasts ached so much... they had had to stop and let her rest, she felt faint now from her repeated orgasms and being held tied and outstretched for so long.

'Please... enough...uhh...'

Serena gave a gasp and jerked her arms frantically against the straps as one of the men rubbed then squeezed her clitoris between his fingertips. It was enough, combined with the effect of the berry juice to make her come yet again and this time as she screamed, her orgasm sweeping through her body like a flame, the man smothered her mouth with his hand, intensifying her sensation of breathlessness.

It was then, as she hung, gasping for breath and crying

plaintively that the Emerald Tiger returned to the torture chamber. His smile showed how pleased he was with her pitiful condition and experimentally he stroked his thumb across one of her nipples drawing a gasp of pleasure from Serena.

'Lick it,' he ordered, holding his thumb out before her mouth. Serena obeyed, tasting for the first time her own milk. Glancing down as she sucked the man's thumb she saw that the swollen tit was shiny with a pale white tear of fluid which when the man squeezed her breast, dripped onto the floor between her spread and tethered legs.

'I think you're ready to be milked, aren't you?'

The man didn't bother to wait for a reply and the truth was that Serena was desperate to be milked.

In the last few days of being the Doctor's prisoner, he had brought her to this condition. Her breasts had swollen and grown more sensitive and then he had fastened a milking machine to her. Her arms and legs bound so she was helpless, all Serena could do was watch in nervous fascination as the clear plastic tubes had been attached to her tits and when the suction pump had been switched on she felt the pressure like an invisible hand squeezing her tits repeatedly. The feeling, to her shame her been exquisite and she'd gazed at the tubes as they had filled with her milk and her panting had grown harder and faster as the sensation aroused her so much that by the end of it she was begging the Doctor to fuck her. He had been delighted with the effect and her response and once a day he subjected her to the treatment and secretly Serena had longed for that time each day when she would be strapped and then milked. Once the tubes were removed from her aching breasts, she was all too willing to submit to MacKennan who wasted no time in ramming his massive into her pussy.

'This machine looks different to the one the Doctor used on me,' Serena said, gazing down nervous but eager as the Emerald Tiger's henchmen brought their master's new acquisition into place.

'Why are there wires inside the tubes?' Serena asked,

watching wide eyed with curiosity as the two men fastened the plastic tubes over the nipples of her distended breasts.

'Why are there wires? You are just going to milk me, aren't you?' Serena asked, glancing at the two servants and then at the master who stood watching a broad smile on his face.

'Please... what are you going to do?' Serena looked apprehensively at the machine and a shiver of fear ran down her back. She glanced sideways at her outstretched arms and tugged urgently against the straps that held her limbs spread and immobile.

'Uhhh...'A gasp was dragged from her lips as a button was pressed on the machine and the air was extracted from the tubes, creating a vacuum, forcibly stretching her breasts so that more of the tits were drawn into each tube.

'Do you want me to tell you want is about to happen to you, Serena?' the Emerald Tiger grinned mischievously, his hand hovering above the machine's control panel. Serena swallowed the lump that had risen in her throat, glancing down at the tubes that were now tightly fastened upon her tender breasts and seeing the fine copper wires spiralling inside the clear plastic.

'I think I can guess,'she answered, glaring at the man furiously.

'Doctor MacKennan took the trouble to tell me that you had a penchant for a little gentle electric stimulation.... I thought it would be a more satisfying experience for you if each time you were milked your breasts enjoyed a little extra stimulation.'

'You bastard....'Serena glowered at the man then held her breath as she saw his fingers close around a switch on the machine and flick it on.

'Uhhh!'

Immediately she felt the pumping begin and as the first spurt of milk was coaxed from her tit and it splashed against the inside of the tube Serena experienced the sharp bite- like sensation of an electric current shoot through her nipple into her breast.

'Uhhh!'

She shook her head urgently as a second jet of milk was squeezed from her tits and simultaneously she received another sharp shock through her already achingly sensitive breasts.

'No…uhh…stop…'

Serena shook her head urgently, dragging her arms and legs frantically against the straps that restrained her.

'Enjoying your milking session, Serena?'

The Emerald Tiger smiled smugly as he watched her struggling more and more desperately.

'Please…stop… too much…uhh…'

A gasp was dragged from Serena with each little shock that ran through her distended and aching tits. Her body was bathed in perspiration and her breathing was coming in ragged gasps as the repeated shocks brought her nipples to an unbearable degree of sensitivity.

'No…uhh…no more...'

Serena shook her head, biting down on her lip and blinking back the tears as the sensation, which already seemed too much to stand, got more and more intense.

'Good girl, not too much longer to go, I imagine.'

The Emerald Tiger stroked her tousled hair clear from her face so he could see more clearly her anguished features. Serena looked balefully at him, tears now streaming down her cheeks as her tits were subjected to shock after shock.

'How does it make you feel Serena? Let me feel…'

A hand touched between her legs and the man laughed softly as he felt stroked her folds of soft flesh around her sex that were soaking with arousal juices.

'You're loving it aren't you?'

Lifting her head by her damp hair, the man met her gaze, helplessly and shamefully Serena nodded in admission.

'But can't… take… much… more…'Serena gasped plaintively, her body writhing against the straps as her breasts were forced to yield more milk and with each spurt she gave she was rewarded with the sharp taste of an electric shock rippling through her achingly sensitive breasts.

'I'm sure you won't have much more milk to come Serena and then the pain will stop, can you last just a little longer?'

'Uhhh...please...enough...'

Serena shook her head, gasping then biting down on her lip before another cry was torn from her by the shocks that came with each splash of milk hitting the copper wires inside the tubes fastened around her tits.

'Can 't... uhhh... take... any... more...'

Serena gasped, gazing down helplessly at her tethered body and staring at her breasts, trapped in the plastic cones. Another spurt of milk was drawn from her tits and another shock ran from her nipples through her breasts. She shook her head urgently and gazed imploringly at the man watching her. The Emerald Tiger gave an understanding smile and nodded.

'Please... make...it... stop...'Serena begged breathlessly.

'I'm sure it will be over soon now my dear girl.'

Serena shook her head despondently. The torment, as the man had guessed was nearly at an end and after a few more moments the tubes were removed from her throbbing breasts, which had yielded all the milk they had stored for the present.

By the time Serena had recovered her senses sufficiently to appreciate that her first electric milking session was concluded, the henchmen of her new sadistic master were already preparing her for the second phase of her torture and she found herself gazing down in dismay as clamps were fastened upon her throbbing tits.

The Emerald Tiger turned to one of his henchmen.

'Gag her.'

'No!' Serena shook her head despairingly as the two henchmen forced a ball-gag into her mouth. The gag was fastened tightly against her nape. Serena stared wide-eyed at her tormentors as they proceeded to fasten weights to the clamps. As her breasts were pulled down painfully hard Serena tried to let out a cry of anguish but the gag reduced her howl to a muffled groan. Gazing with tearful eyes at the man standing before her, Serena shook her head urgently.

'Is this too much for you?' the man asked, smiling sadistically as he watched her writhing and twisting helplessly against the straps that held her pinned to the cross. Serena nodded urgently, tears rolling down her pretty cheeks.

'What a pity, because you know my dear Serena, this is just the beginning…'

Serena looked balefully at the man who moved closer to her, smiling sympathetically. A hand touched between her spread legs and fingers slid into the wet folds of her aching pussy making her arch her back in pleasure as best as her restraints permitted.

She gazed longingly at the man, her tethered body trembling on the edge of a climax. The man slid his fingers deeper into her sex. Serena groaned through the gag, closing her eyes for a moment. The man stepped back and withdrew his hand, making her open her eyes in frustration and disappointment. The man's gaze lingered on her naked body then he idly stroked one of her breasts. Serena sighed then gave a plaintive cry as he lightly tapped the weight dangling from the clasp that was tightly fastened upon her nipple.

'You will be treated like this every day, because it is what you deserve and because it's what you want, isn't it?' he said.

Serena, blinking away her tears, nodded in shameful admission. The man smiled triumphantly and turned to one of his henchmen.

'I thought the last one was the perfect slave but I think this girl may prove to be even more pleasing!'